Text Classics

T0358009

AMY WITTING was the pen name of Joan Austral Fraser, born on 26 January 1918 in the inner-Sydney suburb of Annandale. After attending Fort Street Girls' High School she studied arts at the University of Sydney.

She married Les Levick, a teacher, in 1948 and they had a son. Witting spent her working life teaching, but began writing seriously while recovering from tuberculosis in the 1950s.

Two stories appeared in the *New Yorker* in the mid-1960s, leading to *The Visit* (1977), an acclaimed novel about small-town life in New South Wales. Two years later Witting completed her masterpiece, *I for Isobel*, which was rejected by publishers troubled by its depiction of a mother tormenting her child.

When *I for Isobel* was eventually published, in 1989, it became a bestseller. Witting was lauded for the power and acuity of her portrait of the artist as a young woman. In 1993 she won the Patrick White Award.

Witting published prolifically in her final decade. After two more novels, her *Collected Poems* appeared in 1998 and her collected stories, *Faces and Voices*, in 2000.

Between these volumes came *Isobel on the Way to the Corner Shop*, the sequel to *I for Isobel*. Both *Isobel* novels were shortlisted for the Miles Franklin Award; the latter was the 2000 *Age* Book of the Year.

Amy Witting died in 2001, weeks before her novel *After Cynthia* was published and while she was in the early stages of writing the third *Isobel* book. She was made a Member of the Order of Australia and a street in Canberra bears her name.

MELANIE JOOSTEN's most recent novel is *Gravity Well*. Her debut novel, *Berlin Syndrome*, saw her named a *Sydney Morning Herald* Best Young Novelist and receive the Kathleen Mitchell Award; it has since been made into a motion picture directed by Cate Shortland. In 2016 she published the essay collection *A Long Time Coming: Essays on Old Age*.

ALSO BY AMY WITTING

I for Isobel
The Visit
Marriages (stories)
A Change in the Lighting
In and Out the Window (stories)
Maria's War
Isobel on the Way to the Corner Shop
Faces and Voices (stories)
After Cynthia

Selected Stories
Amy Witting

Text Publishing Melbourne Australia

textclassics.com.au
textpublishing.com.au

The Text Publishing Company
Swann House
22 William Street
Melbourne Victoria 3000
Australia

All of the stories in this edition were published in *Faces and Voices* (Penguin Books Australia, 2000); many were published in *Marriages* (1990) and *In and Out the Window* (1995), and in various magazines, journals and anthologies.

First published by The Text Publishing Company 2017

Cover design by Imogen Stubbs
Series design by W. H. Chong
Typeset by Midland Typesetters

Printed and bound in Australia by Griffin Press, an accredited ISO/NZS 1401:2004 Environmental Management System printer

National Library of Australia Cataloguing-in-Publication entry
ISBN: 9781925498158 (paperback)
ISBN: 9781925410495 (ebook)
Creator: Witting, Amy, 1918–2001, author.
Title: Selected stories / by Amy Witting ; introduced by Melanie Joosten.
Subject: Short stories.

CONTENTS

INTRODUCTION

*Amy Witting and the
Art of the Long Game*
by Melanie Joosten
VII

Selected Stories
1

Amy Witting and the
Art of the Long Game
by Melanie Joosten

WITH A HINT of a sorrow akin to regret it is often noted that Amy Witting only received public recognition and critical acclaim for her work towards the end of her life. Her late blooming is usually accounted for with mention of how the pressures of a teaching career and the responsibilities of bringing up a family stymied her creative output in a manner not unusual for women, then and now. The truth, as it so often is, is a little more complicated.

Joan Levick, who wrote under the pseudonym Amy Witting, had been publishing short stories in literary journals (including the *New Yorker*) since 1956 and her first novel, *The Visit*, appeared in 1977. She did not claim any real success for her writing, however, until the age of seventy-one, with the publication of her long-rejected second novel,

I for Isobel (1989). Highly successful and popular with readers and critics alike, *I for Isobel* was followed over the next twelve years by two collections of short stories, *Marriages* (1990) and *In and Out the Window* (1995), and further novels and poetry. Both collections, along with other published and unpublished stories, were reprised in *Faces and Voices* (2000), from which this new, shorter selection has been drawn.

Rather than a late rush of proliferation, Witting's trajectory should be considered an extensive and comprehensive apprenticeship. Written throughout her life and recording Australia's changing social landscape, her short stories— distinct in tone and varied in plot—are second to none. With a lightness of touch and an ability to swap perspectives with great subtlety, Witting records both complex psychology and base emotion while prioritising neither. She acknowledges the whole person, every facet of their thinking. Without apologising for their behaviour or attempting to elicit empathy, she tells it how it is. She is both endearingly honest and merciless in her depictions, which makes her characters appear as people rather than ciphers of the writer's imagination. As her pen name suggests, Witting's writing is far from unwitting: it is done in full awareness or consciousness. Her characters face up to the circumstance of life and, in doing so, request that the reader must as well.

Critics usually focus on the aspects of Witting's novels that were autobiographical, depicting a childhood marked by a mother capable of unusual cruelty. Despite the dark subject matter, Witting's deceptively jaunty voice—particularly as worn by the unforgettably arch character of Isobel

Callaghan—captures readers' imaginations. When Witting takes flight in long form her brilliance is undeniable, yet it is her short stories that really flaunt her skill as a storyteller and, more strikingly, as a truth teller.

While the short story was not Witting's first love, over the course of a lifetime it became the genre in which she felt 'most at home'. In her preface to *Faces and Voices*, Witting offers the following as a statement of fact rather than an apology or justification: 'I began to write short stories because I could not get a novel finished. In my mid-thirties it became clear that I had neither the creative energy nor the physical strength to combine novel-writing with full-time teaching and the care of a household.'

At first glance, her explanation reads as one common to many women artists, including those such as Virginia Woolf who, even with house help and no children, still longed for a room of one's own. Witting wanted to write novels, but she also had to live: to earn money, nurture a marriage, survive an illness, run a household, bring up a child, build a career. Early on she made a pragmatic decision: in order to write well (and she wrote so exceptionally well!) she made what initially felt like a compromise on form, from long to short fiction.

It is a shift I can understand, for a story can be held in the mind in the way a novel cannot—all those words, all those possible directions. A short story can be attended to in small moments: I imagine Witting going about her other tasks while mulling over a phrase, mentally editing out the superfluous words that fall onto the page when a writer is desperate to make progress. Or perhaps she built her stories as paragraphs, one after the other, small adjustments made here and there? Or wrote in a flurry, capturing the essence before pruning and revising the telling? However she did it, Witting ended up with a wonderful array of keenly observed stories while also developing a unique style. This style, hinging on brevity and a clear-eyed realism, was then readily applied to the writing of novels when retirement afforded her the time.

'My idea is, to be a good parent you have to be yourself as successfully as you can,' says Isobel Callaghan, Witting's much-loved protagonist who returns for the last time— Witting did not live to complete the third Isobel novel—in this collection's first story, 'Soft Toys'. The line can be taken as a hint that Witting was not bitter at the prolonged approach to her writing career. As Yvonne Miels explains on her excellent biographical website, Joan Levick was a French teacher, and a very good one at that, who made her way up the career ladder to the prestigious position of Mistress of Modern Languages at North Sydney Girls High School and published French textbooks. She also taught English as a second language and wrote a book, *Each One Teach One* (1988), detailing the techniques she used. Passionate about teaching English to migrants, she was made a life member of the Smith Family for her work in this area.

By all accounts Levick was loved and appreciated by her students, while Thea Astley, a friend and teaching colleague, was intrigued by how well Witting managed her happy marriage alongside her writing. 'Somewhere I've picked up the notion that life is worth living. Don't ask me where,' says the irrepressible Isobel, much to the consternation of her dining companion, and despite (or perhaps because of) the predicament she finds herself in. 'Soft Toys' is, like many of Witting's stories, a defiant meditation on the restrictions society places on both men and women through the performance of gender roles.

It is unusual for authors today to speak of any job that is not writing as anything more than a means to an end. As the potential money to be made from writing plummets, many authors lament their need for an income that takes them away from the page; often a marker of career success is to have reached a point where one's time can be entirely devoted to writing. Without presuming there was no such struggle for Witting, particularly as she was a woman writing in a landscape that prioritised the words and thoughts of men, I am cheered by how she bucked the trend in balancing life, work and writing. It seems that Witting took pride and care in her career and family, rather than resenting them; she strived to succeed in these areas and she enjoyed this success. Levick the teacher, mother and wife were not in constant opposition to Witting the writer. She wrote in tandem with her career and life, rather than in conflict.

*

The stories collected here are a powerful testament to a lifetime's dedication. The masterly 'The Weight of a Man', set within the classroom Witting knew so well, demonstrates an uncanny ability to follow the true erratic nature of a person's train of thought. Far from a cool and logical rationalism, her protagonist's mind hurtles from one decision to the next as if encountering a series of switchbacks: 'Of course!' cries the reader at every turn. It comes as no surprise to discover that upon reading this story Patrick White wrote to ask Witting's advice on short-story technique, as he was keen to attempt the form.

I don't suppose that many people would think of Amy Witting and David Foster Wallace as contemporaries, though they published story collections within a year of one another. With his verbose, rolling style expertly juggling unruly, tangential narratives and profound insights into the human condition, Wallace is still considered by many to be at the avant-garde of the literary world. Meanwhile, the *New Yorker* described Witting's style as one of 'shocking economy'—the two writers could not be more different.

And yet, when I read Witting's superbly restrained story 'Knight in Armour', a hellish descent into the everyday evil born of disregard (a sentiment she revisits in the heartbreaking novella-length 'The Survivors'), I felt the same growing queasiness followed by a sucker punch to the gut as when reading the penultimate, titular story in Wallace's collection *Brief Interviews with Hideous Men* (1999). Both tell confronting stories of opportunistic rape, without resorting to cliché. Both demonstrate the capacity of the author to describe the worst aspect of ourselves, without tacking on a hackneyed denouement to dole out the punishment any good-hearted reader hopes for.

In 'The Survivors', a young shearer is forced to marry, and cannot understand how his callous disregard has led to this:

> He wasn't thinking about the girl at all, words like
> son-in-law and wedding coming at him like fists

from nowhere, and there she was in the doorway, the past on her face and the future in her great belly, and it shattered him, for he didn't give thought to either but travelled in the lighted cabin of the moment.

Witting and Wallace share an ability to make us reckon with our most unattractive emotions and behaviours, and to baldly consider how these two things—how we feel and how we act—so rarely intersect.

In 'A Bottle of Tears', Witting explores the ambivalence of what it is to be human, to want to be loved and to be alone. It is crude to cherry-pick quotations out of context, but who can resist such phrasing as: they had 'begun to make love readily and without grace, like awkward swimmers getting into water where there is no danger'?

Thea Astley encouraged Witting to submit 'Goodbye, Ady, Goodbye, Joe' to the *New Yorker*, where it was published in 1965. In brief exchanges between Joe and Ady, who are self-aware but never self-involved, Witting insinuates the ebbs and flows of a lifelong marriage, while fleeting images such as a son-in-law bobbing about floodwaters in an army duck, or Ady asleep with her false teeth clasped to her chest, give more character backstory than chapters of explanation.

Ady turned on him a look of morbid gentleness; it filled him with pity to see how fear had hold of her poor old sagging body. He ought to encourage her to talk, if it made her feel better. The trouble was that what seemed to help her was the very thing he couldn't stand—to have her soft, monotonous voice go on and on, not mentioning death but taking it for granted, not really facing it but thrusting the idea at him with sly, unconscious cruelty.

Witting is a joy to read, but I also find her a comfort. I wrote this introduction in stops and starts, snatching quiet moments as my one-year-old daughter slept, at each sitting not sure whether I would have the time to complete a paragraph or edit out my praise when it risked reaching saturation point. Each time I stopped to reread one of Witting's brilliant stories, I saw anew a perfect line here, an unvarnished truth there. As I send a recently finished novel to print and embark on a happily anticipated new job that is unrelated to my writing practice, I silently thank Witting for schooling me in writing's long game: for reminding me that effort pays off on the page rather than through publication, that writing is for life, but life is for living.

Selected Stories

SOFT TOYS

Phillip was finding it difficult to maintain his air of elegant detachment as he strode out among the lunch-time crowds in the thick, hot January air. The jacket of his expensive lightweight suit was clinging damp to his shoulderblades, making him wonder how well the cut of it was surviving the ordeal, and he was embarrassed by the bulky parcel under his arm, not only because it spoiled his outline – it was troubling his thoughts, too. It was Isobel's birthday present, not bought to please, a message rather than a present: this birthday business gave him the creeps and he wanted her to know it. When he had bought the present, it had seemed to him a stylish hint, but now he feared it was devious and hurtful.

You could hurt Isobel once and never again, that was certain – she would curl up fast like one of those little South American whathaveyous into an armour-plated ball and roll smartly away. If she did, he would miss her. He had been missing her badly enough for the past month – the birthday idea got on his nerves so much he had been keeping out of her way, but she certainly left a gap.

He walked into a woman who was standing gazing into a shop-window, was shocked by the thud and the contact of flesh, muttered 'Sorry', and walked on shaken. She had been standing almost in midstream but that was no excuse for him.

Style and presence. Watch yourself.

The birthday business was bad style, which finished it for him.

Why hadn't he said No, in that first conversation, when they could have told each other anything? There in Sean's living-room, with the party expiring round them, a strange corpse on the sofa, a couple or two upstairs, the faint sound of tired voices and the chinking of crockery coming from the kitchen, Isobel had sat on the hearthrug laughing quietly, unpacking the horrors of childhood with calm detachment as if she was looking through an old album of grotesqueries found in the attic – his own stance entirely, which he had never expected to find in anyone else.

'My mother could turn on a three-hour screaming match if you brought home the wrong brand of cleaning powder. Think what she must have been like, getting a girl when she was counting on a boy! I was lucky I got through the first twelve months.' She had laughed a cheerful survivor's laugh.

'And mine, of course, got neither. Or both.' He had added, with controlled amusement, 'My father used to call

4

me Phillipa, because I liked music better than football. The joke, I think, is on him.'

She had nodded in unspoken sympathy. 'My mother used to call me *child*. *Child, child, child*. And that is the thing she would never let me be.'

They had matched memories in a cheerful, non-competitive game of dominoes. Even when she talked about the real damage, she was calm, if not cheerful.

'You loathe and despise them but you have to keep trying to get a kind word out of them. There's a gulf between your feelings and your actions that you never close again. It makes you a non-person.'

That had brought them close to the nub, the inability to love that had set them both adrift.

She had come closer, saying, 'I thought being homosexual would be better, because you'd have made that effort to discover yourself, which must get you a bit farther along, and then, you'd be together against the world – I'd think that would be a good thing.'

'It's no better,' he had said without further comment. 'Oh, well!'

She had not sounded so careless when she said, 'The worst thing, you know, was the birthday – not getting a birthday present, when my sister did. That's the primal insult. I felt so fond of George Orwell when he wrote about his birthday at school – every boy in the school had a cake on his birthday, except him, and he never forgot that.'

Phillip had been startled. 'I used to get presents – quite lavish ones, but they always dodged the day, gave them the day before or promised them for the next day.'

5

'I tell you what – we'll have an arrangement. I'll celebrate your birthday and you celebrate mine. When's yours?'

'The twelfth of August.' He had felt sorry as he said it. He should have said, instead, 'Forget it. That sort of thing never works. You can't go back. Detach! Cut your losses and detach!'

She wouldn't have minded, then. He had been taken off guard, adjusting to the new insight about his birthday.

'Oh, good. Yours is first. Mine's in January. I'll buy you lunch.'

So she had, and had bought him a funny book. If her birthday had come first, he would quietly have forgotten the arrangement. This birthday idea was so unlike her – she was tough and sophisticated, yet she couldn't see how wet this was. It was girlish, that was the trouble – there were things he wasn't detached about, either.

Keeping out of her way hadn't done any good. She had rung him up and said, so happily, 'You haven't forgotten, have you? I turn twenty-nine on the twenty-third.' She was so confident of his friendship that he winced, thinking how little confidence she had in most things.

'I hadn't forgotten.' Deceiving truth.

Then he had gone out and bought the present, which he now regretted, thinking that it was bitchy, that is, girlish and poisonous too – out of the frying-pan into the fire.

She was there already and had got a table by the wall. He edged his way through the crowded room, wondering at the change in her appearance. It was that loose thing she was wearing, which didn't suit her – what an odd, stocky look it gave her.

6

'Hullo.' She sounded bright but uneasy – perhaps she hadn't liked having to ring him up and remind him, which showed how set she must be on the idea, to do it just the same.

This was going to be nasty. She'd get the message, all right. Isobel never missed a message – at least, a disagreeable one. He would have to pretend good faith and end up deeper in than ever.

'Happy birthday,' he said, handed her the parcel and sat down. He watched tensely as she unwrapped the winsome-faced white woolly dog.

Well, she wasn't offended. When she looked up at him, he was puzzled to see the relief in her expression.

'Oh, that's great. You know then. Who told you?'

'Told me what?'

'That I'm pregnant.'

That knocked the style out of him. He said, 'Oh, my God!' so loudly that people at other tables looked round at them.

The unforgivable sin. Style must be maintained under stress.

Even when he had assimilated the news, he had to consider the calmness of her tone, which was horrifying. He was not sure she had not gone insane.

'How far? How long?' But he knew now, from the look of her, that it was too late to do anything about it.

'A bit over half-way.' As if it was a journey she was looking forward to the end of.

'How could you? How could you just let it go on? If you didn't have the money, why didn't you ask me? I'd have given it to you.'

7

She smiled at that. He was sure now she had gone insane. Lost touch with reality, at least.

'All this time, you've known and said nothing about it.'

Sitting in the pictures, watching the Marx Brothers, laughing and laughing. Deceitful, treacherous.

The waitress was standing beside the table. He took the menu and stared at it. Since Isobel seemed to be composed, though mad, he said, 'What are you having?'

'Wiener Schnitzel.'

'For two, thanks. Black coffee?'

'Chocolate milk for me, please.'

Ugh.

When the waitress had left, he said, 'I can't understand you. It's bloody irresponsible.'

'Well, yes, I knew.' Sitting calm and thoughtful on the rim of the volcano, the very lip of the crater, she analysed the fatal irresponsibility. 'I suppose I must have known, but I managed to keep myself in the dark for longer than you'd imagine. My mind was curled up in the foetal position. Acquiescent, you might say.' She confessed, 'There wasn't any way I was going to have an abortion.'

He could not control his voice, on which style so much depended. He could only shout or murmur. Now it failed him altogether so that he produced a spinsterish click of the tongue.

'What about the man?'

She shrugged. 'The usual flash in the pan.'

'But what does he think about it?'

'I haven't told him. I suppose it's pretty obvious who it is, but if I'm not telling him, I don't think I ought to mention his name to anyone else, do you?'

8

She seemed to think that this trifle of moral delicacy quite made up for any hardship she was imposing on the man.

'You don't think it might be his concern?'

She made an uneasy gesture, clasping her hands together and pressing them to her chin.

'He could find out easily, if he wanted to. I think it's best to leave it at that. If he asks me, I won't deny it. I hope he doesn't, though.' She noted his expression. 'I'm shocking you.'

'Yes, you are. It's a dreadful thing to do to the man. The responsibility . . .'

'I'm not giving him any responsibility.'

'He can't help having it in his mind.'

'In his mind! Minds are tough.'

'It's shocking. It's a kind of rape.'

She stammered with laughter. 'You must admit, there's been plenty of the other kind. I'm just redressing the balance a bit.'

Rape had been a silly word to use – that showed how shattered he was.

'You're not . . . you're not thinking, are you, about keeping it? Trying to look after it yourself?'

'Yes, I am.' She looked past him, indicating that the waitress was coming.

While the waitress served the lunch, he sat rigid, frowning with distress. He had not known till now how deep Isobel's trouble was; because she had laughed at her history and her nature, he had supposed her to be somehow free of them.

'You can't. You can't. You'd never make a go of it. You'll finish yourself, that's all. Self-destruction, that's all

9

it is. That's your story, all the way. All those dreary, worth-less men, to start with – did you ever have anything to do with a man who wasn't an absolute penance? I don't know where you find them.'

'They find me.' Her voice was light, but tremulous. 'No, you're right. Being a born loser, you see, I only take on what I can afford to lose.'

'Oh, yes, you know, you know all right. You're a great one for knowledge, but where does, it get you?' He stopped. 'I'm sorry, I shouldn't have said that, about the men – it doesn't matter, anyhow.'

'It must have been in your mind.'

'Well, I must say, with that last one, I couldn't help thinking you must be punishing yourself for something.'

She laughed and said, laughing and shaking her head, 'It wasn't the last one.'

'I'm glad to hear it.'

'I wish you'd eat your lunch.'

She had been eating hers, calmly, stoking up, eating for two.

Feeling as if he was accepting defeat, he picked up his knife and fork. 'But it's no laughing matter. You're self-destructive, Isobel. This is the first chance you've had to do for yourself completely, and you're taking it.'

And that explained why she was so calm and smiling, like a suicide who has made the decision at last.

He had made her falter.

'It's not. It's not. It's quite the other way.'

'How do you think you're going to live and support a child? Have you thought about that?'

'Calm down, it's not going to be so bad. My aunt has come good, remarkably. I went and told her – I have to have somebody to turn to, if I get sick, or the baby does, and Aunt Noelene isn't a bad sort. She was a lot more sympathetic than I expected, she said she wished she'd had my nerve, instead of going through life with nothing. It gives you pause, doesn't it, the thought that your maiden aunt is no maiden? She said she'd take us in in a crisis' – the word 'us' jarred him – 'then she wrote me a letter, very businesslike, typical of her, she said she was putting it in writing so that I could think it over carefully before I answered. She offered to settle some money on me, enough to bring in twenty-five shillings a week, if I'd promise to look after her when she was old.'

'And you accepted, of course. You'd never miss a chance like that to bugger up your life for ever. Thirty years perhaps of waiting on an aged tyrant, carrying bedpans . . .'

She made a sour face. 'Not while I'm eating, if you don't mind. Look, if anyone offers me twenty-five shillings a week, in my present situation, I'm going to take it, aren't I? Of course I said yes. And once I've taken her money, I'll have to look after her anyhow, so I'm not losing anything by promising. I have looked after her before, that's how I caught up with her again. Margaret wrote and told me she was in hospital, a couple of years ago, so I turned up and did her washing and fed the cat, and when she got out of hospital I stayed with her for a while. It wasn't too bad. After that, she made an arrangement.' She grinned. 'Aunt Noelene tends to be businesslike. I go there to tea the first Sunday of every month, unless one of us calls it off.

11

It's good really – she calls it tea but she serves up dinner, claret and percolated coffee and liqueur chocolates and all. She's a good cook too. She's got some ideas about enjoying life. Besides, I think it's meant to mean something. And she's turned up all right about this, hasn't she? My little acid test.'

He ceased to chew for a moment, fearing she would pat her rising belly as if it was a pet dog.

'Life's hard enough, without being illegitimate.'

'Being legitimate didn't do you and me much good. Besides, it doesn't have to know it's illegitimate. You can always depend on me for a good story. That's one reason I don't want to tell him. I'd rather have a good lie than an indifferent father.'

Phillip had given up eating again. 'You're still bringing up a child without a father.'

'You're comparing with perfection, and who gets that? Plenty of children have terrible fathers – as I shan't fail to point out when the subject comes up. And life is difficult, all right, but surely the place is worth a look, if just for the scenery. I often think that. The play's a disaster, but the staging – bloody marvellous.' She paused, chewed and reflected. 'I see your point, all right. But I don't know . . . somewhere I've picked up the notion that life is worth living. Don't ask me where.'

He said, 'It's probably hormones. One of Nature's dirty tricks.'

'You're probably right. One of Nature's tricks but not necessarily dirty – at least you'll admit she knows dirtier ones.'

12

'Oh, sure. No limit in that direction. You've got all your arguments at the ready.'

'Of course I have. Been using them on myself, haven't I?'

It gave her an unfair advantage, he thought, as they ate in silence.

Isobel set down her knife and fork on her empty plate.

'I don't think Aunt Noelene would be such a tyrant. After all, she's settling the money on me instead of doling it out. I liked what she said, too – I said I had to have a house where the child could bring its friends, it wasn't going to work if she objected to the noise of children, and she said, "I don't know what I may be objecting to by that time. You will have to ignore me." I liked that.'

She could not win a word of approval from him.

'It's not just the money. I'll need Aunt Noelene, to get in with the family again.'

'I should think you would have had enough of your family.'

'But that was in another country and besides . . .' For the first time, she looked weighed down. 'Oh, I know what you must be thinking, don't think I haven't thought of it myself. I just have to hope that the wench is dead.' She shivered and steadied. 'I have to get in with the family. Cousins, Christmas presents, holidays in the country. Anyhow, suppose I die young?'

'I was wondering if you'd thought of that.' He was beginning to accept that she had thought of everything, but he tried again. 'Twenty-five shillings a week isn't going to get you far, you know.'

'We'll have food and shelter.'

That pronoun again.

From her elbow, the woolly dog simpered at him; he wished he had never set eyes on it.

'Shelter,' she said. 'It's a wash-house. With set-in tubs and an old fuel copper, and full of lumber, but it's a roof. So long as it doesn't leak. I went to Mrs Dean, I wanted to know if I could keep my room when the baby was born. She was very nice about it – everyone has been, except you – she said she couldn't let me have the room, there'd be too many complaints if the baby cried at night, but she couldn't turn out a girl with a baby, not a nice quiet little thing like me. Then she showed me this . . . outbuilding. It's got advantages . . .'

She embarked, if 'embarked' was the word, her voice being more river than traveller, on a long discourse on the wash-house: dark, but it would be better when she'd cleaned the windows; a concrete floor, but the Samaritans would give her an old carpet and some furniture . . .

'I thought I'd feel terrible, taking handouts from charity, but I don't. I think it's wonderful, people caring what happens to you. Perhaps I've found my niche.'

In the wall of the vault, he thought bitterly.

The wash-house would be cold in winter, not being lined; she was making wall-panels out of hessian . . . it was really interesting, all the different techniques for applying wool to hessian . . .

'Right now, I'm crocheting clouds. It's fun.'

Listening to her tone rather than her words, he perceived that she was happy. Not insane, just happy. He could fight no more.

14

Absent-minded, he became himself again. 'Sheer arrogance, bringing up a child in a wash-house.'

She laughed. That laugh of hers! She didn't just acknowledge wisecracks, she celebrated them – and prompted them, too. He was always wittier in her company.

'Believe me, I'll never draw the parallel. Well, Mrs Dean says I can have the place for nine shillings a week, if I get it cleaned out. I've got a man coming in on Saturday to take the stuff away to the tip. That's an economy, really – the sooner I can move in and start saving on rent, the better.'

He tried to step back on to the dais of disapproval.

'You still won't manage on twenty-five shillings a week.'

Her tone became reserved and she stared into the remains of the chocolate milk. 'Mrs Dean says I can get plenty of work cleaning the flats round about.'

'Oh, my God, Isobel! Cleaning!'

She answered him firmly. 'If you meet me with my pail and my rag, you have my permission to ignore me.'

He saw that he too could be judged.

'I'm not being snobbish. It's such a hideous waste of your time.'

'The only other thing I could do is take in typing, and I don't want to do that because it takes away from writing. It's writing that's going to come first, not the child. That'll come a close second. My idea is, to be a good parent you have to be yourself as successfully as you can. And I know, you don't have to tell me, I haven't made much of a go of that so far but now I've got a motive, and I will. I'll work twice as hard at writing, you'll see. I thought I might pick up a short story or two on my cleaning round.'

'So long as you find this way of life conducive to literary effort . . .'

'It'll be the only way out of the wash-house, won't it?' She looked at her watch. 'I have got to get back. I was hoping you'd come and help me hang the wall-panels. I can't climb ladders in my present delicate condition.'

She was nervous, waiting for his answer, yet she looked at him steadily.

He grumbled, 'If you had any decent feeling, you'd be jumping off the copper.'

She leaned forward, grinning, cupped her mouth and murmured, 'Not in front of the f-o-e-t-u-s.'

He laughed, and that was that.

'I'll come and help you hang your panels. I'll help you clean the place, but don't expect me to babysit or play uncle.'

Shining with relief, she got up, tucked the white woolly dog under her arm and patted it on the head, insolently, saying, 'You haven't made a bad start.'

Looking at her great-grandfather, it was hard for Frances to see why, old as he was, he should not live forever. What was perishable in him had dwindled. His hair was scanty, and his flesh had shrunk so that his bony wrists seemed to protrude from his skin like a schoolboy's from an outgrown coat. Around him, the surfaces of the furniture had disappeared under a homemade lichen of rugs, throws, doilies, and antimacassars, the slow growth of decades, among which he sat as solid as a crag – unimpaired, it seemed, in the more lasting elements of bone and spirit, for though there was a stick resting against his armchair, he held his great frame so erect that the stick seemed only another of the room's superfluous accumulations, and the look in his lashless tortoise eyes as he studied the tape recorder Frances had brought to the farm from Sydney was cheerful, inquisitive and bright with intelligence.

17

His daughter Ann, Frances's great-aunt, stood behind him, looking older than he and aged further by the gloomy look she fixed on the tape recorder, as if suspecting it of strange habits and of needing to be fed.

'It's not mine, Grandpa,' Frances said. 'It belongs to Mr Blount, the head librarian where I work.'

'What do you mean to do with it, girl?'

When she heard her great-grandfather's faint, labouring voice, Frances was reminded that one of the perishable things that had dwindled in him was life itself. Trying to keep her awareness of his frailty from him, she said, 'Well, Mr Blount is interested in Australian history, and I was telling him some of your stories about the early days. He wants you to talk about them, into the microphone, so that I can record what you say.' She heard herself speaking with the fierce sprightliness of a nurse.

The enterprise made her uneasy. She had objected to Harry Blount that recording the old man's memories, being too much like making a will, might frighten him with the thought of his death. That was a pretext, though she thought there was some truth in it. Her real objection was inadmissible – a selfish aversion to the effort of getting in touch with her great-grandfather on the far promontory where the aged stand. Mr Blount had dismissed her pretext. 'Nonsense,' he had said. 'The old gentleman will be delighted.' What had finally decided her to come, though, was the thought that she should not withhold Mr Blount's offer of a kind of immortality, even if it was an obscure immortality among the whining aboriginal music and the ballads sung by shearers in his collection of tapes – important to Australian history, no doubt, but dreaded by Harry's dinner guests.

The old man seemed, indeed, to be pleased. 'How do you work it, girl?' he said. 'What do I have to do?'

Frances set the machine on a low table beside him and removed the lid. 'Well, here's the microphone,' she said, putting it into his hand. 'All you do is hold it and talk into it. When you're ready, I press this button. I can stop it whenever you like.' Holding the microphone, he sat stiffly, looking shy and eager to please. 'What do you want me to say?' he asked her.

'Begin by telling us when you were born, and where.'

She pressed a button, and the reel began to turn. The old man took a deep breath and said, carefully and respectfully, to the microphone, 'I was born on the sixteenth of February, 1871, in a farmhouse on the Dingo Creek in the north of New South Wales. When I was five years old, we left the Dingo and went to live on the Camden Haven River.' He paused, looking at Frances for help.

'Do you remember living on the Dingo Creek?' she said.

Forgetting the machine, he said, laughing, 'One thing I remember, for sure. A cow butted me off the fence. Well, not so much butted me as came up behind me and nudged me off with her forehead, so down I tumbled.'

'That's marvellous, Grandpa!' The moment of physical sensation bobbing up so strongly in Time's unlighted waters made Frances laugh with pleasure.

Her laughter gratified him, and he smiled.

'Do you remember anything else about the Dingo?' she asked him.

19

The smile vanished and he shook his head. 'Too long ago, girl,' he said.

He was tired already. Frances switched off the machine and looked at her great-aunt for advice, but she could make nothing of the frown and the shrug the old woman gave. 'I'll play it back now and make sure it's recording properly,' she said.

When the old voice rose from the machine – a straining whisper, the voice of a ghost – saying, 'I was born on the sixteenth of February, 1871,' she thought angrily, What a damned fool thing to do!

But Grandpa was leaning forward, enchanted. 'Do you hear that, Ann?' he said to his daughter. 'My own voice.' With the delight one takes in a toy, he put his hand on the machine, repeating, 'My own voice.' He looked at Frances. 'Are they very expensive, girl, these machines?' he asked her. 'Are they beyond the reach of the ordinary person?'

Behind him, Great-Aunt Ann began a lively dumb show of disapproval. What nonsense, Frances thought. Why shouldn't he have one if it amused him? Old age should be a time of frivolity, like the great ball on the eve of Waterloo. Ignoring her great-aunt, she answered, 'Oh, no. Dozens of people have them. Young people have little ones as toys, even – though, of course, they are expensive for toys.'

He leaned back in his chair, smiled, and set the tips of his fingers together. 'I shall buy one,' he said.

After the unusual effort of making a decision, he rested for a moment, wearing a contented look, while behind him Ann shook her head, tightened her lips, and frowned. Then he looked toward the machine again with silent admiration. 'Girl,' he said at length, 'I'd like to think first what I'm going to say. I see that thing turning, and I can't collect my thoughts to keep up with it.'

'If you like, Grandpa,' Frances said. 'But it's better to talk as you always do and forget about the machine if you can.'

'Suppose I make a mistake.'

'It doesn't matter if you do. I can wipe it out easily enough. If I wind it back and press the button, it wipes out whatever you've said.'

He did not speak for a minute. 'And you're going to wipe this out when your friend has heard it?' he said finally.

The pause had been so long, his tone was so casual, that Frances knew the answer to this was important, though she did not know what the answer ought to be. In doubt and confusion, she decided on the truth. 'No, he means to keep it,' she said, aware as soon as she saw the old man's expression change that she had made a mistake. It was of his death that he had been thinking, and of his voice surviving his death.

As the old man's determined air faded into a look of doubt, Great-Aunt Ann said, 'Tell about the convicts. You know the stories your father used to tell – about that Miss O'Brien on horseback, and the convicts on foot, driving them over to Port Macquarie to be flogged.'

Gently astonished, he said, 'I don't know anything like that.' He paused, and framed a statement intended to dispose of the subject. 'There may have been convicts. I never saw any,' he said.

21

That could not be true, Frances decided, thinking of Port Macquarie, not twenty miles to the north – a penal settlement, with its convict-built church and, behind the church pews, the red brick floor where the convicts used to stand during the service. Transportation would have stopped, of course, years before Grandpa was born, but there would still be convicts alive to stand there when he was a boy. He was lying, calmly and with authority, as adults lie to children.

So much for Mr Blount's oral history, Frances thought. Among her acquaintances, it was the fashion to take a frivolous tone when speaking of the transportation of convicts from Britain. One usually quoted the lines

> True patriots all, for be it understood
> We left our country for our country's good.

She knew one or two people, even, who could advance to the end of the first verse, responding:

> And none will doubt but that our emigration
> Has prov'd most useful to the British nation.

How much closer to the truth, she thought, was Grandpa's lie, which made transportation seem real and terrible beyond words.

'I think I can remember the journey from the Dingo to the Camden Haven,' the old man said to Frances. 'Don't you turn that machine on, girl, till I'm ready. Give me a little time.' He held the microphone in his lap.

'All the time you like, Grandpa,' she said. 'Only don't tire yourself.'

'We went by bullock wagon, of course. Four days it took us.'

'Four days for fifty miles,' said Aunt Ann, shaking her head.

'There were no bridges. No people, either, between Port Macquarie and the Camden Haven. We had to go to the head of every river, to ford it. And my mother quarrelled with my father – the only quarrel I ever remember between them, and over such a little thing. She would not set the table without a tablecloth. He set up a table, driving forked sticks into the ground and laying planks across, and then she would have a tablecloth. Angry she was, at leaving her home on the Dingo, having to begin again. I can see her yet, in her long skirts, climbing up on the load and opening the bundle of linen . . . But she came to like Camden Haven. When the supply ship came in, she would walk down to the landing with four dozen eggs in a bucket, with me behind her, too small to carry a bucket, carrying eggs in a billycan.'

'Fourpence a dozen for eggs,' said Aunt Ann.

'But they didn't give cash. You had to take the price of eggs in goods the ship brought. Two little sailing ships that came up the river with supplies. One of them was called the Root Hog or Die – because of the little waves, girl. Those choppy little waves in the river. She had to put her head down into them like a hog rooting.'

'Tell us more about your mother,' Frances said. She put her hand discreetly on the tape recorder, trying to have it admitted again to the conversation.

23

This time, the old man looked at it with a reserve in which there was some coolness.

'She was a very ordinary person,' he said, removing his mother to a private room of memory out of reach of the machine, and the warmth and animation that had been in his voice and his expression as he told his story drained suddenly away. Now, as he sat concentrating, searching his memory, it was clear that he was really tired. His eyes became dull and his face strained with anxiety.

'It doesn't matter, Grandpa,' Frances said, beginning to be anxious herself, but he did not seem to hear her. At a sign from her great-aunt, she began quietly to close the tape recorder.

He looked round at it sharply, in such distress that she left it alone. 'Give me a minute, girl,' he said. Returning to his drifting thoughts, he sat absent-eyed with his hands clenched. Now and then his lips moved as if he were about to speak, but their movement sketched not the word but its silent flight, and he would shake his head, discouraged again.

He will make himself ill, Frances thought with dismay.

'It was something about the Dingo Creek you wanted?' he said.

Tired, too, from watching his struggle and wanting only to release him from the task he had set himself, Frances would have shaken her head but for the thought that if he must rack his brains so it had better be for something concrete. 'That would be very nice,' she said.

'Of all the people living on the Camden Haven then,' he said carefully, 'I am the only one left alive.' Then he was silent, until at last he seemed to seize on an idea and hold

24

it fast, leaning forward in excitement. But it escaped him, and he sank back in absolute dejection.

'Another day, Grandpa,' Frances said. He relaxed. She had discovered the words that released him from his anxiety. 'Another day,' she repeated, relieved of her worst fear – that he would exhaust his little remnant of life in the effort he was making.

'Girl, I wouldn't know what to tell you about it,' he said with painful resignation. 'It was just life, just ordinary living. There's nothing to tell.'

Aunt Ann broke in on him. 'It's time for your rest,' she said.

'What a foolish life I've lived,' he said. 'A life of constant, senseless striving. When I was sixty, I had four farms and not a thought in my mind but to own five. What could a man want with five farms?' He seemed to be asking the question of himself. 'And when I was a young man, it was to own my own bullock team. That filled my thoughts. I spent my days in the bush, splitting timber, to get together the money for a team. You could always sell split lumber before the sawmills came; that was what the supply ships took back to Sydney. Then working with a team, and paying half my wages every month to buy it . . . Till I was seventy, I never stopped to ask myself why I was doing all that.'

'You just lie down and have your nap on the sofa,' Ann said in the tone of one who had heard it all a thousand times. 'Frances can go across and visit her cousins.'

'No, you stay there, girl,' he said to Frances. 'I won't sleep long.' He gave her the microphone, then grasped her hand to lift himself out of his chair, took his stick, and crossed the room to lie down. As Frances put a rug across his knees, he closed his eyes and drifted into sleep.

'Auntie,' she whispered. 'Have I overtired him? I didn't mean to.'

'Goodness, no. He always talks himself to a standstill if there's anyone to listen.'

Aunt Ann didn't know everything about her father, Frances thought. She watched the old man breathing quietly and thought, with relief, that he was not going to die today.

'You ought to go over to the other house now,' Aunt Ann said.

'But he asked me to stay.'

'You'll be wanting a cup of tea then.'

'No, thanks. I'll wait and have something at the other house,' Frances said. A stiff drink, she added silently. How tired she was!

She was glad she had stayed, for soon the old man stirred and said, 'Frances.'

'Yes, Grandpa?'

'Frances, I remember. I remember waking up and hearing people move outside in the dark, and seeing a lantern swinging. They were loading the wagons, the night before we left for the Camden Haven. So that was on the Dingo Creek. The eleventh of December, 1875.'

He closed his eyes. She thought he was asleep, but he opened them again and said, 'You bring that machine back, one day, and I'll tell you all about it.'

Retreating without haste, Joe paused at the door of the private office, looked back and said, 'If you change your mind and want to place an order, I'll be seeing you about.'

He was crossing the outer office, wearing the placid look with which he concealed defeat, when the muttered words reached him: 'Not if I see him first.' The little girl at the desk raised her head sharply; her mischievous glance flew at him like a bright insect, but there was no sign of strain in the lazy, indulgent smile that went with his farewell nod.

The words rankled, nevertheless. Hours later the grievance rose like a cry to the surface of his thoughts, and he said to himself, 'What kind of salesman would I be if I gave up half-way?'

He was taking old Petheridge's order at that moment; the old fellow glanced at his face and said, 'Not yourself today, Joe?'

27

'Old age, my boy, old age,' Joe answered woodenly. Petheridge laughed heartily, but Joe was aware that his face had shown his thoughts, and was angry with himself.

That was the last call of the day. He had left his bags at the Royal and as he was crossing the hall Irma, the publican's wife, fatter than ever, but neat and pretty, came to meet him, taking quick short steps on her tiny feet, like a goldfish swimming vertical.

'Joe, darling, I missed you this morning.'

'I missed you more than I can say, my love.'

Joe hardly moved a muscle when he spoke, and the stillness of his face offset the extravagance of his words. It was a trick that delighted Irma, and she began to laugh as she took his arm.

'They gave you room 10, love, but I'll move your things into 16 before dinner. Coming in tonight?'

'Do I ever miss?'

The warmth of Irma's welcome was comforting, the bathwater was hot, and he had a bright evening in the little private bar to look forward to; he was almost himself again when he went down to the dining-room.

In the private bar, after dinner, he found the usual half-dozen people, and a pale, long-nosed girl perched on a stool, looking at a tall glass of gin and ginger on the counter in front of her.

'Now,' said Irma firmly to the girl, 'here's the man to cheer you up. For God's sake, Joe, try to brighten her up a bit. She sits in her room night after night with her bloody library book; twice a week she goes to the bloody library to change her books, and I'll stand no more of it. Wait till you die to get buried, I say. So she's coming in here for a bit of life whether she likes it or not.'

Out of politeness Joe sat on the next stool and ran the heel of his hand along the girl's too palpable backbone.

'Don't do that, please. I don't like it.'

'I grow on you, baby. I grow on you.'

'What'll you have, Joe?'

'A long, cold beer, love. I think I've earned it.'

The girl's harsh, determined voice was still ringing in Joe's ear. It started a thought in his mind. Too determined, maybe? Just for devilment, he ran his fingers along her spine, and was rewarded by a baffled and helpless look in her eyes.

'Afraid of mice, dear?'

He ignored her then, and began to talk to Clive and Irma. Irma kept her eye on the girl, saying now and then, 'Come on, Betty, drink up,' as if she could pour youth, joy and company down her neck.

The party was beginning to go well, and someone said, 'Come on, Clive. Give us "McDermott's Sulky".'

This was Clive's special party performance, which was tolerated as a tradition and asked for as a compliment to Clive. He began at once in the fine voice that grew more cultivated as he grew drunker:

'Now, McDermott had a sulky, and a daughter,
	rather bulky,
Unattractive, but a most obliging girl.'

Joe had heard it so often that his attention wandered; he looked at the girl and saw how pale she was. At first

29

he thought she was going to vomit, then he realised she was sick with disgust at Clive's recitation.

> 'And I bring to your attention, what I hardly like
>   to mention,
> There were heel-marks on the ceiling, upside-down.'

The girl stared into her glass in such misery that he said to himself, 'Why doesn't she go, then?' After years of dealing with that race of people, he still was astonished at them. Happening to catch Clive's eye, he gave him a confidential glance, placed an explanatory fingertip on the girl's half-empty glass, and then with the familiarity of old love put his hand under her elbow and took her outside.

She wasn't so healthy, either. She stood at the back door, dazed by the cold air, but she shook her head a little and said, 'I'm all right.'

'Yes, I know.'

At this she looked at him, surprised by the sensation of being not alone.

She said, 'Will you excuse me?'

'Sure. Coming back?'

'Oh, yes. I won't be a minute.'

Joe felt like asking, 'Why don't you say no, if that's what you mean?' He'd never gone so far as to wonder whether that was what they did mean.

He let her go and when she had reached the shadow of the opposite wing, he went to his car, fetched his flashlight, lit a cigarette and waited. At last he heard footsteps on the wooden stair that led to the bedrooms and switched on his light, catching her straight away in its beam. Being invisible to her gave him a feeling of power and he was so grateful to her for being where he had expected to find her that his voice was full of tenderness when he said, 'Where are you off to?'

Hearing the loving note in his voice she relaxed and answered confidentially, 'I suddenly felt I had to go and lie down.'

She didn't look too bad, leaning against the rail of the stair, the colourless feathery hair shining in the light, looking moth-like enough to rouse a vague poetic association in his mind.

'Lying down is the worst thing you can do. What you need is fresh air.'

She frowned, looking for him behind the beam of light. He switched it off and said indifferently, 'Let's hop in my car and go for a spin.'

'No, thank you.'

'Frightened?' he asked with sarcasm.

'Of course not.'

Oh, ho, a lucky strike. Got her sensitive point, he thought, perceiving the vanity that prided itself on having no vanity. There was authority in his tone as he said, 'Come on, then. It'll do you good.'

Hearing her come slowly down the wooden steps Joe felt the consciousness of his power in which he was most intensely alive: the rest of life was nothing, beside moments like that. The girl advanced into the moonlight and in spite of her words couldn't help looking uneasily into his face. She found his glance so indifferent that she flushed,

31

mortified again, and followed him to the car without a word.

As soon as she had shut the door she leaned her head in the angle between door and seat and apparently went to sleep. As Joe turned into the coast road the moonlight shone into the car and he glanced at the girl, seeing her again not transfigured but revealed. A silver spider, she looked like, and some fools might tell her so, but not Joe.

She straightened up after a while and he leaned across her to wind down the window, noting that she didn't move away from his arm when it brushed against her. Ten minutes later, he decided that it was time to get her talking. The fresh air would have done as much as it was going to do for her; they'd be there in twenty minutes and he had a long way to travel before then.

'Funny girl, aren't you?'

She opened her eyes and said, 'I don't think I am.'

'No. Perhaps funny isn't the word. Perhaps I mean different.'

He took care to suggest scientific interest, rather than flirtation.

'Different from whom?'

Joe laughed. 'There you are, you see. How many girls would say that? I've been in a lot of places, but I never met a girl just like you before.'

'You haven't been everywhere. For all you know there's a place where everyone is exactly like me.'

'I'd certainly like to see that place.' Good for Joe. That was the approach exactly.

32

'It's near the South Pole. You must come and sell us some refrigerators.'

This chilled him like a wind from the cold regions. He didn't see how to go on, for the moment; he didn't even know that he wanted to. He was tempted to say to himself, 'What the hell, she's not my type,' and take her straight back to town. He knew the next moment that if he did, his vision of himself would be altered forever, and then, looking at the girl, he saw that his silence had turned defeat to his advantage. She was looking at him anxiously, upset because her attempt at light conversation had miscarried.

'I'm sorry. I hurt your feelings.'

He didn't try to reassure her, but said, 'Think nothing of it,' distantly.

'It's a lovely night, isn't it?' she said after a while, and he let a moment pass before he spoke.

'The view from the headland ought to be good tonight. We'll go and have a look at the sea.'

She was like a kid, so relieved at being forgiven that she began to talk quite easily. She'd never been out to the headland before – how long had she been in the town? – five months – and never been so far? Funny girl – the library books and how Irma hated them. She laughed over that.

'Books take you further, though,' she said confidingly. 'Anywhere you want to go.'

'It's a lonely life, kid.' There he expected a break-through, but she didn't even look at him, simply shook her head and smiled.

'It'll be tough if you ever run out of books.'

She looked as if that would never happen. Funny girl, all right, he thought.

They were driving through the gateway of the deserted reserve then, and Joe drew up a few yards from the cliff edge in time to say, 'There you are. Better than all your books.'

She leaned forward and he slipped his arm behind her.

'The water's like a fish; a tremendous silver fish swimming for its life.'

'Is that out of one of your books?'

He saw what she meant, just the same. The moon shone on the broken surface of the water like a million scales flashing life and movement.

'What a night,' he said respectfully.

She leaned back, discovered his arm and straightened up as if it had burnt her.

'Cigarette?'

She nodded and took one, but she didn't relax.

'What are the lights over there?' she asked in a careful social tone.

'Falkiner's Bay. Never been there either, I suppose.'

'No. Is there anything worth seeing?'

This was painful. It could go on all night. Joe ran his fingers along her spine.

'An old church and a decent surfing beach, take your choice.'

He tried it again and found that she went on making conversation as if nothing were happening. He was wondering how much she was prepared to ignore, when he saw by her confused, uneasy look that she wasn't ignoring it.

34

She was afraid he'd ridicule her if she protested; and that's just what he would do, of course.

He let it go for a while and started again; under the thin dress he felt the back fastening of her brassiere and his heart began to beat harder, though he went on saying casually, 'I like the northern beaches better myself.' This was a real test of skill; if he could bring it off, why, he deserved to win out. She didn't seem to notice anything different about the movement of his fingers; he took his time and went on talking calmly. Suddenly the catch gave way under his fingers and she swung round towards him in a movement of protest he misinterpreted deliberately as an advance, taking her into an embrace from which she would never be resolute enough to extricate herself, saying (half-promise, half-apology), 'Better than all your books, darling, better than all your books,' as he began to unbutton her dress. There was a moment when everything was doubtful, and she might still begin to scream and fight, then he heard her sigh of acquiescence and it lifted the weight that had been on his heart all day.

With the clatter of young horses the members of the senior French class came into the classroom. They were nine large boys. Their teacher, Jenny Brundall, knew them well. She never looked at their closed adolescent faces without being glad she had taught them since childhood, could see in Colin's dark face the serious intelligent child he would carry safe into old age, could remember when the kingfisher glance of Alan Potter's beautiful eyes flashed in a round baby-face. Alan had changed so much that only the glance remained in a bony, irregular, secretive face which would have frightened her if she had been a stranger; after all, the rosy, solemn countenance of his childhood, disarming as it was, was only another expression of his reserve, for it had concealed mischief and intelligence. Of the nine, only Peter Leonard was a stranger, lately arrived from a boys' school in the city.

She handed out the corrected proses, and discussed the commonest errors which she had already listed on the blackboard. The class settled down to work.

In the silence Peter Leonard said, 'What's the matter with this, miss? I've got *capote* here, and you've crossed it out. "Without even taking off his overcoat," it says. What's the matter with *capote,* miss?'

Oh, damn, she thought. It was obscene, that was the matter with it.

'The word for "overcoat" is *pardessus* in this case.'

'What's the matter with *capote,* miss? It says *capote* in the dictionary.'

It gave him some satisfaction to repeat the word. She looked up and saw on his face a slight gleam that told her the obscenity was not accidental, and she felt a sudden intimate shock. When the length of old piping in the grass near one's feet comes to writhing, sliding life it is the lapse of the eye's vigilance that terrifies, more than the presence of the snake. For an instant she stood petrified, her confidence shattered, receiving the impression, from the absolute stillness of the others, that they were forewarned.

'It means military greatcoat, Peter. That isn't what is meant here.' She was tempted to smile, simply because to smile would be disastrous. 'I'm sorry you had to look up such a common word,' she added, speaking smoothly but too quickly, 'and I think you should have been able to find it in your own vocabulary note-book.' To the class she added, 'This is a very good example of the danger of using the dictionary carelessly.' She assumed a bleak,

37

set expression, trying to ward off the idiotic butterfly smile that persisted in trying to alight on her mouth. 'Supposing that one word is as good as another is like supposing that any coat will do, though you know quite well that one doesn't wear a military greatcoat to the office. Words have to be chosen according to circumstances too, so there is a limit to the use of dictionaries. If you use them wrongly you will only confuse your ignorance.' Deplorable, that; she was answering the boy's concealed insolence with concealed spite.

Alan Potter turned on Leonard a bright-eyed, uncommunicative look that indicated secret laughter, and Colin Ellis said easily, 'Would you mind explaining these six lines you've put under this trifling error of mine?' This familiarity was unusual for Colin, and she took it rightly as a gesture of friendship. 'Consider,' his tone said, 'how long we have known you.' This virtue which she had met once or twice before in Colin was the flower of intelligence; stupid people have other virtues, but not that one, thought Jenny. When she had dealt with Colin's mistake, she took up Alan Potter's book. Alan was her best pupil. He was taking Honours French, and she was overjoyed to discover that he was not going to escape enlightenment. As she wrote a correction in his book she said, 'The books have come, Alan. I got a parcels slip from the station this morning.'

All at once she was back with Ivan in the studio on the last day of the vacation. For the first weeks of the term she was haunted by the presence of Ivan and the atmosphere of the studio, but on that last day of the vacation when she was with Ivan her thoughts had been occupied with Potter and the books he needed from the Public Library.

'I absolutely must go and order those books,' she was saying to Ivan, who wanted her to go on posing for the drawing he was finishing.

'A lot of use you are, with that bloody, harried, self-important look on your face,' he grumbled. 'You might as well go.'

Obviously he didn't expect to be taken seriously, for he roared in protest when she got up.

'It won't take an hour, and it's really important. The boy won't be able to follow the course if he doesn't get the books. We don't have Villon and Mallarmé at the School of Arts, you know.'

Ivan probably didn't know what a School of Arts was, but he made no attempt to find out. He had no curiosity at all about the lives of other people.

'Oh, come back and sit down, for God's sake,' he said, with a burst of irritability like tears.

Jenny shook her head. She was painting her face in front of the mirror which reflected Ivan looking at her with a strained, uneasy frown, like an illiterate staring at a newspaper headline that might contain a threat. The claims of a boy in a country town seemed to him completely meaningless.

Jenny was shocked. She had never maintained the importance of anything in comparison with Ivan's work, but that was because it belonged to a whole class of things important enough to devote one's life to, and Potter's reading belonged to it too. She felt strongly that to fail one was to fail all, and was astonished that Ivan didn't think so too. It occurred to her that perhaps Ivan's paintings were important to him simply as things that Ivan did.

It was one of those moments the mind retains for a long time. Ivan, so deep in the mirror, appeared to have receded into the past, and Jenny thought that this might be the beginning of the end.

Meanwhile, with the detachment of the experienced teacher, she was writing notes in Potter's prose book. After all, she thought, Ivan's work, so austere and so convincing, stated those values she lived by and he seemed not to know. 'The summer's flower,' she said to herself, suddenly interpreting something that had escaped her before. 'The summer's flower is to the summer sweet, though to itself it only live and die.' She was expecting too much of Ivan, who was only called upon to live and die.

'You need the past anterior tense here, Alan, because of the tense in the main clause,' she said, and thought how good it was, after the uncertainties and tyrannies of art, to be back in a world where she knew the rules and applied them.

'If you give me the parcels slip, Miss B, I'll ride over and get the books at lunchtime.'

'I left it in the staffroom.' Just then the recess bell went, and she added, 'Come with me now and I'll get it for you.'

She was careful to conceal her gratification as he was to conceal his eagerness. For years she had practised such tact, had taken care always to be just, to be trustworthy, to be an acceptable authority, and she could not face the thought that one boy like Leonard could frustrate all her efforts, but she knew it was so, and under her discussions of grammar and her thoughts of Ivan she felt the drag of depression and anxiety. In the staffroom she searched her briefcase for the parcels slip with such a look of misery that her friend Margaret said, 'What's the matter, Jen? You look upset.'

She nodded towards the door to indicate the presence of Potter waiting outside as she took the parcels slip out to him, called after him, 'Bring your Honours prose round after school, Alan,' and came back sighing and rubbing her forehead.

'That new boy Leonard wrote some dirt in his French prose. I crossed the word out, thinking it was an accident, you see, and he cross-questioned me about it with a great smirk on his face, so I realised he did it on purpose.'

'The little beast! What did you do?'

'What could I do? I ignored it. If I'd realised when I was marking it I never would have marked the word out, but I've never struck anything like that before. I hope I never do again.'

There was so much anxiety in her voice that Margaret made haste to comfort her.

'The others would never play a trick like that. Imagine Colin Ellis!'

'I'm certain Colin wouldn't, but he's always been a bit of an outsider, and I don't think he has any influence. I don't know what the others would do. I don't really know them. Do you ever really get to know the children in your class?'

41

'But after years, Jenny?'

'I would have thought so too, but I'm sure they were all in on it. They were as still as stones while he was talking. Mind you, they wouldn't have the slightest idea that I knew what was going on.' She frowned. 'What's the point of it, then? It's like a story I read about some Oriental aristocrat who was offended by some people so he invited them to dinner and served them food mixed with human excrement.'

Quickly, Margaret put down her half-eaten biscuit.

'Thank you for telling me that.'

'Well, I wondered at the time what satisfaction he got out of it, seeing that they never found out. It's rather the same thing, isn't it?'

'No, it isn't the same thing at all. He isn't trying to insult you particularly, he's just trying to be smart.' She eyed her biscuit and decided to be hardy. 'It will all pass over; the others won't be in it because they like you.'

'Oh, as for liking!' Jenny shrugged her shoulders. She wanted something more dependable than that.

Looking at her severe, handsome face, Margaret thought with dislike of Ivan, as if Jenny's exclamation referred to him too. The two girls were so intimate that Jenny guessed the thought. Once she used to talk a great deal about Ivan to Margaret, but she had stopped because Margaret translated into a limited language of her own the painstakingly accurate information that Jenny gave her, and Jenny in consequence found herself involved in false-hood. Once Margaret, who found the situation exciting and agonising, had said, 'Suppose he met someone else while you were away?' Jenny had considered this as carefully as she considered everything.

'Well, I don't think he'd do any active courting, love. I don't think he'd go to the trouble. If some beautiful passive mermaid came in on the tide, well . . .' She shrugged her shoulders. 'I don't suppose I'd die of it.' I shouldn't like it very much either, she admitted to herself.

Carefully as she had answered the question, Margaret had asked it again, so she realised that it was actually a devious and timid defence of marriage, and ceased to give serious thought to her answers. Time and again she had said, 'I'm not in love with him,' but Margaret's ears rejected the words, and at last Jenny realised that this was her moral limit, and she could accept Jenny's affair with Ivan only so long as Jenny was too much in love to help herself. That was a pity, for Jenny very much wanted to talk about her feeling for Ivan and to demonstrate that it wasn't love. Ivan's value for her was that he let her into the world in which she wanted to live; to be near him when he was working was to be near the centre of the world. She admired the work so much that weaknesses in the man shocked her; he was a good artist, but sometimes she thought that given his choice he might have been a bad one. 'I know exactly what it would be like to lose someone you love,' she told herself. 'It would be like a fire's going out for ever. It would be like closing a window, to lose Ivan.'

Jenny knew all about love, for she had invented it. Her parents had been bound together by the real needs of hatred and the false comforts of respectability, and quite early in her childhood she had distinguished the real from the false.

As soon as she understood the characters of her parents, she saw that they were bound to make each other suffer. Her mother had no troubles she could display, but was convinced that pity was the only feeling worth inspiring, and her fantasies were so intense that she drew on the air the frail, romantic shape she longed to be. Frantically she tried to make her husband into the villain this situation demanded; if he were five minutes late for dinner there was a clamour, a rehearsal of grievances that rose to a climax of shrieking and sobbing. There was no living in peace with such a woman, for peace was not what she wanted. Jenny often wondered how perfect virtue would have confronted her, but she could not see any answer, and that gave her her first idea of the terrible severity of love, that as soon as one partner failed, both were punished.

To most people her father's behaviour seemed like perfect virtue. It was the cruellest part of her mother's fate, to be told often that she was lucky to have married a good-tempered, easy-going man like Stan. Stan took a quiet pleasure in substituting for the appearance of suffering that would have given his wife a temporary satisfaction, a real suffering she could neither understand nor express. He observed her agitation calmly, prompting occasionally when she omitted an item of her litany, attacking the delicate phantom, his wife's vital part, with no feeling apparent except contempt for such an easy mark. Once or twice a cruelty that seemed innocent but was carefully planned showed the tension of hatred and anger beneath his calm, and compared with this forethought her mother's raging seemed harmless to Jenny.

Love had to exist and to be as strong as hatred, or life would be intolerable. So Jenny set about inventing love, and modelled it on her parents' hatred, an intense demanding passion ruling every moment, requiring her mother's intensity of feeling and her father's diligence. Knowing nothing about social pressure, or the sexual passion and its mysterious connection with one's secret desire to suffer or to inflict suffering, to be extinguished or to live for ever, she supposed love had brought her parents together, which made it seem an unreliable and perilous arrangement. When she grew up she professed the belief that human love was the greatest good, but she thought of it as a beautiful and complicated piece of music, quite beyond her powers of execution; to attempt it and play one wrong note would bring down on one's head an overwhelming curse. So she was always setting tests for love and being relieved when she failed them. If I loved Ivan, she thought, I wouldn't care whether he was a good artist or a bad one. But I do care. It is really the only thing that matters to me.

She was tempted to tell Margaret that Ivan had proposed to her, but she wasn't quite sure that it was true. Certainly, just before she had left to catch her train, he had looked gloomily at the unfinished drawing and had said, 'Can't you get a move to the city? Would they move you if we got married?'

'Not before the end of the year,' she had answered, which meant perhaps that she was engaged. She should, of course, have pounced in a ladylike way, and obliged him to make his meaning plain, but that would have meant making her own meaning plain, which she was, after all, not ready to do. She had never experienced and could not imagine a love that would withstand the rigours of marriage, yet the prompt, whole-hearted refusal hadn't risen to her lips as she had expected.

With the parcels slip in his pocket, Alan Potter went to join the others at the end of the playground. They slouched on the grass, their minds so idle that they stared at him simply because he was moving.

'How's Miss B?' said Leonard, emphasising the initial in a pointed manner.

To show his opinion of this insinuation, Potter allowed his face to sag in a look of idiot amazement while he stared at Leonard.

'She wouldn't change much in two minutes, I suppose.'

'Thought she might have found out what a *capote* was.'

'She was on to you about that,' said Ellis.

'Oh, rot!'

'Yes, she was. She got that gloomy, set look. Always does when she's keeping a straight face.'

'You rave, Ellis, you rave. Where would she find out about a thing like that?'

'There's always the dictionary, son.'

Perceiving the taunt, Leonard muttered in rage, 'Only place she'll ever see one.'

'Shut up,' said Potter sharply, moved not by loyalty to the teacher but by the painful confusion he felt from time to time, when it came over him that a carnival of grotesque behaviour rioted under the sober surface of the world he knew.

'The Honours boy,' said Leonard.

Potter let this pass. It was useless and unnecessary to explain to fools like Leonard the satisfaction that Honours French gave him, the feeling of carrying a gold coin in his pocket and now and then running his thumb over its reassuring milled edge. He needed such a talisman at the moment, since existence was complicated and uneasy; life appeared inviting, yet punished his advances, and he twisted sometimes for slight reasons on the skewers of shame, while every new thing attracted him so strongly that he could never live cautiously. In books he found the passions and the oddities of human behaviour and the words of love and anger safely written down, losing nothing but their power to hurt and to alarm, gaining something that made them more satisfying than they were in life. There was another satisfaction too. The work was hard, and he was pleased to find that he could do it; it made demands, and when he met them he gained not maturity but entry into a world where one did not have to prove maturity or virility, because they were of no account. Voltaire and Verlaine spoke as freely to him as to anyone else; all he needed to bring was the understanding mind.

At the end of the day Jenny was really too tired for the French Honours lesson. During the last lesson of that afternoon she had to concentrate on preserving her self-respect in front of a rowdy Second Year class, in front of which she stood like a desperate matador evading the mortal thrust of ridicule. She came back to the staffroom where the others were getting ready to leave, and the quick succession of small sounds, the whirr of a zip-fastener on a briefcase, the snap of a locker door, the scrape of a chair, which marked the end of every day, convinced her that all days were the same, and she longed to be married, but not to Ivan; she dreamed of a hero of legend intervening between her and 2B.

'Potter left a parcel for you just after lunch, Jenny. I told him to leave it on your table,' said the English master.

Unwrapping the parcel and finding the shabby, sound old volumes with names as familiar as the names of friends, she decided she could give another lesson after all.

'Put your head in as you go past Fifth Year room and tell Potter I'll be five minutes, will you? I must have another cigarette.'

'Don't work yourself into the ground, my girl. How is Potter going?'

'All right, I think. He can when he likes, you know.'

She opened the volume of Madame de Sévigné's letters, reading here and there while she looked for one that would appeal to Potter. All at once she realised that for Potter the barrier of language had disappeared, and she was thinking only of limits in his taste and his experience. I did that, she thought, taking heart, and she stubbed out her cigarette and went to Fifth Year room.

Potter had left his prose book open on the table. She nodded to him, and picked up the prose. He came and stood beside her to watch the correction. It was a difficult piece of translation, an elaborate and formal dialogue between a ladylike but sprightly Victorian miss and a worthy suitor whose proposal of marriage she was determined to parry. As usual, Jenny did not refer to the text book but read quickly through Potter's version, translating it into English mentally as a test of expression. Suddenly she stopped. '"Pray rise, sir," said Miss Lydia, no longer able to support so heavy a lover.' '– *Veuillez-vous lever, monsieur, dit mademoiselle Lydia, ne pouvant plus supporter un amant si lourd*.'

Dreamily she turned to the original. '"Pray rise, sir," said Miss Lydia, no longer able to endure so tedious a suitor', and as she read it she saw again the look of drowned merriment Potter had turned on Leonard that morning. She knew now that it was not ridicule it had conveyed, but complicity, for this was the same thing, though a hundred times as clever. Shock had paralysed her for a moment this morning; now it was the weight of sadness that slowed her thoughts. My life is too narrow, she thought. I invent consolations, I delude myself. She had believed she was communicating something of great value, and now she was crushed by disappointment. That the joke was clever seemed to her the hardest thing to bear; the sentence shed its ludicrous impropriety over the distinguished sentiments the couple were expressing, and made their artificiality ridiculous. It was her kind of joke, aimed at her in hostility or at least with crushing indifference.

Then the boy said, 'What's the matter?' in such a natural voice, so free from guilt, that the world righted itself. After all, it was an innocent mistranslation.

How could she ever have thought he would embarrass himself by embarrassing her? Besides, she thought, it wasn't a boy's joke. Boys weren't much inclined to put themselves in the other person's place. Oh, lord, she thought, I believe I am going to laugh. Miss Lydia and her ponderous suitor appeared more ridiculous every moment, and her sudden intense relief seemed to have weakened her self-control. As she advanced from line to line, underlining and discussing mistakes, aware all the time of the approach of the deadly ambiguous sentence, she set her face in a stern, unresponsive expression. 'Not *lourd*, I think; *ennuyeux* might be better,' she said. There was something in her voice that made the boy look into her face, and though she was certain it was quite expressionless whatever he read there made him look at the sentence, staring until slowly its hidden meaning occurred to him. No matter how slowly, there was no way of stopping it. At last he stood up, snatched his book and said, 'I hate you,' with bitter authority.

What a fuss! Jenny thought angrily, at first, then as slowly as he had deciphered the sentence, she read the meaning of that strange mixture of grief, disgust and indignation in his face. It wasn't a boy's joke; it wasn't the joke of an innocent woman either. It was the coarse, comfortable chuckle of old Margaret in *Much Ado*, when Hero talked of the heaviness of her heart: ''Twill be heavier soon, by the weight of a man.' Oh, there was no hiding it; she knew to an ounce what a gentleman weighed.

So there she stood, naked and hideous in the boy's eyes, and likely to remain so for ever, since time had stopped. There was room for everything in that extended moment; she could trace events backwards and lay the blame on Peter Leonard, reflect on the irony of her remark to Margaret, 'Oh, as for liking!' 'Poor kid,' she said to herself now, 'I hope he likes me.' Nothing else could interpret the situation for Potter but a particle of real affection. She even had a vague, surprising idea about love, but it slipped away from her without words. She would have said to the boy, 'Can't you see that it makes no difference what I am?' but she could not say what she was.

As if his own words had just reached his ears, Potter's look of anger changed to a touching look of worry and confusion, and he hurried out of the room.

In ten years' time he'll look back and laugh at himself, she thought. How unfair it was that she should know what it was like to be seventeen and he have no idea what it was like to be thirty-two. Only too well she knew what it was like to be seventeen: was seventeen again herself and tasting disgust, feeling the wretchedness of adolescence giddy in the void of inexperience. Life was dirty, drab and miserable, and she had an anguished feeling of being lost in time, lost in herself. She longed intently for Ivan, and thought her inconsistency comic. Wasn't Ivan the cause of this self-disgust? But the feeling was so extreme that the vision of Ivan rose incongruously innocent, and she thought of everything she liked about him and would like for ever, the simplicity and directness that took the place of humour in his nature, the hardy indifference he felt about making himself ridiculous, and the mildness of temper he tried to disguise with blunder; she thought of the freedom with which they told each other their thoughts and the complete lack of malice in their dealings, and realised that their relationship was thoroughly respectable.

Meanwhile her misery assembled its context from the past, and she recognised herself at seventeen, trying with nausea to reconcile what she knew of her parents with what she had learned about sex.

Love was going to save me, she thought. Love was going to gild the woodwork and repaint the furniture. But I'm like them, though I'm luckier. I never found love, and I did without it.

At least I won't marry. I'll never risk that. She had never liked Ivan better, but she had to be done with confusion and difficult decisions, and, having given her sadness a home in the present, she felt unhappy but secure. It seemed a noble frame of mind, a victory at least over the sordid, and peace of mind seemed to be worth the price she was paying.

The next day in class Potter engaged Jenny's glance, discreetly and deliberately. His look was shy but determined, and there was a gleam in it that indicated his willingness to laugh at himself if she would laugh too. At her faint reassuring grin his face relaxed, invaded by happiness, and Jenny thought with wonder, I could never have done that. She hadn't loved her parents, and this was the first time in her life that she had admitted it. Not because they didn't love each other, but because I didn't love them. What a little prig I was, that I couldn't admit it!

She had a light-hearted feeling that difficulties had disappeared, and the boy had given her something of permanent value, and at last she realised that her old idea of love had vanished. She had discovered something easier, more commonplace, that would do just as well. With amusement she looked at the ponderous old vehicle, high-built and armour-plated, which had carried her across the dangerous desert of childhood, haunted by the sly, deadly serpent and the fierce bird with the poisoned beak. It was time to get down now; the country had changed and the natives were friendly. She was going to marry Ivan, after all.

A BOTTLE OF TEARS

While Rita was waiting in the corridor outside the doctor's office the door opened and the doctor himself came out, shepherding a tall, thin man on whose face there was a look of intense concentration.

The doctor recognised her and said, rather irritably, 'Are you next? Go in,' so she went into the little room and stood looking aimlessly about at the desk, the examination couch, the lighted screen on which a chest x-ray was hanging, her mind quite occupied by the question of whether or not she should sit down, when the doctor came back and hurried across to the screen, exclaiming, 'It isn't yours!'

'I wasn't looking,' she answered, 'so it doesn't matter.'

He put his hand on the frame of the x-ray, meaning to remove it, but it drew his gaze again and he looked at it with pain and anger, muttering, 'I wouldn't want to see that in your chest, never,' unconsciously revealing his affection and giving her the impersonal joy one feels at the sight of a fragile-looking plant growing in conditions that bear witness to the toughness of the species. He was indiscreet, she perceived, because he was concentrating so much on the x-ray that he wasn't quite aware of her presence.

With an effort he put it away and, setting Rita's in its place, he produced a complete change of atmosphere, like an Elizabethan scene-shifter.

'Why don't you stop wasting my time?' he asked, pretending severity in order to subdue a smile of joy which would have been really excessive.

'As good as that?'

'Couldn't be much better.'

He opened a book and began to ask routine questions more seriously, and Rita gave the expected answers, but when their eyes met they both smiled, and as Rita was walking to the door her feet performed an irrepressible dance step. She looked back smiling at the doctor, who said, 'No silliness, now.'

'Everything in moderation, even silliness,' she answered, and closed the door behind her.

Outside the weather was splendid, with warm sunshine and a small wind playing in the street. A wonderful day for a walk, she thought, and set off to walk down Oxford Street to Foy's, meaning to drink a cup of coffee on the piazza and look at the park. On her way she paused outside the secondhand shop to smile over a framed panel of looking-glass decorated with a painted white swan, green reeds and a pink waterlily, and decided with surprise that it was pretty.

Suddenly, the money she had saved during months of austerity began to run in her veins and she went in to ask its price. Inside, on a table covered with dusty china ornaments, she found a narrow silver vase and bought that too. She promised to call for the panel and left, quite unrepentant, carrying the vase and planning the redecoration of her room: a dark floor – get rid of that dirty old carpet and polish the boards, she thought, drawing on her energy as freely as on her bank account – no whatnot, no epergne, no jokes except the glass panel, a Lalique swan on the mantel and a white rug with some pink and some green in it. She walked on, planning happily, without noticing her progress, until the laughter of children on the piazza reminded her that the schools were on holiday.

There were only half a dozen children after all, darting about and laughing with upward glances. Then she saw the bubbles, puffed out of a pipe masked with flowers high on the shopfront. The breeze was juggling them and letting them fall, and a little girl who had caught one opened her hand and looked into it with a painless cry of disappointment.

One bubble – how bright it was in the sunlight, outlined sharply with blue and purple – performed a slow descending dance and drifted past a young woman at one of the tables, who let it go and turned smiling to speak to her companion in a language Rita didn't recognise. This was a moment of poetry, a compound of the sunlight and the greenery that framed the woman's head, the foreign voice at home and at ease and the memory of an old map of the Terra

Australis that had always prompted her imagination; and she thought, they are the real inhabitants, the migrants, the first since great-grandfather.

How did that thought bring Matt so close beside her that his absence was really a shock? Almost, she had turned to speak to him. It was one of those strange moments when one feels that a previous experience is repeating itself, but she had never been here with Matt. Of course, of course, the woman at the zoo.

Rita sat at the table drinking her coffee, seeing again the tall fair woman in the checked topcoat, standing at the top of a rise, looking down at the basinful of blue water flagged with white sails, saying 'Wunderschön' with quiet satisfaction. It was then that Matt had been standing beside her.

There is something about that trick of the mind, fusing past and present, that moves the heart extraordinarily. Is it oneself one greets with such sadness and astonishment? Rita drank her coffee thoughtfully, gazing at the park but after all without seeing it. Only the stream of traffic that flowed past the park, with the weaving of movement and the flashing of sunlight complicating its surface, drew her gaze and entered her thoughts. When she had drunk her coffee, she went inside to the telephone and rang Matt's office.

When he came to the phone, she said uncertainly, 'Matt? This is Rita.'

The silence that followed was just what she expected, for the underground river of malice ran so far beneath

57

the surface in Matt that he could never be nasty at will; but she was frightened by it for all that, feeling that nothing she knew of Matt was of any value and that at the other end of the line there was an unknown, unlimited power to harm her.

'I don't see much point in this.' Matt was angry, but only Matt, after all.

'I changed my mind, that's all. You don't have to change yours on that account, of course,' she added in a false and arrogant tone that dismayed her. 'I just thought I'd tell you, that's all.' She waited, exposed to the abominable black receiver, feeling tired all at once, thinking that it would be a relief if the blow fell now. How easy it would be not to love at all!

'You really mean it?' Matt's voice was full of reverence, not for her nor for love, but for good luck, which he respected as other men respect money and fame. It was true that Fate was strict with him, and his wit, his kindness and his good looks were slightly tarnished by an amiable resignation.

'Is it all right?' With joy and relief, Rita began to laugh.

'Where are you?'

'I'm in town, at Foy's.'

'I can get the afternoon off.'

'I can't believe that. I'm sure this is just the day you have to work back.'

'No fooling, this is my day. Can you stay where you are? Half an hour, not much more anyhow.'

'All right. I can do some shopping and meet you on the terrace.' She was inclined to laugh at Matt, the scientist ruled by the stars (ruled by every bloody thing, kid: the stars and science, prenatal influences, economic laws, the boss and what have you), but there did seem to be some magic about the day which allowed her to repair so quickly that moment of loss and isolation.

Upstairs in the dress department she found a green and gold dress that seemed to be made for her, and when she tried it on she considered her reflection in the fitting-room glass, that reflection of a reflection one never sees otherwise, the profile of a stranger about to walk away, and was astonished as usual by its beauty.

She had been a plain girl and had become a beauty unexpectedly when she grew up, and the only thing in her face that she recognised as her own was the mark of her inward anxiety, which remained like the ghost of a frown when her face was in repose and gave her a gentle, sympathetic expression. Today for the first time she could accept her good looks without uneasiness as an accidental glory like the weather and the new dress, having discovered transience as the flaw in everything that made it her own. Matt, too, she thought – remembering the urgency of his question, 'Can you stay where you are?' – wanting that one moment kept for him till he came; having just embarked on the current, she thought, of course I can't, and felt wise, experienced and full of courage.

But, as Matt was walking up the steps towards her, she felt quite deformed by nervousness, marooned in a nightmare on a stage to play a part she didn't know and feeling that everything she said to him from now on would be a desperate guess.

She looked at him for a cue, but he took her parcels in silence, looking happy but remote, and his happiness weighed her down with responsibility as if he had given her something fragile to carry.

'New dress,' she said as she handed over the big box. He grinned and took a slip of paper from his pocket, saying, 'Lottery ticket.' He was nervous too, and their laughter sounded forced.

They didn't talk much until they had closed the door of Matt's room behind them and begun to make love readily and without grace, like awkward swimmers getting into water where there is no danger. Rita said then, 'I had the experience of losing you suddenly. It was one of those moments, you know, that you seem to have lived through before, and I thought you were with me for a minute. It wasn't that I found I couldn't live without you, you see – it's so easy to begin to falsify things —'

'Is that what you're afraid of?'

'Oh, the things I'm afraid of,' she was shaking her head, 'they're too ridiculous to mention. Missing the train, losing the key, not understanding the directions, not hearing what the man says. You could overcome any one of them but there are too many.' Her face was bright and heavy with embarrassment, and Matt, quite startled, said, 'Nothing to be ashamed of.'

'What you're ashamed of is just the thing you are. You'll cover it up even with something worse.' She was silent for a moment, then she added, 'Gulliver tied down with threads.'

'What's that?'

'Gulliver tied down with threads, that's what I am.'

Matt didn't quite follow but he was glad to see her beauty restored.

'You know, Matt, I think I could change, perhaps, but I couldn't bear to have it expected of me.'

'I suppose I can stand you as you are.' He added, 'What you don't see is that happiness is pretty commonplace really. Anyone can have it, even people like you and me.'

This was said without irony and Rita could find no word for it except politeness, but it extended the meaning of the word.

'There's nothing new, is there? About being lovers, I mean. It's all in the past, like a graph that's been plotted already.'

'What was I trying to tell you?'

'And now I know.'

Matt said, 'Let's go out to dinner tonight. Somewhere really good, where we can dance. I'll ring up and book a table.'

'Somewhere with a view of the harbour. I could wear my new dress. You know, I never knew what those places were for, before.'

'Some people eat there regularly.'

'Very nice of them, too, to dress up and dance divinely and eat lobster thermidor on our account.'

'Probably they don't look at it like that.'

'Probably not.' Rita was smiling. She had always felt most alone in crowds and in public places, and now she was thinking that she would never really belong to a crowd again.

It was a wonderful evening, and in the elegant restaurant they did not seem out of place. 'Nothing went wrong,' Rita said when they were back in Matt's room, 'but if anything had, it wouldn't have mattered, and that will always be the main part of love for me. All the talk about what love is,' she added, yawning, very slightly drunk, 'I can tell you what it isn't. It isn't an abstraction. I love you has meaning, but the word love has no meaning; it's a participle, particle, something or other.'

'Grammar, for God's sake,' Matt said, laughing and putting his arms around her.

They fell asleep so close together that Matt woke up, hours later when the room was beginning to grow lighter in the dawn, because her sobs were shaking his chest like a grief of his own.

He whispered, 'Old girl, what's the matter?' But she shook her head and went on crying.

When she tried to speak, the man at the clinic appeared on the surface of the storm like flotsam and was drowned again.

'What man?'

He thought he heard the word 'dying', or was it the end of a sob followed by a brief sigh? No; she said coherently then, 'It's a man I saw at the clinic today, a man who's dying.'

For Christ's sake, he thought angrily, why bring that up now? He said, 'How do you know he was dying? Nobody would tell you a thing like that.' But he knew it in spite of himself, for the conviction that had been in the man's eyes and the doctor's voice was in Rita's crying too.

'An accident.' The word was cast up broken. She said again, 'An accident. I connected a face with an x-ray. Something the doctor said.'

There will always be someone dying somewhere, he thought, astonished at this simple device for destroying happiness, and his memory returned to him something it had kept intact, Rita saying in a queer, affected voice, 'I don't think I'm capable of happiness.' At the time he had shouted, 'What damned sickening nonsense,' but after all it was the queerness of truth, a deepsea fish hauled to the surface.

'If you'd seen his face –' Rita sat up to look for a handkerchief, and in the twilight he saw a relationship of chin and shoulder that was like the first glimpse of the person one is going to love. Oh, well, he had promised to love her as she was, and now he knew what that meant.

'It seems terrible that I didn't think of him all day,' she said, still wiping away tears. 'It was such a wonderful day.'

'Your crying won't help him, kid.'

'No, I know. If I put my tears in a bottle and sent them to him, it would be nothing, a bottle of salt water. He'd look at it and wonder what the hell. What else is pity, anyhow? If I knew him, if I knew what to say to him better than anyone else, it would all be the same to him. Not because he's dying but for what he is now, cut off.' She took his hand, saying, 'Matt?'

'Yes, my darling?'

'I've been an absolute fool, haven't I?'

As he realised what she meant, his love extended to include the dying man, who was not, after all, an intruder.

GOODBYE, ADY, GOODBYE, JOE

The low hill on which Joe's and Ady's old farmhouse stood lay in a loop of a little river, which had been growing bigger during three days of rain. In front of the house and a hundred yards below it, the banks were flat and covered with round stones, and there, the river had been spreading into a shallow lake with ripples visible at its advancing edge. Since the rain had stopped, shortly after noon, Joe had spent long periods at the kitchen window, watching. Where the river ran behind the hill, the banks were steep and the bed narrow; he knew the spot, out of sight five hundred yards away, where the water would spill over into the gully and run down to join the new lake, turning their hill into an island. This was the event that established the flood for him as a full-sized one with its modest place in history, so when the swimming water advanced round the side of the hill he called out to Ady with a note of satisfaction in his voice, 'It's through the gully, Ma. Here it comes.' Plenty of go in it still, he thought. He had had to wade through floodwater on his way back from seeing the cows onto high ground, and, feeling it clutch and drag at his high rubber boots, imperious and cold as death, he had been astonished at the force of it.

The old woman came shuffling to stand beside him at the window. 'Stay out of my garden, you devil,' she said angrily to the advancing streak of water. They stood then, staring while the new river ran down into the new lake, and Joe, who had lived for nearly seventy years on this farm at the centre of the world, thought of the two miles that separated them from their neighbours across the river, the eight miles between the farm and the town where their daughter Roslyn lived with her husband and children, the hundred and ninety miles of railway that connected the town with the remote, humming and glittering city of Sydney, and saw himself and Ady at the edge of all that distance – not at the world's centre, after all, but at its edge. He felt prompted to turn and speak to his wife, but idleness had made them shy with each other. They lived alone unless one of the grandchildren was spending a holiday at the farm, but they were always busy; now, with nothing to do, they were bashful, though full of goodwill, like young lovers.

'I'll put on a cup of tea,' said Ady, 'if you'll stay put to drink it.'

Joe grinned at the reproach. The flood attracted him constantly, so that he had left cups of tea standing to go cold and forgotten food on the table, to walk down the hill and gaze at the sheet of water welling towards them.

'Looking won't help,' she said. 'You ought to take your chance to get a good rest,' – as if the flood were a hostile neighbour against whom one must score what one could. She stoked the fire in the kitchen stove, lifted one of the stove lids and dragged the kettle over the circle of flames. 'It'll be in the town by this, I suppose.'

'Ros and Arnold never need to worry, living on the hill. Highest it ever came in the town was the window sills of the Commonwealth Bank, and that was the big one in 1920.'

Ady knew this as well as Joe, but, history being the man's province, she would have thought it unbecoming to mention it. She listened with respect while Joe talked, as he drank his tea, about the big 1920 flood and compared it with the flood of 1932, which they called their own, recalling, too, what he had been told about the flood of 1889. During the 1920 one, while they sat isolated in the farmhouse, the talk had been of the 1889, and of this talk Joe now told all that he remembered, Ady helping him with a question when he paused. Only the far-off, freakish deaths were passed over in silence. The calamities they recalled were small ones – 'Every plate in the cupboard broken.' These were offset by marvellous lucky escapes – 'But not a chip out of the cut glass in the sideboard. She picked it up and she put it down like a mother cat with its kittens.' What they liked best were the comic stories of survival, and Joe was telling one of them as he finished his second cup of tea. 'Rolled his clothes in a bundle, see, to swim it, and lost the bundle half-way. So, no help for it, in he came, mother naked, and there stood the Reverend's wife. Come over to help with the cleaning up, and she stood there with the mop and the bucket like she was turned to stone. I don't think she ever got over it.' Blushing and grinning, he set down his cup and went across to the kitchen window, where his smile was extinguished.

'My word, she's moving, Mother. She'll be in your garden, all right.'

'Oh, the devil,' Ady wailed with temper. 'Oh, the dirty devil. My poor flowers.'

'Flowers are tougher than you think. My mother said the first thing through the mud after the '89 were the sweet peas. The old lady never forgot those sweet peas, standing up there pink and white with not a mark on them.'

'Don't mention mud to me,' said Ady.

'No use getting cranky with it, Mother,' he said, but, watching the water creep under the garden gate and wreathe around the gateposts, he thought it was easy to give it an evil character, and when it began to lick the walls of the small shed near the fence he nearly gave vent to an exclamation of temper, and only the thought of what he had just said to Ady made him suppress it.

They stood without moving and without noticing the passing of time, which the movement of the flood, in fact, replaced – the large, silent, reliable timekeeper that made clocks insignificant and the progress of daylight irrelevant. Joe thought of nothing while he stood there – watching was work enough – until Ady, in a thin, irritable voice, as if she were exasperated by a long argument, said, 'It's never been into the house.'

68

'There's always a first time. Reckon I might take up the carpet in the front room. Just in case.'

This was intended only as a formal recognition of outside events, however. He did not believe the water would come in, but he had begun to need a little insurance against it – like taking an umbrella to scare away the rain. 'You put a meal on, Ady, while I'm at it,' he said.

It was hard work pushing and lifting the old cedar furniture to free the carpet and then rolling the carpet up, but he worked off his nervous feeling doing it and took pleasure in the smell of eggs and bacon frying on the kitchen stove.

When Ady called him to eat, she did not mention the rising water until he started towards the window. Then she said, 'It's past the old high-water mark.'

'Only takes a minute to stop.' He sat down at the table and began to eat slowly and steadily. 'I'm going to curse myself for taking that carpet up. The old bookcase gets heavier every year, like a man's bones. I'll lay the carpet across the table here and put a couple of chairs under the ends.'

'It's moving so fast,' said Ady. 'I never knew it move so fast before.'

It had to be said sometime, of course, but Joe thought it could have been put off for a while yet. 'Always runs fast and runs away fast,' he said, choosing with composure the losing side of the argument. 'It's to do with the lie of the land. Not like the flat country, where it lies stinking for weeks.'

'Not as fast as this,' she said, stubborn and peevish.

69

'You be right and I'll be wrong,' he answered with belittling good humour, intending to annoy her. She should have held her tongue in the first place. Pushing his empty plate away, he said, 'Call me when the tea's made. I'll finish with the carpet.'

Before he had finished, Ady was at the door, saying, 'Joe . . .' in a timid voice. 'Joe, come and look at it.'

He would not hurry. He was pushing a chair under one end of the heavy roll of carpet and he finished what he was doing before he followed her to the back door, but, once there, he stared for a long time in the last of the daylight at the water sliding and caressing round the lowest step. There was plenty of go in it yet, that was certain, and the rain had come again as quietly as the dark.

'Could you manage a trip to the roof, Mother?' he said at last.

Immediately, Ady began to weep with childlike anguish. 'I'll die in my bed. Get on the roof as soon as you like. I'll die in my bed.'

'Now then, Mother,' Joe said, and reflected. Ady, with her arthritic hip, would scarcely be able to get out on the roof; with her bronchitis, she would not survive a night there in the rain.

'We'll bring the bed out of the spare bedroom and raise it on the table. You'll have to give me a hand. The rate she's coming, we'll have to move to keep our feet dry.'

It was such a relief to begin hurrying that they rushed at the bed and scrambled round it, pulling off the bedclothes and the mattress. They turned the bedstead on its side and tried to push it through the doorway into the hall, but they

70

jammed it, blundering about like a couple of heavy old moths. Joe saw then that hurrying was a mistake, and he paused to get hold of himself.

'Better knock it to pieces. We're just wasting time,' he said.

'We had it out before. When we laid the linoleum. We took it straight back up the hall, feet first like.'

'So we did. Let me think now.'

For a moment, he stood leaning against the tilted bedstead jammed in the doorway, and what he thought was how quickly they had gone to pieces, wasting their strength in a stupid struggle with the heavy iron frame and letting darkness fall without lighting the lamp, as if they had already given in to the water and the night.

'We'll have a bit of light and start again.'

He made himself move steadily as he lit the pressure lamp. He would not forget again how easily panic started. To Ady, who stood watching him with scared eyes, he said, 'Keep the fire up, Mother. We'll be needing our cup of tea.'

Back in the hall, with the lamp set high on the hall stand, Joe talked to the bedstead as if it were a frightened horse. He was not going to admit anymore the existence of large, inanimate obstacles that reared up as if they had the devil in them. Somewhere in the situation there was a frightened horse to be soothed and talked into control. 'This way, now. Give her a little push, there, Mother. There you go, now.' The heavy frame slid into the hall and the difficulty of the removal was over, but the work had begun to tell on them. Ady stood ready to push, wearing a sour

71

and fretful look that showed she was calling on the last of her strength.

'What about stopping for that cup of tea?' he asked.

'We'll just finish this first, if you don't mind. You and your cups of tea!' She gave the bedstead an angry push that did not budge it.

'Give it the rough side of your tongue; it might trot along and hop up on the table by itself.' He used the mean mildness of tone that always put her in a fury, and though in a way he was doing it for her, knowing her anger was all she had to drive her, it was a pleasure to him to be mean.

As soon as the bed was up on the table, Ady went down into the old leather chair in the kitchen. While Joe fetched the pressure lamp and put it on the mantelpiece, she sat there, staring at the boiling kettle as if she were trying to remember her connection with it. Joe had to make the tea, and when he took her a cup she accepted it as her right, like a bereaved person, saying only, 'You'd better open the door and take a look.' Even her weariness was nothing compared with her horror at the coming invasion of her house.

Joe was surprised that the water wasn't in already, they seemed to have been so long moving the bed, but when he looked at his watch he saw it was just on seven o'clock, so it had taken them only thirty-five minutes after all. He opened the door. Looking into the outside world was like looking into a pitch-dark curtained room. The timekeeper there had been moving as steadily as a clock. The water was brimming up to the doorway, and Joe wondered with sudden alarm what he was about, sitting drinking

72

tea, with the mattress not on the bed yet. He had learned, however, how closely panic followed hurry.

'You make a thermos of tea and get something to eat ready to take up with us, and I'll bring the mattress out,' he said. 'Don't get your feet wet. I'll put my boots on. If it starts to come in, you leave everything and get up on a chair, and I'll finish.'

Though he told himself it was better to do a bit of wading than to get flustered, he couldn't help running for the bedding, and to disguise his urgency he put on a wild good humour, hurling up the mattress, saying, 'Heave ho, here she goes!' 'We'll be snug as bugs,' he said as he smoothed the blankets and stacked the pillows. Then he saw the first long, dark ribbon of water spring through the doorway and felt the sudden general weakness of fear.

'Come along. Up with you, Mother,' he said gaily. His feelings were in such confusion that when he climbed onto the table to lift her up he felt an irrelevant flash of high spirits, like a twenty-year-old on holiday. As he poured into a thermos flask the tea Ady had made, and put cake and biscuits into a basket, he experienced from time to time an extravagant delight at paddling about in the water on the kitchen floor, as if he were eight years old. He couldn't seem to keep hold of his mind, which went on bolting into childhood or the summer days of young manhood, and the water was over his instep, running cold and strong, when he handed the basket of supplies and a pocket torch up to Ady.

He put up the chairs, and on the seat of one of them he laid the hatchet from the woodbox, setting it down quietly so as not to draw her attention to it. If he climbed on a chair – Ady would have to steady it on the bed – he could knock a sheet of iron out of the roof, lift himself out, and somehow lift and drag her out, too. Otherwise, they were climbing into a hole with no way of escape.

As soon as he got up and settled himself beside her, he began to grin. 'Proper pair of fools we look, playing king of the castle,' he said.

She did not answer, because she was absorbed in looking at the water, and once Joe began to look there was no room for thought in his mind, either. It was sensational news, the water inching up the kitchen walls, disarranging household goods upon which a forgotten law had imposed places, making visible and extraordinary objects that custom had made invisible. Kindling tilted and began to float out of the woodbox; the boot-cleaning box shifted, swung sideways, and began to travel; the hearthrug grew sodden and sank out of sight.

'Cows'll be up to their bellies in this,' Joe grumbled. 'We won't be milking for months.'

Just then it occurred to him that cows were not the only perishable animals involved, that he might never milk again. The thought came as bold as a nightmare and stayed, altering his breathing and making his skin tighten on his body. He looked at Ady and saw that she had had the thought for some time already, and was sitting subdued and frowning, her mouth moving all the time as one lip worried the other. He wanted to warn her, saying, 'No, no, don't speak,' but it was too late for that.

As if he had been the first to speak, Ady said, 'I never wanted to be left.' She would not look at him, and her

74

uneasy, shifting glance as she watched the water gave her a look of insincerity. 'That was the thing I never liked the idea of, you going first and leaving me alone.'

Now it was said and there was no going back. Joe was so shocked that for a moment he could not think clearly. Trust Ady, trust Ady to open her mouth and say what ought never to be said.

'I always thought I'd have to go and live in town with Ros and Arnold. I never could live under the same roof with Arnold, or under any roof but my own.'

It seemed to him that she got some relief from talking, and he was filled with envious anger at first, but he soon travelled through the thought of her relief to the thought of her fear, and then to the knowledge that she, too, had to die. This knowledge offered him no escape from his solitude – poor Ady on her separate precipice was no company – but it brought on a black sadness that steadied him in his own fear.

'You wouldn't ever need to do that,' he said.

'You know what they'd be like – at you and at you to do it, and all the time thinking you were a nuisance. They'd be worrying about how it looked to other people – that Arnold especially, always worrying about how things look.'

It was dreadful to Joe that the prospect of death made no change in Ady. She thought of death, too, as a hostile neighbour against whom she must score small triumphs, and the expression on her face, superimposed on its look of trouble, was the ghost of an expression long familiar to him. That brought it home to him clearly that there would be no unknown resources in them to meet the moment.

The people they were now must die. It horrified him, too, that he went on thinking about life, thinking new thoughts that were soon to be extinguished.

'It's bound to stop,' he said, with such authority that he believed his own words; for a minute his fear lay down like a dog. 'It's got a long way to go yet. Nothing to get in a panic about.'

Ady turned on him a look of morbid gentleness; it filled him with pity to see how fear had hold of her poor old sagging body. He ought to encourage her to talk, if it made her feel better. The trouble was that what seemed to help her was the very thing he couldn't stand – to have her soft, monotonous voice go on and on, not mentioning death but taking it for granted, not really facing it but thrusting the idea at him with sly, unconscious cruelty. For a moment, he looked at her, reflecting; then he swung off the bed and dropped down into the water.

'Where are you going?' she asked.

Without answering, he set out through calf-deep water towards the dining room. The current would have had him off his feet if he hadn't worked his way along the wall. Now the ruin and disorder of the furniture made him feel sick and angry; without looking round him, he worked his way to the corner cabinet, seized their two bottles of liquor and turned back.

The way back was difficult. The current running against him set him to a slow, wrenching dance that looked comic and made him sad. When he reached their fantastic temporary tower, he leaned against it with a feeling of affection, as if it were home and represented permanence and security. He handed up the bottles and paused a moment before he set off for the sink to fetch a bottle of drinking water and glasses. He had to control his movements so that Ady would not see how strong the current was. Hard as that was for him, as he came back holding the bottle and the glasses like a tightrope walker, concentrating on keeping his balance, he lived for a minute like a man in control of circumstances. It was a short release from the fear that had ceased to be terror and become a straining of the mind at a thought it could not hold.

'Here you are, Ma,' he said cheerfully. He handed up the bottle and the glasses, climbed onto the table and pulled off his boots.

Ady was staring at the bottles with disappointment, as if she had been expecting something more like a miracle.

'Come on, have a drink. It'll warm you.'

The bottle of whisky was nearly full, and there was two-thirds of a bottle of the brandy Ady used for her Christmas cakes. The whisky was most likely to do the trick, he thought, and he poured some into a glass, added water and gave it to her.

Looking askance at the glass, she said, 'I can't drink that stuff,' and then turned to him with a shy, disturbed look that moved something in his memory.

'It'll do you good. Come on.' He poured himself a drink and waited for her.

'Nasty stuff.' She sipped and looked down into the glass with a sour grimace.

'Keep at it, now. You might get a real liking for it.'

'That would be a nice thing.'

At this, the absence of future pressed on them suddenly, the vast terminal brick wall of death reared in front of them and they gulped down the whisky. Then Joe poured them each a tumblerful and they gulped that, too – so open and shameful an action that each resented the presence of the other. In a moment, Joe put his hand over hers in remorse; her soft, shamed glance made him blush suddenly while it travelled in the dark lumber room of memory like a thin, hesitant beam of light. He poured her another drink and said, 'Come on, down with it,' sternly, to cover the shame of her willingness, and was all at once enveloped by a past day, as fresh as paint: cold sunlight and fine slippery grass growing on a steep bank like a wall behind them, Ady red and downcast as she straightened her dress, and himself saying miserably, 'After all, we're getting married Saturday,' and Ady – how astonishing it was, what a splendid present, to see that young face again – saying, 'It won't be the same now,' fretfully, so that he realised that what for him had been a sin against love was for her a domestic disaster in which her bridal finery had suffered. Being romantic, he had thought of love as a secret wonder Ady held in her keeping and feared that his lust, which had sprung on him like a lion, had done it a mortal injury – but Ady did not understand his bitter remorse or his need for comfort. His disappointment was deep, but he bore it with patience and put his arm round her tenderly. Since then the lion had grown old and died, become a disregarded old lion skin warm to the body in cold weather, but that mixture of tenderness and disappointment remained; it was the closest he had come to love.

Ady began to talk in a strange tone, irritable yet dreamy. 'I don't see why she had to change her name. That Arnold and his notions. I thought Rosaleen was a lovely name. Everyone used to say, "What a pretty name you've got, Rosaleen." I was set on her having a pretty name, mine being so plain. The first day she went to school, I remember, the teacher said to her, "Rosaleen. My, what a pretty name you have, Rosaleen." When she got home that day, I said to her, "Well, what did they tell you at school?" and that's what she told me – the teacher said, "My, what a pretty name you have, Rosaleen." '

'Kids always hate their names,' Joe said appeasingly, but he didn't really mind Ady's complaining, for he knew she was finding her way along the beaten path of grievance back to the past.

'I took a dislike to him the first day he set foot in this house. It wasn't my business and I held my tongue, but I never could like him. You're a cold fish, I thought to myself. You'll never let your heart rule your head. And so he's turned out. It was his job that took Rosaleen's fancy. She wanted to be the solicitor's wife and live in the town, that's the long and the short of it.'

'She's got her life, Mother, and she's happy enough in it.'

He wished he could find a door to the past again himself, for it was the only way left to go. He tried to summon up the face of the child Rosaleen, but the stout, cultured matron she had become obstructed his view. He thought again of young Ady, but her face, too, was gone; nothing was left of the picture but the tall bank and the tough, shining grass. The thought that the bank was still there struck him a strange, painless blow, a sensation that first he shrank from and then accepted. It grieved him to think of the grassy bank being drowned under the water, and that, too, was a remote and painless kind of grieving.

Suppose he said to Ady, 'Do you remember that Saturday before we were married?' He had a longing to meet her in the past, but it would frighten her, and she was absorbed, besides, in her lament, which was full of the same kind of comfortable sorrow as Joe's sadness for the grassy bank. Another drink would fix Ady, he thought and poured it for her.

He didn't have another himself, being rather uneasy at the odd thoughts that were drifting through his mind. When a man began fretting about grass being under the water . . . Then he looked at the flood as it rose, quiet and punctual, full of power, and felt in his smallness ashamed of supposing that it mattered whether he was drunk or sober. Something was required of him, some way of looking at the situation, but all he could feel was wonder that the water should be there, drowning the lounge suite and the kitchen clock. Because he found it difficult to believe what he saw, he looked round at Ady and found her lying asleep. Her withered eyelids, not weathered like the rest of her face, were as white as petals, her white hair lay loose about her face and she had clasped her false teeth to her bosom like a child's treasure. She was the link between reality and unreality. Now he believed it all.

The lamp on the mantelpiece went out and blackness invaded his eyes. He sat without stirring. The sound of the water was as quiet as a man's breathing, broken now and then by a gulping noise. He groped for the torch, disturbing Ady, who muttered angrily in her sleep, but when he found it and had his finger on the switch he paused. What good would that do? It was only for comfort that he wanted the light, and comfort was a sickly drink he had drunk enough of. Though his breathing was heavy and fear had a clenching hold on his intestines, he sat in the dark and tried to remember how high the water was. He studied the luminous face of his wristwatch. It was ten after ten – seven o'clock or nearly, just after dark, when the water first came in. Say two foot eight to the tabletop and two foot more to the wire mattress – she was past the tabletop all right. He would look in a minute. If he had thought of it before, he could have been calculating the rate of the flow. It would have done no good, but a man felt better when he could set himself to work. It gave him the feeling he was in control. That was a lie, too, but it kept a man upright on his feet. My God, he thought, seeing life from a new and shocking angle, that was a lie that walked with a man every day of his life.

He had chosen death for them when he went and got the liquor. He had not known it nor intended it; he had only, for a moment, stopped thinking about survival and begun to think of fear as the enemy. What a large, unexplored country lay inside a man – who would have thought he could be responsible for Ady's death? It was because he was an old man; a young man's grip on life was fierce, and he would grudge no suffering that kept him alive. Fear would have saved them if they had been able to endure it, would have given him the strength and the ruthlessness to drag and bully Ady out onto the roof, but he had put fear to sleep.

When he switched on the torch, the water had reached the wire mattress, and the sight of it turned him cold. He looked at his watch and saw it was a quarter to eleven. Then he thought, 'Why die?' It would be so easy, still, to climb onto a chair and escape to the roof. To lie down and die now seemed insane and disgusting, like a man's lying in filth when he could get up. He turned and seized Ady, shouted and shook her, but she did not stir. It was a long time before he could make himself believe that he could not lift her, and he did not stop trying until she uttered a pathetic long moan of protest. Then he lay panting, with his heart beating hard, and thought what he had to do. The thing he must not do was climb out on that roof alone. He groped for the whisky bottle and took a swallow of it where he lay; then he sat up and drank what was left. He found the brandy bottle beside him and sat waiting, thinking of nothing, till a moment of purpose arrived and he uncorked the bottle and began to drink. It was a small bottle and it was not full, but it took a surprising time to drink it out. He let the empty bottle drop into the water, but it stayed beside the bed and nudged his limp fingers like a hungry pet. He switched the torch on then, out of curiosity, and watched the bottle as it heaved and nuzzled among the trailing blankets, showing there was more movement in the water than showed on its surface, which looked like the shining black floor of the cavern of light. Joe looked at the water for a moment with idiot interest and then switched off the torch, because the light was keeping him awake.

The Army duck advanced steadily through mud and water, the soldier at the wheel frowning with concentration as he steered his course, his younger companion gazing about with a tourist's interest at the weird effects of the flood. It was early morning. They had started out from their barracks to the town at midnight and after two hours' sleep had been called from their beds to begin rescue work. In the circumstances, they were inclined to exchange jokes and make cheerful conversation – though it had to be shouted above the noise of the duck's engine – since they did not wish to entertain the thought of what they might find. They were subdued, however, by the bearing of the passenger in the back seat, who sat upright, wearing already the awful dignity of bereavement, looking with calm authority at the devastation round him as if he owned a considerable share of it. He was a middle-aged man with pale, serious eyes, regular features too firmly padded under his rough, shining pink skin, and fair, tightly curling hair. The elder soldier thought of him as Curlylocks in spite of the sad circumstances. Both soldiers disliked him and were ashamed of their dislike, which deepened the unreasonable shame they felt at not being involved in the disaster. When they came in sight of the farmhouse and saw no sign of life there, they were full of remorse and pity.

'You stay there, sir,' the driver said quickly, with some tenderness in his tone, as he got down. He tried to walk with a confident bearing through the open door, but his tread was heavy.

Almost at once, he appeared again and said with a radiant grin, 'Come and have a look at this.'

Joe opened his eyes and reflected deeply. Someone close to him had said, 'Boy, what a party!' He turned his head slightly and saw the grinning face of a stranger, who said, 'Sleeping it off, Dad?'

He closed his eyes again to give privacy to his thoughts. Something quite astonishing had to be taken into account – what was it?

He was alive. If he was alive, Ady was alive, too. That thought brought a little warmth into his brain; he opened his eyes again and tried to lift his head but a fierce pain drove through it and pinned it to the pillow. Then he made sense of what the stranger had said. He was alive and he had a hangover. This time he rolled over and got up more carefully, bringing his head slowly erect – and, by God, there was Ady, sleeping like a baby, with her false teeth held against her chest like a rosebud. He realised then that he was holding the whisky bottle, which he must have found and clung to in his sleep. Looking down carefully, with respect for the condition of his head, he saw his son-in-law Arnold. The old leather chair was leaning drunkenly against the stove, with the upturned brandy bottle resting on its arm. Arnold looked at it with a mild, wondering look, but so intently Joe thought he was going to speak to it, and then Arnold looked round him. The soldiers were studying the high-water mark on the wall, and the elder one said to Joe, 'Only just kept your feet dry that time.' Quickly, with an apologetic smile directed at no one, Arnold hid the brandy bottle in the sink.

'As close as I want to go,' Joe agreed. He shook Ady by the shoulder. 'Hey, Mother, we've got company. Here's Arnold come to see us.'

He could swear she had her teeth in before her eyes were open. As soon as she was sitting up, he took off his socks, rolled up his trouser legs and, stepping down into the mud, made for the door.

'There'll be plenty of damage done,' he thought nervously, trying to prepare himself, but 'damage' was only a word, and he was not ready for the physical shock that struck him through his eyes. He felt a great cry of outrage and protest rise in him, as if he were looking at the corpse of a friend.

'Six inches more and you wouldn't have known a thing about it,' the soldier said behind them, and he seemed to be far away.

How hideous the grey-black mud was, lying as heavy as flesh on the sagging fence. The small shed was lying on its side; slowly and with effort, Joe moved his eyes away from it. There was a great raw scar along the edge of the gully where the land was torn away, and tumbled across it there was an uprooted tree as ugly as a pulled tooth.

'Someone else would be cleaning up this mess,' he said. 'It's no job for an old man.'

He wished from his heart he had not awakened and need never wake again. It seemed to him that the instinct that made an old man turn away from life was the right one; but he was quickly ashamed of the bitter, complaining

85

tone in his voice and of the despair that prompted it. He had not turned his head to speak to the soldier, and that was because he was concealing the look that he felt was set like a mask on his face – exactly that mild and wondering look he had seen on Arnold when Arnold saw the brandy bottle. Reality, with its unaccountable surprises, had always been too much for Arnold, and just now it was too much for Joe. Seeing this likeness between himself and his son-in-law, he felt a disagreeable small shock that woke him out of the great one. 'What were you expecting?' he said to himself angrily. 'You knew there was a flood, I suppose. Had long enough to think about it.'

As for Arnold, Joe knew from long experience, not needing to use words, what it was that Arnold longed for and had this morning allowed himself to expect – a moment entirely free from absurdity. In his mind's eye, Joe saw himself and Ady snoring on their wet, bedraggled, elevated bed, he with his bottle, Ady with her teeth, and slowly he began to smile. Some day he'd be dignified enough to suit Arnold, but, by Heaven, not yet.

He turned away from the door and went back to Ady.

'Come along, Mother,' he said, setting down a chair to make a step for her. 'You better start remembering how we move that bed back again.'

That Sunday morning Father had an argument with my younger sister Nell because Nell had brought home a baby parrot again. Nell wanted to rear a tame parrot and from time to time she appeared bearing a haggard fledgling which she fed and tended for a week and then usually neglected. Even if she didn't neglect them, they died, and Father had told her not to do it again, but here was Nell, looking rapt, remote and extremely dirty, carrying a tiny bird close to her chin and chewing a mouthful of rolled oats.

'Where did you get it?' Father asked. He was standing in front of the glass that hung on the back verandah, tying his tie and frowning at his reflection.

Frowning too with concentration Nell mumbled, 'Found it on the ground. Must have fallen out of the tree.' Very carefully she projected a small quantity of the moist and masticated rolled oats onto her lower lip and lifted the baby bird to nibble at it. She always said she found baby parrots lying under trees; she lied boldly and serenely and refused to accept improbability as evidence against her.

Father was confused for a moment, hesitated between justice to Nell and justice to parrots and said, 'Next time you find one on the ground you'd better leave it there.' The rolled oats disappeared while Nell whispered, 'Cruel!' Then she went on feeding the bird with insolent tenderness. Father recovered and reached the crux of the matter. 'If that bird dies, my girl, and I find out that you've neglected it, you'll be in real trouble.'

It was not like Father to miss the point even for a minute, but he was in his Sunday morning mood. Every Sunday we went to the homestead – so the whole family called my grandfather's house – for midday dinner, and every Sunday morning Father was absentminded, cut himself shaving and said, 'Oh Sunday morning!' like a curse, and made odd jokes which Mother seemed to understand but at which they never smiled.

Nell looked at him resentfully and said nothing. She was engaged at that time in a struggle with Father which I don't believe he ever noticed. If she was meditating an answer, Mother prevented it by coming in at that moment, discovering that Nell wasn't ready and hurrying her off to be washed and dressed. Eventually, she was ready before I was; I had just begun to write poetry then, and half an hour vanished between the polishing and the lacing of my shoes.

'She looks a different girl, doesn't she?' Mother said as Nell came out to the car, but really she looked exactly the same, for she still wore the remote expression which made changes like starch and polish, smooth hair and blue ribbon quite negligible.

She was still looking remote when we went to take our places at the long table in the dining room of the homestead, and I envied her. The conversation rose round me like the smell of dreary cooking, as it rises now when I think of it, though I can't remember a word that was said. The diary I was keeping at the time is no help; on Sunday evenings I used to make spiteful entries like, 'Dinner at Grandpa's. Nobody quoted Proust.' I see now that I was spiteful because I was frightened. Grandpa was a terrifying man, quite unapproachable because he found it as difficult to distinguish between human beings as between sheep. He could recognise qualities – strength, fineness of wool, intelligence and so on – and he did observe that some were younger than others and took the difference of the sexes into consideration quite as much as if people were sheep, but that was the limit of differentiation.

Grandpa sat at the head of the table carving mutton, the plates for the whole company of uncles, aunts and cousins piled in front of him, and now and then lifted his head to make a remark about the price of wool or the weather. The remark fell among the company and some adult felt it his duty to answer. That was not alarming; what frightened me was the dreadful game of musical chairs in which Grandpa's glance ranged the table and came to rest on one; having observed that this was a young one and a male, he would utter a suitable but quite unanswerable question like, 'What do they teach you at school, hey?' I should have liked to begin a singsong 'Five fives are twenty-five, five sixes are thirty', but instead I used to blush and stammer, and for that I could never forgive Grandpa. 'That boy of yours is a fool, Molly,' he said sometimes. He knew pedigrees, as well as age and sex.

Dinner at Grandpa's was what is usually called a ritual, and one part of it really was one. As he carved the mutton, even to a slice for the Hugh Desmonds' baby, Aunt Lenore beside him dished out baked potato, baked pumpkin and beans until every plate but one was supplied. Then he handed down the last plate empty and carried the dishes over to the sideboard; when the empty plate came to Father's place he got up and served himself. Today while Grandpa was carving the mutton my cousin Ronnie, sitting next to Nell, shrieked suddenly, and Grandpa said to his daughter-in-law at the other end of the table, 'What's the matter with that boy of yours, Edna?' He didn't wait for an answer and the business proceeded quickly: Grandpa carved, Aunt Lenore dished out, plates were handed, Father stood up and Nell said clearly, 'Grandpa, why don't you ever cut the meat for Daddy?'

I would never have asked that question, but as soon as it was asked I knew that I was longing to hear the answer. I looked at my parents and realised how alike they looked. Though she was thin, dark and serious and he was stocky, pale and redheaded, with the urchin look men of that colouring still have in middle age, they met moments of crisis with an identical expression, this time of steady serenity which they seemed to maintain without effort. I had always taken it for granted that my parents loved

90

each other – though the word 'love' was never spoken in our house, I think I measured their love for each other by their remoteness from us – and I knew, even, how love had announced itself to them as the subconscious stirring that makes the traveller gather his belongings together as his destination approaches. But I realised then that my parents were special people, and love not a common thing.

'Why, I reckon your father knows how to help himself,' said Grandpa and then burst out laughing. 'Knows how to help himself, I reckon,' he repeated and laughed louder still.

At this, a story that had been told to me in infinitesimal instalments throughout my life cohered at last. The word 'elopement', which had always been in the air around me, attached itself to my parents – and then there was Father greeting a blazing, whitish Sunday morning as 'good weather for running', the mysterious inferiority of our position, Mother's guilt and defiance when she talked about her rights – 'I've worked like a man on that property ever since I could ride' – and her warning, 'Walk straight up to your grandfather. It's the only way.'

Father wouldn't have been an acceptable suitor, of course, for in Grandpa's mind a man's relationship to his land was precisely the same as his relationship to his trousers, without which it is possible to be virtuous, but never respectable. As for women – I don't think his feelings about women had ever crystallised into contempt – they married men with land and provided its inheritors or they stayed home, like Aunt Lenore, and made themselves useful. But that strange two-headed monster, a couple in love, being outside his experience, had somehow defeated him. I didn't have to reconstruct the day because time had stopped there: in Grandpa's roar of laughter was his roar of rage, the wild chase across the paddocks and the high blood pressure that anguished female voices shouted to him to remember, and if every Sunday morning my parents renewed the day, the armour they had worn then was as good as new. This moment, strange and familiar, near and remote, was as exciting to me as that sudden change of focus in 'The Eve of St Agnes' – '. . . Aye, ages long ago, These lovers fled away into the storm' – and it excites me still, as if it kept something about love or time or poetry not yet revealed.

'Knows how to help himself,' Grandpa repeated and set off on a fresh burst of laughter as if the idea was a new one, but one couldn't grudge him all the enjoyment he could wring from a joke that had cost him several hundred acres and came his way only once or twice in twenty years. If Grandpa had known of my talent for poetry, he would certainly have blamed Father for it, but that would have been an injustice. I hope he never does discover where I got it, for with his blood pressure it might be the end of him.

THE CASUAL AFFAIR

I

Sex with no strings to it, no complications. That was the story of Malcolm with Lois. Though they had never talked about it, he was sure it was the story of Lois with Malcolm, also. It was an advantageous arrangement but it imposed restrictions. For example, he couldn't ring up beforehand – that would have put the affair on a different footing. He had to be the casual dropper-in, so he ran the risk of finding the house empty, which didn't happen often, or having her room-mate Madeleine exuding disapproval while she thwarted his plan for the evening. If that happened, he would drink a cup of coffee, make a little difficult conversation, pretend to like the dachshund and leave. Lois would come to the door with him and say, 'What about tomorrow?' or 'Are you free Friday night?'

with decorous composure, as if she had no idea of the purpose of the appointment.

When he arrived, she would put the dog out. That always amused him. Marguerite Gautier carried her white camellias, Lois put the dog out. It was unjust to compare her with Marguerite Gautier – Lois was seriously interested in money, but she would have been angry if a man had threatened her independence with an expensive gift. It was for Madeleine, who presumed to disapprove of him, to dangle after rich men and dream of diamonds.

It was important not to go there too often, not to cross the line that separated the occasional sexual partner from the regular.

This was the question that waited for an answer while he stacked his books and returned them to the desk in Fisher, saying goodbye to Huysmans for the day: twice in ten days – was it too soon? His body said, 'No, not too soon,' but he didn't intend to let his body dictate. That was another restriction he meant to observe.

He crossed to Wentworth for dinner, found no one to talk to, contemplated the empty evening, entertained and dismissed the thought of going back to Fisher to work on Huysmans. That was another question waiting for an answer – a much more serious one. Seeing that he was saying goodbye to him with too much relief every day, had he made a mistake in selecting Huysmans for study? If your subject bored you, you bored your readers. On the other hand, it would be a shameful lapse in discipline to abandon a project once begun. Needing to make a decision about something, he made up his mind to call on Lois.

There was one moment of the bus trip that he savoured: the bus swung round the corner, passed below the lighted hoarding and there she was, upper lip shortened in the radiant, life-affirming smile while she held out to all comers the bottle of fizzy drink which was the elixir of youth and gaiety, ladies and gentlemen. Illusion and reality. Puffed up with private knowledge, he meditated an address to the other passengers. 'She's not like that at all.' It was deflating that he never saw anyone else look up at the hoarding. 'She gets her emotional kicks out of watching soap operas, she loves a nasty fat dachshund, she talks about safe investments and reducible interest on mortgage' – he liked that; he thought it rather Balzacian – 'and she likes her sex dressed up with a whiff of poetry, a dash of myth and legend.' That, of course, was where he came in. Herrick got quite a workout – she thought Julia was a very nice name – and so did John Donne in his youth. In his youth, after all, he wouldn't have minded.

He skipped the bits that mentioned love.

When she opened the door to him, dressed for the evening at home in tee-shirt, trousers and battered scuffs, he felt the usual faint, pleasant shock, after seeing the girl on the hoarding, at the gap between illusion and reality, at the insignificance of her neatly modelled, well-featured face. He was always intrigued by the mystic union with the camera that invested her with radiance.

She greeted him with a smile that was quite unlike the million-dollar fizzy-drink model but did well enough.

'Hello. I'm glad you dropped in tonight. I'm all alone. Nice to have a bit of company.'

95

In the tiny sitting room the television was playing, as ever. The dachshund lifted its head from its paws and snarled at him.

'You'll have to go outside, Wolf, if you can't be polite to the visitor. Come on, out you go.'

The dog shuffled out, protesting. She shut the door on it.

He delighted in the ritual with which she maintained propriety to its very limit.

'I'm watching *A Country Practice*. You don't mind, do you?'

'No. Go ahead.'

He sat beside her on the lounge. She watched the screen without stirring as he moved closer. He slid his hand under her tee-shirt and stroked bare skin without disturbing her concentration. When he slid it into her pants, she frowned and twitched away.

Keep that for the commercials.

One day she'd turn off the TV before the end of the programme and he could crown himself the great lover.

Three commercials and he had the pants unzipped and was troubling her breathing, but she held out to the last word, switched off the machine holding her pants up with one hand and ran laughing into the bedroom.

So there they were together on her narrow bed and he was saluting her breasts with the patter that was her background music, murmuring, 'Oh, they are a witty pair. One nipple pointing south-south-east and the other south-south west, like the perfect answer.' He kissed from left to right. 'Tit for tat.' He kissed from right to left. 'And, that makes two the perfect number.'

He was about to throw in a remark about the single-breasted Amazons, for later elaboration, when she said with a breathy giggle, 'Lucky I'm not your old Diana of the Ephesians, then.'

He couldn't have been more astonished if that dog had lifted its upper lip and said 'Guten Abend' to him when he came in. He didn't have time to stop and wonder, with the tide of sensation rising and carrying them with it, but later as he was dressing he said, 'Who told you about Diana of the Ephesians?'

'Didn't you? The old statue with all the breasts? Yuk. I could have sworn it was you.'

'No. It wasn't me.'

He got his head through the neck of his shirt in time to see enlightenment on her face, then embarrassment, then stillness, closed shutters.

'Must have been some other time.'

It must have been some other man.

She said, 'I'll get us some coffee.'

Of course he had no right to object. He had never supposed that he was her only lover. He didn't want to be her only lover. He did wonder now and then about other men for whom she put the dog out. He could swear one of them was an accountant. Nevertheless, there was a moment in a man's life when he didn't care to be mistaken for somebody else. Feeling humiliated, he drank his coffee in silence. She had let the dog in and disguised what he felt sure was guilty embarrassment by chatting to it as she fed it pieces of biscuit.

97

'No, Wolf. That's the last. You're too fat already.'

It must be someone he knew. Why else should she be so embarrassed?

He had met her at Dickson's the night of the dreadful drunken scene. She had been frightened and had asked him to take her home. That was how it had started, that very night. It hadn't occurred to him to wonder who had brought her there. He had been too stunned, no doubt, at being called a filthy, frustrated peeping Tom of the soul. It must have been one of the drunks, or she wouldn't have been so distressed.

He had no right to question her, he had no right even to wonder, but this was too close for comfort. How vulnerable a man was in the act of sex, naked to the ego, stripped of all defences. It couldn't be Dickson, could it? She had spoken with horror of Dickson. 'He's supposed to be a poet? How could anyone like that be a poet?' He had answered, 'He's a very good poet,' still gagging on that word 'frustrated' and the truth of it. He'd give anything to have written one of Dickson's poems, except perhaps be Dickson.

How could he explain Dickson to her, Dickson possessed by that creative energy which clawed at him in idleness? Come too close and it would claw you too. He had come too close, had thought he had a special understanding of Dickson's poetry which entitled him to approach with intelligent comments. Useful to have that learnt, as Larkin would say. He would keep to dead poets in future.

Remembering how distressed she had been, and how ready to take him to bed, he thought it likely that for her it was the end of a relationship. But had it been the end, after all, or merely an interruption?

Forget it, forget it.

II

Madeleine stood at the door of the darkened bedroom and said softly, 'You awake, love?'

'Yes.' Lois switched on the bedside lamp but turned the light away from her face. 'You're home early.'

'Walked out on him.' Madeleine sat down on her bed and took off her high-heeled silver shoes. 'Ah, that's better. All night, it was on and on about his wife, how much money she spent – I wish I knew how she got it out of him – and how hard he worked to make it, no appreciation and she grudged him a little relaxation. That was me, you understand, the little relaxation. And the last straw was, a carat by carat account of the diamond brooch he gave her for her birthday. Nothing for my birthday, and I made damned sure he knew the date. What did he think I was doing there, getting the warmth off his wallet?'

'Perhaps he thinks you love him for himself.'

'He couldn't be so daft. Well, in the end I said, "Look, if you don't like what your wife does, don't tell me, tell her. And if you don't mind, I have a headache and I want to go home. Would you call me a taxi, please?" He didn't even offer to pay for the taxi, and I know damn well he runs an account.'

'He didn't get rich by giving it away.'

'That one won't get poor giving it away, either.'

She switched on the ceiling light. It showed Lois's face, bloated and shabby with weeping.

'Hey, what's the matter? You've been crying.'

'Malcolm was here.'

'And he's another one. Just making use of you, that's all.'

'No. No. You're wrong about him. It's nothing to do with Malcolm, really. Something he said, and I answered, and I realised all at once that it was a joke I used to have with Jack, not Malcolm at all, and I thought I was talking to Jack. It was a terrible feeling. It all came back to me.'

'Oh, love!' Madeleine was halfway out of her dress; she put it on again in order to speak with more authority. 'It's more than a year. It's getting on eighteen months. You have to put that bastard out of your mind and do some real living. He's gone, married to somebody else, living in Adelaide. Are you going to sit mooning in front of the television all your life because of a rat like that? And this other one, dropping in whenever he feels like a bit . . .'

Lois winced.

'I wish you wouldn't talk like that. He isn't making use of me. It's mutual. It's just sex with him and it's just sex with me. What's wrong with that? It's part of life, isn't it?'

'It's never just sex,' said Madeleine, sighing. 'Never. There's always something else they're after.'

'He's all right, really. You're never fair to him. I like his approach, it's refined. He's never vulgar.'

Madeleine hooted. 'It's the most vulgar thing out and words'll never change it.' She began to undress again.

100

'All I have against him is that he's the same type as the other. It doesn't make him a rat, I suppose.'

'You could say I'm using him, making him a substitute for Jack. I never saw it before. If he'd looked like Jack, I'd have run for my life.'

'He looks harmless, I'll say that for him,' said Madeleine obscurely. 'You ought to stay away from those book-readers. Stick to your own type.'

'Listen to who's talking!'

'I'll pay that one. Better take my own advice, eh?'

'That fellow has a very big account with the agency. I hope he doesn't get a set against you. He might be able to do you some harm.'

Madeleine began to giggle. 'Not very good at it, am I? Oh, well, I don't need him right now and, a character like that, if you were on the way out he wouldn't want to know you.'

The way out. They paid it a moment's tribute.

'You've made a mess of your face. Do you want an icepack?'

'I don't have a session tomorrow. I'll see to it in the morning.'

In the dark, Madeleine said, 'Chris was asking me again about setting up a double date. That friend of his is still crazy to meet you. What about it?'

Lois pondered, then said with resolution, 'Right, I will.'

'Great. I'll just check first and make sure that he's never read a book in his life. Lois?'

'I said yes. Go to sleep, will you?'

'Do you ever feel that there should be a bit more to show for it?'

'Yes, often. Go to sleep.'

III

At the lunch table, Malcolm said, 'Who was Diana of the Ephesians?'

The other young men looked at him, astonished.

'What are you playing at, Trivial Pursuit?'

'What is this, some kind of survey?'

'That's right. Standard of cultural knowledge among University staff.'

'I think I did know once. It sounds familiar.'

'"Great is Diana of the Ephesians." Got quite a ring to it, hasn't it? I don't know what it means, though. What's the second question.'

'Who are you working for?'

'Confidential. I take it nobody knows. Five misses.'

It seemed a splendid cover. He went to fetch coffee and stopped by another table on the way back.

'Can anyone help with a general knowledge question? Who was Diana of the Ephesians?'

Three young men stared in silence. The fourth said contemptuously, 'Diana the many-breasted. A statue in the Temple of Ephesus, reputed to have fallen from Heaven.'

That was Tully. Tully was squat; his thin neck stemming from rounded shoulders gave him a resemblance to a tortoise, he had thick padded eyelids and a bulbous nose.

102

For these misfortunes he took revenge on the rest of humanity with savage wit. He was brilliant; he wrote epigrams and travelled with Dickson and Purvis though he did not call them friend.

Someone was muttering, 'Fancy that, now. Not a chip out of it. Amazing,' while Malcolm reconstructed that dreadful evening and saw Tully silent in a corner grinning at his humiliation.

In the washroom he looked at himself in the glass and straightened his shoulders. He was tall, at least. He thought his face was sensitive and intelligent, though hardly handsome. He saw no resemblance to Tully.

This was nonsense. The other knows of Diana of the Ephesians. Tully knows of Diana of the Ephesians. Therefore . . . That would get you drummed out of Logic One.

An unknown had come to stand at the neighbouring washbasin.

'Who was Diana of the Ephesians?'

'Statue in the Temple of Ephesus, wasn't it? One of the wonders of the ancient world. What brought that on?'

'Oh, just a quiz.'

The stranger looked at him with some astonishment.

'Be my guest.'

IV

The television game went well, but when they got to the bedroom, he found he couldn't manage the commentary,

103

being haunted by a feeling of being overheard. Apparently it was part of his talent as a lover, for it was not one of their happiest encounters, though he managed to save it from disaster.

She said, 'You're quiet tonight.'

'Mmm.' He let a moment pass. 'Did it come back to you, where you heard about Diana of the Ephesians?'

She turned her head to look at him steadily and coldly.

'I read it in a book.'

He tried to grin.

'Funny time to be reading a book.'

Lois sat upright.

'Listen. I don't ask you any questions. For all I know, you're a married man. That's your business. Don't you ask me questions either.'

'In the normal way, I agree. I have been married, by the way. I am not now.' Four words for a long, dreary story. 'Of course I'm not entitled to question you about your relationships. But when you confuse me with somebody else, you see, it comes too close for comfort. I hoped you would understand that.'

She was silent for a few seconds, making a decision. Then she said, 'Nobody you know. Nobody you've ever seen, so far as I know. And please don't talk to me about it again.'

The look on her face, remote in a private passion, daunted and humbled him. Well, it wasn't Tully. Tully could never bring such a look to a woman's face. Neither could he.

V

Lois said to Madeleine, 'Who does he think he is, asking me questions? He's got no right to ask me questions.'

'Well, I don't suppose he thought he was another man's stand-in.' She giggled briefly. 'Not a bad word, that, stand-in. I think you're being rough on him, I do. I knew of a girl who wrecked her marriage that way, moaning "Ken" when she should have moaned "Graham". Never talked her way out of that one.'

'He's not married to me!'

With assumed primness Madeleine said, 'I had supposed that something of that nature was occurring at the time.'

'Oh, well, yes. I see what you mean. It was rude.'

'Tactless, to say the least. Why don't you explain?'

'It's too late now. Nothing I said would make any difference. If I'd explained straight away – but now it's too important. I was too upset at the time. Besides, it's no fun any more. He's changed. And I know he isn't Jack. I just want to forget the whole thing, and Jack too. Like you said, change the scene.'

'Well, that's something gained.'

VI

Malcolm had gone back once, and found the house empty and accepted Fate's verdict with relief. It had been an adventure, a charming one, but it had no future. He would finish the study of Huysmans, make a friend or two – how he had laid waste his time in pursuit of Dickson – perhaps find a lover who was also a friend.

Unfortunately, his indecision about Huysmans was getting worse and had developed symptoms. He forgot titles he needed, mislaid papers, left books and notes in his office, so that he spent time on trivial errands going back to fetch them. Sometimes his eye travelled through a paragraph without conveying meaning to his brain.

He had reached the third novel *En Route*. The irony he perceived in the title convinced him that he was stalled. Another month of his precious fellowship had passed without profit, but if he dropped Huysmans now, there were three months wasted.

Yielding to boredom was a luxury he couldn't afford. He had to impose some plan on his shifting mind and carry it out for the sake of his self-respect.

He resolved to write an outline of his thesis, add the best of his notes, take it all to Prof Walsh and ask for a decision. If dear old Walsh saw promise in the work he would persist; otherwise he would cut his losses, courageously. He was so cheered by the prospect of discussing something with another man that he saw what a great part loneliness played in his trouble.

This was a bad patch. He must work his way through it.

The outline went well and there seemed to be more worth in the early notes than he had remembered. He worked in

Fisher after dinner till nine, then went back to his office to leave his papers.

There was a hand-delivered letter in his pigeonhole, another hopeful sign that he was not alone in the world. He put his papers on his desk and opened the envelope.

The message was typewritten, too.

WHO WAS DIANA OF THE EPHESIANS?

WHO GIVES A FUCK?

Dickson and Purvis, the eternal larrikins. Were they never going to forgive his innocent enthusiasm?

He folded the paper and put it in his shirt pocket, locked the room, walked back to his lodgings, sat on the bed and began to consider his situation.

It might not be serious. He had made himself slightly ridiculous – an easy thing to do in these parts – with his culture survey. He had desisted, but it seemed not soon enough. Dickson and Purvis might well think it worthwhile, in half-an-hour of atrabilious idleness, to resurrect the event in order to torment him. If so, it meant little. It would pass.

If they had found out why he was asking the question, they would never let such a savoury gobbet go. He foresaw comic short stories with a quite recognisable anti-hero, epigrams from Tully, limericks . . .

Lois. What a fool he had been, going naked in unknown territory. Hostile territory, since he had met her at Tully's. Nobody you know, she had said, but why should she have told the truth, since she had made it clear that she resented the question? She would never tell the story in malice, that was certain, but she might tell it out of innocence. She had more than her share of that. There was the room-mate, besides, to whom no doubt she told everything . . .

This wasn't normal life. This was a terrarium where seedlings grew into monstrous plants.

This one was too much for him. It was no use trying to rise above it with analysis of the creative temperament, understanding and lordly forgiveness. If Dickson and Purvis, with a little help from Tully, took it into their fevered heads to make him an object of ridicule, they could do it, and brilliantly.

If I had had such a talent, he thought bitterly, I'd have made better use of it.

He did not think he could endure it. He would take flight.

That would settle the matter of Huysmans. It would settle the matter of Malcolm, too, for what else could he do with his life?

He had taken flight once, from heartbreak and humiliation. Must he run again?

Was he running still? Was this the same flight – no love, but a ritual of sex with a stranger, no friendship, but the contempt of men he had pursued – admit it – for the purpose of study?

It would be absurd, shameful to be chased away by malice, no matter how much talent there might be in it. That couldn't happen to a man who had a proper sense of his own worth. That was the truth of it; he had brought his wound with him and it was festering still. That explained his problem with Huysmans, too. He was expecting too much of the study, wanting to use it to prove his own worth. It would be easy to finish it if he aimed only at a little modest usefulness.

He had to find out how much Dickson knew; then he could face it out.

VII

He needed to see Lois again, of course. He'd made a mistake in asking the direct question, but it would be easy to find out if she had kept any connection with the group. It wasn't what she would think of as classified information – they needn't be sexual partners. Just a tactful remark, at the right time, drop Dickson's name, perhaps – she was candid about everything but her lovers. (It must be the room-mate. He was sure it was the room-mate.)

At the florist's he bought one yellow rose. On the card he wrote: 'Go, lovely rose . . .' (feeling ridiculous, looking furtively about him), signed it 'Apologies, Malcolm', and had it sent to her. He did not know why he felt so ashamed. He meant her no harm. He hoped Madeleine would be in when he called, so there would be no sex. His body, of course, hoped otherwise.

He rang her up early in the evening. That was new. Her voice sounded unfamiliar, much lighter and livelier.

'Thanks for the lovely rose. It came just at the right time to cheer me up.'

'I hated to leave you on a bad note. I thought we could be friends.'

'Of course we can. Why don't you come out to see me? I'm all alone. I could do with some company. Big changes here, Madeleine's getting married. I'm happy for her, of course,' she said woefully, 'but I'll miss her terribly and I'll have to look for a new lodger. Are you busy? Can you come over?'

'I'd like to.' He thought with dismay that nothing had changed; Lois expected to go to bed with her friends. Well, the rest of the poem would have to see him through it.

It's the loss of innocence, he thought. Odd though it sounded, that was the truth of it. It was the loss of innocence that made him reluctant to go to her, yet he went.

The television wasn't on, which disconcerted him. He felt like saying to her, 'The rules! You've forgotten the rules!' She was feeling quite wretched. She came straight to him and put her arms round him, looking for comfort in what was familiar, but as soon as he responded, she thought, He's changed. He was holding her too tight and kissing too hard, hurting her a bit. She said, 'Take it easy!' but he didn't seem to hear. She pulled away and he walked his mouth down her chin to her neck and kept it there, nibbling gently at her throat. It wasn't a bit like him. Then she felt his teeth take hold lightly.

'Oh, be careful,' she said urgently. 'Don't mark me. Oh, for Heaven's sake, do be sensible. I won't be able to work if you mark me.'

The frightened note in her voice was having a dreadful effect on him. Amusement, that's what it was – heartless, disgraceful amusement.

'Tell me who it was,' he murmured.

She said, 'I think you are mad!'

She felt his teeth nip her flesh and shouted 'You bastard!' pushing him away with closed fists. 'Get out of here and don't come back. Do you hear me?'

'Oh, I hear you,' he said vaguely, straightening his jacket, smoothing his hair.

She had run to the telephone and dialled – at random, he supposed – and was standing now with the receiver at her ear, glaring at him, one hand at her throat.

'If you don't get out, I'll get help.'

'I'm going. I'm going.'

He walked out slowly, too tired to move faster.

VIII

When Madeleine and Chris came in from their dinner, Lois was sitting in front of the television, staring through the lighted screen. There was a bowl of water on a small table beside her and she was holding a wet cloth against her throat.

'What on earth . . . ?'

'Malcolm bit me.'

'What!'

'What I said. He bit me. He's gone a bit mad, I think. Got some bee in his bonnet about another man. I don't know. Have a look, will you? Does it show much?'

She took the cloth away. Madeleine peered. Her betrothed, representative of the guilty sex, stood silent and embarrassed.

'It's not too bad. It hardly shows at all. I think it'll cover up all right. I'd like to know what was biting him.'

'I don't know and I don't care. I never want to speak to him again. If he rings, say I'm out.'

'Suppose he comes around? Perhaps we'd better stay around in the evening for a while.'

Lois shook her head. 'It's not all that much. Nothing to worry about. I just don't want to talk to him, that's all.'

Chris said, 'But he wouldn't want to come back, would he?'

The two women turned on him an identical, unreadable expression.

'Oh, yes. He'll be back.'

THE RESCUE

In the last carriage of the train Margaret found an empty compartment and put her bag and her coat on the rack above the window seat facing the engine, rejoicing in her luck. No one to give odd looks as she cleaned the seat and the window-sill with tissues, and, if she was lucky and no one got in, silence and peace in which to read *The Way of the Soul*, to practise meditation and perhaps to achieve that longed-for moment of true communion with the Divine. *The Way of the Soul* drew odd looks too, which she accepted as a test of faith, but how pleasant it would be to do without them. She sat with the closed book in her lap, gazing over the parched plain yellowed by the warm sunlight of late afternoon, willing people away as she waited for the train to start. One man paused at the door and looked in but went on further down the carriage. She was lucky. The train moved, she opened her book and began to read with a concentration that blocked out the world.

Once she paused to pray – she wasn't sure, though, that it was a moment of true communion, there might be a truer communion yet – and once to eat her sandwiches, looking out of the window because it didn't seem respectful to meditate while she was eating. It was quite dark now. Wan trees and scattered lighted houses flowed past under a dark starry sky. Then rows of houses, a city glow in the sky. They were coming into Bathurst.

No point in trying to read as the train stopped and people got out, jostling, calling and crowding the refreshment counters. She meditated, withdrawn from the lights, the voices and the clatter. 'Divine Spirit, the human senses which bar me from your presence I dismiss. I dismiss sight, hearing, smell, touch, taste. (Those salmon sandwiches had been a weakness.) I shall eat only to still hunger, not to satisfy appetite. I shall free myself from the bondage of the senses which divide me from you. Divine Spirit . . .'

The train was moving out of the station when she was startled alert by the sound of feet running too close, impossibly close, then the window was suddenly filled with head, shoulders and torso, then the young man fell back, one elbow over the sill, a hand clutching the window frame, a thin dark face meek with panic fixed on hers.

She was going to have to touch him. That gave her skin a funny feeling, until it went cold with fear and she realised she was going to have to lift him in and she felt the weakness in her arms that would surely let him drop.

'Oh God,' she prayed, 'don't let me fail in this.' She knew, as she thrust her arm under the accessible armpit and tried to heave against his weight, that she was being punished. She had failed in brotherly love, wanting to be alone; now she was alone with the frightened dangling young man, without help. There was a terrible slithering yielding moment while she tried to get her other arm round him. She shouted. 'I can't. Grab me, quick. I can't hold.'

His grip on her upper arm was cruel till he got his other arm round her shoulders, hard and warm. He clutched her shoulderstrap, then her shoulder; he was holding now, she need only stand firm. The pain eased as his feet got purchase against the carriage wall. He was coming in; she used her weight to help him, leaning backward, till he came in a long dive that sent them both sprawling on the seat, he on top of her, she with her arms still about him, laughing with joy, crying, 'Oh thank God. Oh thank God.'

'Sorry,' he said. 'Extremely sorry.' His wet pungent breath brought the atmosphere of the rowdy station bar. 'Very sorry indeed.'

'It's all right. It's all right.' She remembered to open her arms and let him go. 'Oh thank God.'

He got to his feet and stood swaying, steadied himself against the wall and said, puzzled, 'You are a swell girl. I thought you would go crook.' She saw now that he was drunk. 'You are a swell girl.'

'No, it's all right. So long as you're safe.'

She got the strength to pull herself upright on the seat and two torn straps fell and dangled while one fat

115

white breast stared naked with its idiot nipple eye at the young man.

It wasn't true. It couldn't be happening. It was too cruel. The blood came up into her face, drowned her eyes, sang in her head. She could not stir.

All at once, he was sober, sat beside her, lifted the straps, caught the great white fish neatly in the cup of the brassiere, held the straps in place at the back of her dress and said, in a business-like tone, 'You got any safety pins?'

She had to move then. Her bag was on the floor. She groped in it and with shaking hands managed to pass him two small safety pins.

Fumbling with the pins, he scolded them and pleaded with them. 'Stay still, will you, you silly little bugger. Stop that, now. You just stay put and stop horsing around. Ah I got you, see. That's fixed you. Now, come on, you . . .'

While he struggled, everything came right for Margaret. The blush cooled, the singing stopped; she was wrapped in a beautiful comforting memory of sitting on someone's knee, small, warm and clean, having her toes dried one by one with a white towel. She felt the pain in her bruised arm as sharp as toothache but it didn't matter; it gave her a feeling of being picked up and comforted when she had fallen over.

When had that ever happened?

'That's fixed it.' He got up triumphant, looked down at her and saw the bruised arm. He was woebegone as a clown. She thought he was going to cry.

'I hurt your arm.'

'It doesn't matter. Truly.'

She didn't want to talk. She wanted to stay sealed in her beautiful memory.

He shook his head, muttering. 'You surely are one swell girl.'

'Were you with friends? Won't they be worrying about you?'

'Oh sure. Yes.' He was astonished to remember that he had friends. 'One swell girl,' he muttered as he walked carefully away.

Could it be a memory of her mother? Her mother had died before she was two – did anyone ever remember back so far? Why not? Why not, and who else could it be, cuddling her and drying her toes?

Her book was lying open on the floor. She shut it and put it in her bag and sat holding her arm to ease the pain, enjoying the strange peace of mind she took for fatigue and relief.

A throat-clearing noise made her look towards the doorway. The young man was standing there rigid and solemn.

'Swell girl.' He made it sound like 'Ladies and gentlemen.' 'We are having a bit of a party and we want you to come. Everybody wants you to come because I told them what a swell girl you are.'

She shook her head. 'No, thank you.'

The rigid pose melted. Holding the door-frame he said mournfully to a friend who must be floating just under the ceiling, 'She won't come. She – won't – come.'

Silly drunk as he was, she couldn't help smiling because he was alive.

117

He pondered, nodded cleverly and wavered away.

Then he was back with a tall blond young man beside him.

'This is Dickie. He isn't drunk. He just got on at Bathurst. Will you come with Dickie because he isn't drunk? You tell her, Dickie. Tell her you're not drunk.'

'Not drunk,' Dickie agreed and enquired with his eyebrows.

She shook her head.

'Come on, Pete. The lady wants her beauty sleep.'

Silently, he promised to keep Pete from disturbing her peace and led him away.

She stretched out on the seat then, holding her arm, and went to sleep.

She woke up uneasy in the cold twilight of daybreak with the train nearing Sydney. Why was she uneasy? There was a safety pin prodding her shoulderblade but that was a healed wound. Her arm was almost comfortable. She sat up and inspected it: purple fingerprints gloriously aureoled.

She remembered then and prayed, 'Lord, forgive me that I did not bear witness. I did not tell the young man the part You played in his rescue.'

And there he was, sober, haggard and serious. Grown up.

'Hello. You awake? I came to get your stuff down for you. Getting off at Hornsby?'

'No. Central.'

He got her case down from the rack and set it on the floor.

'How's the arm?'

'Good. It's quite all right now.'

'That's good.' He looked at the bruise, winced and clutched his hair. Now was her chance.

'Look. It's all right. I bruise easily.'

He laughed then, bent, put his arms round her and kissed her on the mouth.

'Goodbye,' he said tenderly. 'Goodbye, swell girl.'

He was gone, then.

'Lord, forgive my weakness,' she prayed, but absentmindedly. She got out a tissue to wipe away the young man's kiss, but on second thoughts she left it there.

The mood in Staffroom 8 at Browning High was elation subdued by embarrassment: elation because the staffroom syndicate had won a major prize in the lottery, embarrassment at the presence of Garry, who had dropped out of the syndicate a month before. When he took his fixed grin of despair out to the playground to take lunchtime duty, there were one or two long expulsions of breath.

Angela put down her coffee cup, turned her face to the room and said, 'What are we going to do about Garry?'

Since nobody spoke, she continued, 'I do think we have to do something.'

Victor the music teacher said lightly, 'You have to be in it to win it.'

Angela persisted, 'But he has been in it for eighteen months while we never won a cent.'

'Perhaps he was the Jonah.'

'Then we owe him something for being good enough to get out.'

Charlie wished that woman would shut up. People didn't really do such things, did they? Give money away when they didn't have to?

'I agree,' said Peg Hadley. 'He's been having a tough time, with his wife sick and having to pay to get the kids looked after. That's the only reason he got out – plain poverty.'

'I suppose,' said Martin, 'he should get his stake back.'

'What would that be? Sixty dollars, maybe, out of ten thousand. You don't have to insult him.'

Peg said drily, 'He might even have to accept it.'

'Thoughtless of me. Sorry.'

Angela was becoming heated. 'Well, what you do is your business, but I'm going to keep a seventh share and offer him the difference. How much is one-sixth of ten thousand?' She began to scribble on a notepad while the others looked at her with astonishment, unable to believe that she had not done the sum already.

Martin showed his amusement, but indulgently. '1666.6. We have an infinite repeater there. Awkward.'

'Mary Scobie,' murmured Victor.

The laughter was abrupt and loud.

'Oh, forget the cents.' She scribbled and calculated.

'A seventh comes to 1428. So I'll offer Garry the difference. That's 238, isn't it?'

Meddlesome bitch, thought Charlie.

'Worthy of the Maths Department,' said Victor.

Peg said, 'They'd be using their calculators.' She added to Charlie's dismay, 'I'll be with you, Angela. That'll make it a decent sum, worth offering.'

Peg was a widow who supported her three children with difficulty. Her remark was met with silence.

Angela looked towards Martin, with whom she had been pursuing extracurricular activities.

He shrugged. 'All right. I'll be in it.'

I believe I'll cool that situation, he thought. He didn't begrudge the money, but he liked to make his own decisions.

Brian said sulkily, 'I managed to put in my two dollars.'

He was a middle-aged bachelor without dependants. Nobody looked at him.

Victor sighed.

'Dear me. How painful it is to give money away, even when one hasn't seen it. However, I shall join you because Garry has been the victim of one of Fate's dirty tricks, which one should frustrate whenever possible.' He sang softly, 'Frustrate her knavish tricks . . .'

Even muted, his voice was beautiful. Angela looked at him with new interest and he acknowledged the look with a private smile. Round-shouldered, pot-bellied, shaggy-haired, affected shit, Martin said to himself with a fury that shocked him. It's too late. I can't cool it. I'm hooked. I'll go mad if she looks at anyone else.

Brian grumbled, 'All I can say is, you're putting us in an awkward position.'

Us now meant himself and Charlie. Nobody had looked towards Charlie nor thought of him as a contributor. He knew why. Ever since he had made a perfectly reasonable complaint about the amount of the tea bill, intended for everyone's benefit and supported by comparative studies of the amount other staffrooms paid for tea and coffee – an average of 4 cents a cup in Staffroom 3, for example, and 4.3 in Staffroom 1 – he had devoted time and effort to this, had not spoken without preparation, and what had he got for it? Persecution. Fury from Peg Hadley, asking him if he would care to take over, needling from that superior swine Victor, ridicule from one of them whenever the tea bill was put on the notice board.

'Short arms and deep pockets, Charlie? Stretch now!' 'Come on, Charlie! Do it quickly and it won't hurt so much.' Worse than the kids, they were. You'd expect that sort of thing in the playground, not in a staffroom.

Angela said sweetly to Brian, 'You choose your position and I'll choose mine.'

How did this happen to me? thought Martin. I don't like strongminded women. How does she feel about me?

He perceived that his life now depended on her feeling for him, and the loss of his freedom stunned him.

'I'll join you,' said Charlie, his voice thin with strain. Giving away money, painful to Victor, was agony to him.

Brian looked at him with hatred, the others with remorse.

'Thank you very much, Charlie,' Angela said in a subdued tone.

It was worth it, $238 to put an end to that laughter.

'It's not the money,' said Brian. 'It's the principle of the thing.'

'The interest, too,' murmured Victor.

Peg looked at her watch.

'Nobody's pressuring you, Brian. We don't have to name names.'

Charlie looked bleak.

Victor said smoothly, 'I think you owe it to yourself, Brian, to make a public stand in defence of your principles.' He added in a wondering tone, 'Whatever they are.'

Angela was smiling at that bastard again and he was preening himself. He hadn't been so ready to come in, had he?

First bell sounded.

Peg said, 'He'll be back in a minute. What's it to be?'

Brian yelled. 'Oh, all right. I'm not going to be the only one standing out.' He had managed to smooth the glare from his face when the door opened and Garry came in, tense and silent.

Peg spoke for them. 'Garry, we all want you to have an equal share in the prize. Nobody would feel happy,' she lied, 'if you didn't share the good luck. You shared all the bad luck, after all.'

Garry looked quickly round the room, sat down at his desk, put his face in his hands and began to sob deeply.

'I can't say no. It means too much. Wonderful. You are wonderful people.'

Peg put her arm round his shoulders. 'We're happy to do it.'

'The lines will be in in a minute,' said Angela.

Victor looked through the window at the quadrangle.

'It's all right. The boss is on the assembly. If he's on a morals crusade, he's good for ten minutes.'

Charlie waited.

They all fussed round Garry. There was Angela now, hugging and kissing, and Martin saying, 'Give me your roll, Garry. I'll take your rollcall.' Everyone was carrying on as if he was a hero.

Charlie said at last, 'Haven't you forgotten something?'

They all turned and stared at him. Garry blew his nose and began to grin.

'Of course.' He began to search his hip pocket. 'Two dollars makes thirty-five cents each, right?'

Then the laughter started, Brian laughing more loudly than the rest. They sobered to grinning as Garry handed out thirty five cents to each of them with ceremony, making a game of it as he took change and counted out coins, as if it was a joke, as if he didn't owe the money.

They hadn't changed. Charlie was back where he started with $238 gone for nothing. Pack of kids. They hadn't improved at all.

HOME TO ROOST

At ten to nine on Monday morning 3X2 Mathematics, giving in grudgingly to Fate, lined up outside Room 21. Miss Ferris came along the corridor to meet them, tight with fear at the sight of them and shouting down her fear.

'Straighten that line! Stop talking! Stand up straight!'

They shuffled obligingly while she flung open the door, stepped in, hurried out roosterwattle red and pulled it shut.

'Halt! Stop there! Wait quietly!'

At the end of the line somebody muttered 'Stop! Go! Drop . . . dead', the thought of something first-class on the blackboard drifted through the minds of one or two, most stood waiting without thinking at all while she opened the door again carefully, sidled through a thirty-centimetre gap and closed it behind her.

In a moment she came out again, opened the door widely and cried, 'Forward!'

'Backward!' piped the joker at the end of the line, but the class moved slowly in the right direction, resigning itself to tedium.

'A winebottle and two glasses.' Miss Ferris looked accusingly at the headmaster. 'Used.' In agitation she gripped the edge of the table, which was a fine piece of polished teak.

He looked back at her with a concerned expression which she knew meant nothing – it was the effect of a couple of wrinkles and the set of his eyes – leaned back in his black leather chair and asked, 'Did any of the youngsters see them?'

'No. I shut the door straight away and hid them in the table drawer.'

'Not much harm done, then,' he said too lightly. 'What was it, by the way?'

'Invalid port.'

'Good God! At that hour of the morning!'

Seeing the crumpled, desperate little face inflating with rage, he assumed a serious expression and said, 'I'll have a word with Mr Sutton about it.' He would have liked to say 'Sutton' or 'Jim', but the caretaker had a severe inward look which discouraged liberties.

'I hope you will get to the bottom of the matter,' she said in a tone which spoke less of hope than of disillusioning experience.

They looked at each other without enthusiasm, he reflecting on her remoteness from real life as she reflected on his remoteness from 3X2 Mathematics. The prize for innocence was his, since he had no idea what she was thinking, while she saw right into his mind, except for the corner where he was wishing she would take her damp little paws off his polished table. It was Miss Ferris's fate to know a lot about other people but never to know why she annoyed them.

The thought would have pleased her if she had read it. Whenever she came into the office, her face tightened with displeasure at the milk-chocolate carpet, the even milkier walls, the black leather, the shining teak, the biscuit-coloured curtains which hung almost to the floor in stiff folds as rich as an unsuitable dessert, the notes of soft positive blue in the vases and the sunny prints on the walls. When the new wing was built, the ladies of the Auxiliary had undertaken to furnish the office. They had worked hard and spent freely to create a calming and civilising atmosphere, more conducive to reasoning than to corporal punishment. Miss Ferris thought the effect immoral for reasons which maddened her by their elusiveness.

As for the headmaster – the new decor had had a stronger effect on him than could have been expected from mere furniture. Elegance had become his watchword; he banished the sordid and the ridiculous from his carpet with a neat epigram or an inward-turning smile, so that the mothers, when they met on canteen duty, were soon complaining to each other of the flippancy of his judgements. Surely, they grumbled, it was his responsibility to discipline the children, after all.

'Such a funny thing happened this morning,' said Miss Lloyd a week later at the staff morning tea.

The headmaster looked at her glumly, fearing that the funny thing would be a trivial incident which would involve him in tedious exertion. Meanwhile he considered the problem of Miss Lloyd's legs, which were visible to mid-thigh below a long loose red sweater and a short narrow tartan skirt. They were clothed, indeed, in solid black tights, which might be considered sobering, but on the other hand . . . What attitude should a sophisticated male in authority take in this situation? A disapproving glance? Such was the authority of Miss Lloyd's legs that any glance in their direction would be misconstrued. Why couldn't Miss Ferris make a complaint about Miss Lloyd's display of leg? He would be able to take the matter up then in a worldly way – 'There have been complaints' – no names, of course, but a tone that deplored envious disapproval from the less fortunate of her sex.

'I came in early to draw a map on the board in Room 22 and I couldn't get in because the door was locked. So I went looking for Mr Sutton or a cleaner to open it for me. I couldn't find them anywhere so I went to the office for the key but it wasn't there. Back I went, feeling pretty frustrated, and I saw Mr Sutton just going round the corner into the Fourth Form corridor. I called out after him but he can't have heard me. Anyhow when I got back to Room 22 the door was open.'

'Mr Sutton having no doubt opened it as he passed.'

'But here's the odd thing. I went in and started on my map and then I heard somebody in the bookroom, so I looked in. It was one of the cleaners dusting the shelves.

You know the tall bony one who never smiles? The one with the black hair in a bun?'

'Mrs Grimsby. A cleaner cleaning. Very odd, as you say.'

'But how did she get there? If the door was locked? And I was only away a minute.'

With a small, yawning sigh he said, 'I feel sure there is some simple explanation.'

'Isn't there a regulation duster? That pink and yellow thing on a cane handle?'

'Yes, there is. I take it Mrs Grimsby wasn't using one. Great are the sins of Mrs Grimsby. What was she using, then?'

The school flag?

Miss Lloyd consulted her memory, which must suddenly have enlightened her, for she blushed translucent pink and muttered, 'I just thought it was funny.'

'Well, if it's not your job, Mrs Russell, don't you do it,' said Vera Johnson, the senior mistress.

Leaning on the handle of her polishing machine Mrs Russell spoke in a worn and plaintive tone. 'I'm sure it would never be done if I left it. There was chalk trampled into the floor on Tuesday and streaks of it still showing Friday. Never a drop of water nor a bit of polish, nothing but a quick onceover with the broom from one week to the next. And a really nasty thing written on the windowsill that stared you in the face for days. I made up my mind not to do it again but I could stand seeing that word no longer. I went in to clean it off and once I'd started, there I was, doing two people's work and getting no thanks for it. Far from it.'

'Why don't you speak to Mr Sutton about it?'

Since Mrs Russell was looking at her with a strange look that suggested distant laughter, Vera said sharply, 'You'll get nowhere making a martyr of yourself, you know. People just think you enjoy it.' This was a sidelong approach to a well-known weakness in Mrs Russell.

'It goes against the grain with me to leave a room like a pigsty.'

'Leave it just the same,' Vera yielded to the unspoken request. 'If you don't, I won't be able to report it to Mr Blake.'

'Well, if you wouldn't mind, Mrs Johnson. I'm sure I don't see how things can go on as they are.'

Mission accomplished, Mrs Russell switched on her polisher and drifted away in its wake.

Mrs Russell was standing in the corridor with her friend Mrs Wiley when Vera paused beside them and said, in the neutral tone of the mere messenger, 'I spoke to Mr Blake about that matter, Mrs Russell. He has mentioned it to Mr Sutton and Mr Sutton says that he is quite satisfied.'

Mrs Russell's eyes met Mrs Wiley's. Round that steady gaze their faces folded into grins.

'Thank you very much, Mrs Johnson,' said Mrs Russell in a struggling voice, catching and biting at her wavering lips. When she looked back to Mrs Wiley they gave way, leaning on their brooms gasping, sobbing and heaving on a great tide of laughter.

'Satisfied. Oh my God,' sobbed Mrs Wiley. 'Satisfied. That's the word, all right.'

Vera walked on, affronted, leaving them shaking their heads and wiping their eyes. Of course she took their meaning – how could she help it? – but summoning up a mental picture of Mr Sutton and Mrs Grimsby, such a tall, dour, raw-boned, uncommunicative pair, she thought, 'It isn't possible.' They must be laughing because the idea was so outrageous.

With profound gravity, the headmaster said, 'You wish me to understand that Mr Sutton has a *tendre* for Mrs Grimsby' – he pronounced the French word with offensive correctness – 'and that therefore he may be favouring her unduly.'

'It's not beyond the bounds of possibility.'

'That's one department where nothing is beyond the bounds of possibility.'

The headmaster became thoughtful as he took his own words to heart.

'I don't suppose it matters,' said Vera, 'so long as Mrs Russell doesn't have to do Mrs Grimsby's work.'

'I'll have a look at the rooms myself.'

Hadn't Mrs Grimsby become a little too interesting lately? What had someone been saying about her the other day?

Later, he said casually to his deputy, 'You know, I think we'll lock those bookrooms. Miss Ferris is complaining that they reek of cigarette smoke. In fact, it might be a good idea if I kept the keys myself.'

The day the headmaster drove his daughter to the airport he arrived at the school forty minutes early. His office door was locked. Frowning at the lateness of the cleaners, he opened it with his own key, pushed it wide, caught it, pulled it shut and leaned against it, trembling with shock. Then he opened it ten centimetres and spoke through the gap.

'Mr Sutton and Mrs Grimsby, you are to leave the school at once. Take all your personal belongings with you. I shall send whatever money is due to you. Do not come here again.'

Then he leaned against the wall until the lovers came out stiff-faced and walked past him without a glance.

At morning tea, Miss Ferris asked, 'Where's Mr Sutton today? He was going to fix the blind in Room 11, but he hasn't done it and I can't find him anywhere.'

The headmaster turned his answer into a public announcement.

'Mr Sutton has left.'

'You mean for good?'

'I mean for good.'

When someone behind him said in an idiot tone, 'Mrs Grimsby doesn't seem to be here either,' he gave no sign that he had heard it.

As he walked away with the deputy, he thought, Say no more. Dignity. Dignity. What a mistake it would be to say the words that were struggling to be said. Goodbye sophistication, goodbye elegance and imperturbability. He would be a laughing stock.

He said them.

'On my polished table. The pair of them. On my polished table!'

'Oh, the dirty wretches,' said the deputy with a mouthful of gloom.

The headmaster turned to look at him. The profound sorrow of his expression told the worst. Laughter through the staffrooms, demure faces at morning tea.

'There's been a very lax atmosphere lately,' said the headmaster sharply. 'I've been noticing it in the staff. Those skirts of Miss Lloyd's. Most unsuitable. I'm astonished that Mrs Johnson hasn't said something to her about them. See to it, will you, that she has a word with her?'

Worthing Manor
3rd November, 1854

My dearest Jane,

I write this letter in a mood of bitterness, or rather in a passion of indignation against injustice which would do credit to my dear Jane herself.

I am under notice here. The young master, down now permanently from Oxford, has been paying me marked attentions – without, you may be sure, any encouragement from me! But his mamma chooses to believe otherwise and was quite open, to the point of insult, in giving me the reason for my dismissal.

So there the situation is. I am supposed to be attempting to entrap Mr Edmund – such a Puffer Fish, my dear, as no woman would wish to find entangled in her net!

No matter how plain my dress, nor how subdued my manners, I must suffer once more from that caprice of Nature which clothed me in a style quite unsuitable to my station in life. I know that it is most unbecoming in a woman to attribute beauty to her person, but I trust you, my dearest Jane, to hear without misjudging me.

I was so angry at the insolent accusation that I quite forgot to guard my tongue. 'Indeed, Madam,' I said, 'as an affectionate parent, you must wish to spare your son the pain of a rejection which must follow any proposal he might make to me!'

'You forget yourself, Miss!' – looking very much the mother of a Puffer Fish as she spoke.

'No, Madam. It is I who know what respect is owed to a virtuous female, and you who forget it! You forget yourself when you forget that!'

I was asked to leave at once, with a month's salary in lieu of notice. This was, I suppose, for the convenience of Master Edmund, for whose comfort I care not a jot. He glooms about, convinced that his heartless mamma stands between him and his happiness, a position in which I should be quite willing to stand, though the fatuous youth could never be brought to believe such heresy.

I have refused to budge. I shall not be thrown upon the world without a prospect of employment. I am applying for other positions while I continue my duties. At least there will be no heartbreak this time in leaving the children – cold, arrogant and priggish young ladies as they are, with hardly a trace of real childhood about them.

I have little hope of a good reference here. Meanwhile the Puffer Fish sulks, without one thought for the unfortunate young woman he has cast upon the world. How selfish are these animal passions to which those who hold them dare to give the name of love!

Forgive the bitterness of my tone, dear Jane, and write to comfort me!

I am glad that Thornfield Hall promises so well. Mrs Fairfax seems to be an amiable person, and the little French girl quite enchanting.

One thing, however, in the situation does disturb me. You speak of the strange manners and unprepossessing appearance of the servant Grace Poole, but you do not give an adequate reason for her employment in the house. Amiable Mrs Fairfax may be, but I think that she is withholding information which may affect your comfort and even your safety. Such a person, so withdrawn and yet given to this rowdiness, may easily be prone to excesses of rage, or of irrational behaviour. Are there not servants and sempstresses to be found, who can be relied on not to indulge in strange mutterings?

What an odd little person you are, my darling Jane, with a head full of fancies, of legends and goblins, for here is a mystery which I should be compelled to investigate, yet which you seem to accept with great composure.

Remember, dear Jane, that we have no natural protector, that we must look to ourselves for comfort and security. I beg you to inform yourself further about this woman's employment.

The problem is how to inform yourself, since a direct question to Mrs Fairfax will clearly bring a vague and unsatisfactory answer. The social standing of the governess is so precarious that to gossip with the servants may sink it altogether, yet what other source of information can be found?

You do not give me a full account of the staff. I do suggest that if you are reduced to seeking information there, you should avoid the upper servants, who are too close in situation to yourself. A ribbon or a pretty collar to the tweeny, a sixpenny piece to the bootboy, will compromise you less and may be just as productive. These young people are in general so neglected that the approach is in itself rewarding, even if it does not bring the reward of information. The selfless devotion of an under footman is quite beyond price, but cannot always be commanded.

I think I may write a manual, a 'Guide to the Governess in the House of the Mighty'.

But I shall not continue, for I know that these frivolities put you out of sympathy with me. I am not being frivolous, however, when I beg you to be observant. There is some mystery here, and mystery is ever a cause of unease – except, it seems, to one gentle, trusting little Jane Eyre!

I wait for the dear expression of your sympathy. Do not fail.

Your affectionate friend,
Mary Ann Wilson

My dearest Jane,

Thank you for your dear letter. Your indignation on my behalf is a great support to me in this cold and hostile place.

I am firmly resolved not to move until I have found employment, but I am beginning to fear that this may not be easy. I have applied twice for positions for which I felt I was qualified, received promising replies, and travelled to an interview which ended in specious excuses and polite rejection. Alas, that a woman should have so little confidence in the constancy of a husband or the chastity of a son! But I begin to think that there is more than the unintended insolence – I find no better word – of my address that discourages employers. I have had spiteful indications here of a worse cause, questions about my reasons for leaving previous positions, with an undertone of implication which does me no credit.

I know that the sufferings of poor Mrs Fordyce were worsened by her consciousness of the injustice she was forced to inflict on me in dismissing me from my post, an injustice she strove to mitigate by the grant of half a year's salary, and by strenuous efforts to find me a new and favourable situation.

'You know, Mary Ann,' she said falteringly, 'I must think of your welfare also.'

It is strange that a young woman employed mainly for her skill in languages should not be supposed to have at her command the means of rejecting unwanted advances! Yet I knew that in this the poor lady was clinging to a last remnant of pride, so I let the matter pass.

I must protest, dear Jane, at your remark that you are glad to be protected by the plainness and insignificance of your appearance from such trials as mine.

You are not plain nor by any means insignificant. Your features may not be striking, but there is nothing in them to repel, and when they are animated by any interest or affection which may be brought to shine in your quite beautiful eyes, they possess a charm which transcends physical beauty. You are well equipped to inspire love. Let that knowledge guide your conduct.

I remember those weeks at Lowood when we roamed the woods – freed, as I now recall with compunction, by the typhus epidemic which was bringing sickness and death to many of our companions. We were too young to dwell on the thought of death, nor had the atmosphere of that institution promoted the formation of friendships which might have taught us to grieve. So we roamed happily. You sat beside me on that white stone which rose in the centre of the beck – running barefoot through the water to reach it, and thinking then that we had discovered a small kingdom of our own where none could challenge us. It was a pastime somewhat undignified for one of my advanced years, but you took such pleasure in it that it delighted me too. There we sat, safe from the world, and I told you stories of Apsley Park, the great house, the great park, the grand people who visited there unaware that they were scrutinised without indulgence by the servants, whose comments I loved to repeat to you, and when I brought your solemn little face to laughter, I felt both proud and tender.

I think I had never had a real friend before; I had not, since my mother's early death, known such an affection. You could not have known how dear it was to me, nor how I suffered when your solitary grief over the death of Helen Burns removed you from me into a region of sorrow where I could not penetrate.

One must not of course criticise a saint, particularly a dead saint, yet I could not share your reverence for Helen Burns. Indeed, I must feel some sympathy with poor Miss Scatcherd, whose duty it was to impart both knowledge and orderly habits. To say, 'Yes, I have earned this punishment and must bear it with patience,' is an exasperating answer to punishment, which aims towards amendment. Helen never did make a serious effort towards amendment. She did not become more attentive, nor remember to tidy her drawers.

I discern, however, something in you, Jane, which is drawn always to the extreme. Helen Burns was a saint indeed. I shall not further insult your feeling for her, except to remark that there are pupils I should prefer to have in my class.

Please allow these remarks to pass – put them down to the bitterness of a disappointed affection, which at that time caused me suffering. My friendship for you is deeper, I think, than yours for me; I am not formed on that heroic scale which only can command all your love. I know that I have your truest affection when I am unfortunate, and that gives me a little ease in misfortune.

How sententious, how analytical I am today! Believe me, I am prepared to accept truth from you as I hope you accept it from me.

As for the rest of your letter and the other misfortunes you ascribe to me – it was, I suppose, disgraceful that any dependant of a noble house should have been sent to such an institution as Lowood was when first we knew it. You know, my dear, that there is on my birth that shadow which justifies any contempt, any neglect of the innocent issue of sin. Yet there are extenuating circumstances. Money was not plentiful at Apsley Park, for all its outward glory. The estate was much encumbered through the debts left by that dissolute Marquis to whom I must suppose I owe my being. While my parentage was never openly acknowledged in the family, I was nevertheless the living representative of his faults. Many a dark look was directed at me when they were mentioned.

My father had left no heir. The younger brother who succeeded to the title – an honourable and conscientious man – set about paying the debts which threatened ruin to the house. Land was sold; great oaks were felled, to the grief of all. The new Marquis sold his magnificent hunters, dismissed an idle and incompetent steward and undertook the management of the home farm himself. His first efforts at farming were greeted with pity and derision in the servants' hall, but through common sense and application, he mastered his new trade of gentleman farmer; as the supply of poultry, eggs, milk, butter, fruit and vegetables to the kitchen improved in quantity and in quality, contempt gave way to respect and even to emulation. Mrs Bonner managed the kitchen with due regard to economy.

The Marchioness furthered the efforts of the Marquis. I fancy that, being a woman of severe disposition, she felt some satisfaction in imposing restrictions on her two daughters – perhaps to remind them that they were but daughters! There was no son of the house; the estate was entailed upon the heir to the title, a distant cousin named Robert Lorimer.

Her Ladyship's only anxiety was that the economies practised in the household should not damage the family's standing in the world. Economy was practised in stealth; it was never allowed to interfere with the duties of hospitality.

I did not, in these circumstances, regard my consignment to Lowood as an injustice. It was in the breast of the two young ladies, Letitia and Honoria, that the sense of injustice burned fiercely. They had but one maid to attend both – and she an untrained girl who had other duties in the household. This they felt to be a disgrace. They lamented most the loss of the smaller carriage, which had been kept for their use and now was sold 'for the benefit of Mr Lorimer'!

Indeed, the name of Mr Lorimer evoked the same black looks as were so often directed at me.

As for the hardships of Lowood – I took care not to mention them at Apsley Park. I endured cold and hunger without complaint there, for fear of being taken away, since I had decided early that education must be my resource. I could not be invited to share the lessons of their governess with the Ladies Letitia and Honoria (being, you understand, the Very Dishonourable Mary Ann), nor would I have wished to do so, since I had soon advanced far beyond their standard.

My parentage was no romantic dream, I assure you. In the servants' hall, which was then my true home at Apsley Park, the talk was all of my likeness to my infamous Papa. 'That turn of the head she has, it brings His Lordship right to life!' 'She has His Lordship's eyes.'

I have been forced to the conclusion that His Lordship's eyes, set in my innocent countenance, send an invitation to liberties which are foreign to my intentions. This, the only legacy I have from my late unlamented Papa, is not likely to advance my credit in the world. At times I envisage a Supreme Being who has a quite malicious sense of humour. But I must not shock you, dear Jane, for your friendship means much to me. I went once into the picture gallery seeking his likeness, but found only a family group where he figured as a half-grown boy, stiff and solemn, with no hint of the mischief to come.

I never suffered as you suffered in the home of your infamous aunt. There were no terrors, nothing like the terrible red-room, no bullies such as John Reed to torment me. Her Ladyship regarded me with cold dislike; my cousins – if I may take the liberty of claiming them as such – disliked me perhaps more intently, but were too conscious of their own dignity to ill-treat me.

Nor must I ever forget that my dear Mamma was not turned out to die in want. She was maintained by a pension from the family, so that I owe to their bounty nearly eight years of carefree childhood, and when my happy village life was ended by Mamma's early death, they gave me a home, food, clothing and education. Many people would have done less. It was perhaps heartless to leave me at Lowood during the typhus epidemic, but they had after all a great establishment in their charge and were responsible for the health of many. I cannot make a grievance of a neglect which brought me such a time of happiness.

Write again; tell me more of Thornfield – and what of Grace Poole? Is her behaviour still marked by outbursts of wild laughter and by strange mutterings? Have you given some thought to my advice? I wish with all my heart you would do so.

I shall continue my search for employment and tell you how I fare.

Your affectionate friend,

Mary Ann Wilson

Worthing Manor
5th December, 1854

My dearest Jane,

Do not take my reproaches so much to heart! You are quite right; there is in me a lightness of manner, even an air of frivolity, perhaps, which makes it difficult to perceive the depth and sincerity of my affection. You say that it was not until we began to correspond that you knew my true nature. That I understand. It is only with pen in hand that I feel free to express my feelings. Perhaps my situation at Apsley

Park, which required that I conceal anger and humiliation, has given to my demeanour a fashion which might pass for indifference. Indeed, I have often been compelled to cultivate indifference to slights against which I had no defence.

We understand each other better now, and I trust that you value my affection as I value yours.

You ask me why I do not take refuge at Apsley Park, where I must have a claim at least to shelter. Perhaps I shall do so as a last resort, though it would be to me a bitter confession of failure. I have told you that my early childhood there was not unhappy. Below stairs I was much petted. Below stairs I was 'His Lordship's little girl', while above stairs I was 'poor Wilson's child'.

In the servants' hall I was always welcome; it was home to me, but the kitchen was my delight. I spent my happiest hours in that bright, warm, active place – I cannot call it a room, since it had more the air of a busy market or workplace. I was lucky in the tolerance of Mrs Bonner. She had even bought for me from her own wages a miniature pastry board and roller, which I plied busily, making small tarts which Emily the kitchenmaid would put in the oven to bake. This was good training for a cook, and I might have grown to be a good one.

Unfortunately, as I acquired some of Mrs Bonner's skills, I was also acquiring her habits of speech. One afternoon I chanced to meet the Marquis as he crossed the hall and, on his kindly enquiring whether I was happy at Apsley, I answered blithely, 'As happy as a little pig in the muck pail, thank you, my Lord,' thereby pronouncing my own sentence of banishment from the kitchen.

146

When I arrived next morning, ready for the expected task of stalking the currants which had been brought in the day before from the kitchen garden, I found Emily weeping and Mrs Bonner muttering from lips set in anger.

'You can't come here any more, Mary Ann,' said Emily. 'His Lordship says it's not right for you to play in the kitchen. So I'll have to find another kitchen maid for when I'm a cook.'

Mrs Bonner's muttering became louder and more intelligible. 'Too good to be a cook, that's the story. Too good to be a cook, but, mark my words, never good enough to be a lady. If those who have a feeling for the child aren't allowed to concern themselves, then who will, and what's to become of her? That is what I ask and I mean to have an answer from those who take it on themselves . . .'

At this temerity, her voice sank again to a mutter.

Her wrath was Jovian and her influence such – the influence of an excellent cook angry enough to give in her notice at the slightest further provocation is not to be ignored – that it reached above stairs and fetched down an answer. I paid one more visit to the kitchen, escorted by the housekeeper, who was nervous and flurried at facing righteous anger. She told Mrs Bonner, and incidentally myself, that I was to go to school, and that when I was at Apsley Park I was to eat my meals in the nursery wing with Mrs Field and the young ladies.

I should probably not have persisted in my ambition to become Emily's kitchen maid and her apprentice, on my way to becoming a cook, but the nursery wing was a poor substitute for the bright, bustling kitchen, and the company of Miss Field and the young ladies, who clearly resented the intrusion, very dull after the gossip and the laughter of the servants' hall. Miss Field particularly, being set, I think, to correct my speech, resented the task and performed it without concealing her resentment. The poor lady felt herself much compromised by her brush with my vulgarity.

The nursery wing of course no longer housed a nursery. It consisted of a school room, a sitting room where we took our meals, and a small bedroom which had once been occupied by the nursery maid and was now Miss Field's quarters and which later was mine.

Since my own experience as a governess has enlightened me, I understand how painful was Miss Field's experience. The social standing of the governess is in the gift of the employer. Miss Field was given little honour and scant politeness by Her Ladyship, nor did Letitia or Honoria offer that open-hearted affection with which one's pupils can make the position tolerable in spite of slights from the household.

Exiled from the kitchen and left without occupation, I wandered into the library and discovered – with what joy and excitement – the world that was to be mine. Most of the text, of course, was beyond my small domain of literacy; I looked for books with illustrations, works of natural history and travel. It is so strange, to reflect that like you, I found Bewick's *History of British Birds* – but, unlike you, I did not linger on the coasts of Norway, which I found forbidding. There were pleasanter pictures to dwell on: a mother bird in its nest, a robin picking crumbs from a windowsill – my tastes, I fear, tended to the sentimental rather than the heroic.

I did apply myself to the text beneath the engravings and by spelling out and recognising a word here and there; I began to increase my power of reading and to look forward eagerly to the promised arrival at school.

I owed my entrance at Lowood to Lady Forrester, a friend of Her Ladyship who had contributed money to the institution and therefore had the privilege of granting a few places there. To Lady Forrester I was represented as the illegitimate child of a servant – which was of course true, and the whole truth if one accepts that a child has only one parent! I did not blame Her Ladyship for her discretion, but I did dislike the other's admiration of her charity. I was, however, too bent upon the prospect of education to harbour bitterness.

I suffered less than you did at Lowood, being older by two years, well grown and, I fear, aggressive. No one stole my half-slice of bread and, upon my honour, I never deprived a smaller child, although I see now that I did not do enough to protect the younger children – the struggle for survival makes one selfish, indeed.

Besides, I spent my vacations at Apsley Park, where Mrs Bonner set herself to fatten me for the lean term ahead.

'What they feed you in that place I do not know!' she would scold. Nor would I tell!

In those vacations, I was set to help Rachel the sempstress. Sewing, it seemed, was a genteel occupation, though laborious enough to make it a servitude.

Rachel was a quiet, well-looking woman of perhaps thirty, not so much a woman maturing as a pretty girl fading day by day. She worked at a long cutting-table in the sewing room, with no company but a headless, limbless figure of Her ladyship, which I greeted every day with a curtsy and a compliment. 'Your Ladyship is in excellent looks today!', 'I doubt that I have ever seen Your Ladyship look better!'

The purpose of this childish habit was to make Rachel laugh, in which purpose it succeeded, though the little spurt of laughter was always followed by a protest. 'Mary Ann, you are wicked!', 'Mary Ann, you shouldn't say such things!' Yet a small smile lingered when the laugh was gone, so that I was encouraged to persist with my impertinent little ceremony.

It was in the sewing room that the art of keeping up appearances was most effectively combined with economy. Nothing was wasted; handsome trimmings of lace and fur were carefully unpicked and set aside to be used again. Her Ladyship's ball gowns came from a famous house in London, but, after a brief social life and a tactful lapse of time, they were cut again to make evening gowns for the young ladies. Unlike Her Ladyship, they were required to attend the sewing room for fittings, which they did without grace, for they found the contrivance humiliating.

I never acquired Rachel's skill with the needle. The stitching of a long seam, a day's work to me, was for her the work of an hour, and to see her beading a design was to watch a skill which approached artistry. I did, however, show a natural aptitude for cutting and design, and could adapt the master pattern to reproduce a fashion plate from the *Ladies' Journal*. There were times in the sewing room when the work went well and we were happy in our achievements, though they met with little appreciation from those for whom the gowns were made.

It was over the honey-coloured satin that I felt the first stirrings of rebellion on Rachel's account. It was cut as usual from a gown once worn by Her Ladyship. Rachel had gathered the bodice into a standing quilted collar and finished the full sleeves with cuffs of the same quilting. This quilting was Rachel's masterpiece. The great house in London could not have produced its equal, and when we called Lady Letitia for her fitting, we had a sense of anticipation, an expectation of giving pleasure which quite raised our spirits. Letitia however put on the gown without remark, except to say ill-temperedly to Honoria, who of course had accompanied her, 'All this to save a few fields for Mr Lorimer!'

Rachel turned away to hide a tear of mortification and I bit my lip to repress an angry comment. When they had departed, I asked Rachel why she gave herself so much trouble, since it was paid poorly in money and not at all in appreciation.

'But this is the part that I enjoy,' she said, stroking her quilting with a loving touch. 'I only wish, Mary Ann, that I was doing it for you!'

That was the only protest I ever heard from Rachel, but I began to ponder the difference between her condition and that of Mrs Bonner. They both had special skills;

151

Rachel's perhaps were rarer, yet Mrs Bonner had authority, even some power, and certainly earned higher wages than Rachel, whose skills must save the family hundreds of guineas in a year. Mrs Bonner supported the prestige of the house, while Rachel was involved in its private embarrassments – but must the value of a woman's work be judged according to the caprice of others? Should it not have some absolute value, independent of the part it played in their lives?

I began to experience a discontent which was, for the first time, not selfish. Meanwhile, I had cause for selfish discontent. As first Letitia, then Honoria, left the schoolroom to take their place in society, and soon afterwards Miss Field moved to another situation. I was left alone in the nursery wing.

As I sat over my books at night, I heard the sounds of music and laughter from the drawing-room, and oh! how I longed to join that company! How much I resented my exclusion from a society to which I felt, nevertheless, that I belonged. A cold anger was growing in me, which, without my full understanding, was poisoning my tongue. Too often, in the sewing room, I lamented that a shade of sage or amethyst might be unkind to Letitia's complexion, or recommended a cut which might disguise Honoria's corpulence. One day I saw Honoria flinch, while Letitia's lip curved in scorn, and I perceived with shame that I was being possessed by a truly menial spite.

Small as my virtues are, I cling to them. I could endure Letitia's scorn, but not the deserving of it. At that moment, I resolved to leave Apsley Park for ever.

I sought an interview with the Marquis, and informed him that I had decided to make my way in the world as a governess, that therefore I wished to spend my vacations at Lowood, where I should take private lessons in French with Madame Pierrot, and also begin the study of Latin with the rector of the parish – I was, you see, ambitious!

'I think your place is here, Mary Ann,' he objected.

'And where in this house is my place, sir, since I belong neither in the servants' hall nor in the drawing-room?'

At this he nodded unhappily and gave me his blessing, asking only that he should always know where I was and what was my situation. I promised him this and have kept the promise, for I know that he will always be my friend and will help me in need.

So I left Apsley Park. The Marquis gave me twenty guineas, wincing a little at the smallness of the sum. Rachel wept and gave me an embroidered purse, at which I wept too, for since Mamma died, I had had no presents, except for Mrs Bonner's pastry board and the guinea which I received from the Marquis at Christmas and on my birthday. The latter attention I appreciated very much. He had had to ask me for the date, and had given me my first guinea when he found that my eighth birthday had passed unremarked. That small kindness I have never forgotten.

Her Ladyship gave me an almost new mantle which Letitia had particularly disliked, and bade me remember the benefits I had received from the family. My answer to this had been well rehearsed, I assure you.

'Madam,' I said, 'that this family did not fail in its duty to my very dear Mamma is a circumstance which must always command my respect for its name.'

Having delivered this strictly limited measure of praise – which did a little curdle Her Ladyship's complexion – I curtsied and departed.

I tend to forgive my enemies, since I find it the best and safest way of annoying them, but, having delivered my little shaft (long and lovingly polished, I admit), I usually succeed in forgetting them. Her Ladyship has not been much in my thoughts since then.

What a long answer this has been, dear Jane, to your brief question: 'Why do you not take refuge at Apsley Park?'

I hope you have not found it tedious. To me, in the telling there have been some discoveries, some clearing of mist.

Let me have news of you soon!

Your affectionate friend,

Mary Ann

The White Hart
Worthing
20th December, 1854

My dearest Jane,

You will see from the above address that I have left the Manor, I could not endure to spend Christmas where the chill indoors, in spite of log fires, matched the chill without. I have received at this inn an unexpectedly warm welcome.

The family at the Manor is not much loved in the village. Though I have said nothing of my reasons for leaving my employment there, it is taken for granted that it is through no fault of mine; indeed there is much unspoken sympathy for me. It seems that one of the inn servants, a pretty girl named Sarah, has a tale to tell of Mr Edmund.

I mean to have a happy Christmas. I shall go to church on Christmas morning and there try to find goodwill towards all, while I ask for guidance in directing my future. Then I have been promised a merry dinner at the inn, with the family and their guests, relatives from London.

As for my future – I have despaired of finding a new post as governess and mean now to look for employment in a school. I have a little money set aside, which gives me time for reflection.

Miss Temple warned me that I was not suited to the life of a governess. 'I know your qualities, my dear, and I value them,' she told me kindly. 'There is, however . . . a little too much spirit in your address, which some might find challenging.' She did not mention His Lordship's beckoning eyes, which I seem to my misfortune to have inherited, but perhaps she had them also in mind.

I do not quite share your reverence for the virtues of Miss Temple, though I appreciated her kindness and enjoyed her instruction, which was indeed of the first quality. I thought myself lucky in the acquaintance, for all teachers are not so inspiring!

I came, however, to believe that in virtue she fell a little short. I know she defended you against a false accusation, taking a trouble that many would have neglected in your cause, and for that I honour her – yet she did not defend you to Mr Brocklehurst. She did not take that one step further, which would have made her truly heroic.

I cannot forget that in the vacation which followed the typhus epidemic, I was called down from the sewing room to attend Her Ladyship in the small sitting-room. She sat there alone with Lady Forrester – I believe I have told you that Lady Forrester had given money to Lowood and had arranged for my entrance there. The poor lady had suffered much grief over the death of the children during the epidemic, and some disgrace from her connection with the institution. She now sat, pale and red-eyed, languid from weeping, her head resting against the wing of her armchair, an image of desolation.

Her Ladyship spoke to me sharply. 'Mary Ann, why did you not inform us of these dreadful conditions at Lowood? Surely it was your duty to speak of what you saw there!'

Much you would have cared, Milady, thought I, and stood mute.

Poor Lady Forrester roused herself then to take my part. 'Mary Ann cannot be blamed. Children are taught to be silent, to show respect and obedience to their elders. They are told they should be seen and not heard. How then can they be expected to speak against those who hold authority over them, when all their training tells them that it is a fault to do so?

'I cannot escape my responsibility. I have had a terrible lesson. I know now that it is not enough to give money – one must accompany it with care and concern, but were there no adults there, no teachers who observed this regime of semi-starvation and who could have spoken out?' she cried out with sudden indignation. 'Could they not have had some faith, that among the sponsors of Lowood, there would be those who would remedy such conditions, if they had known of them?'

She had shaken her head, then, tired by the outburst, and drooped once more against the wing of her chair.

I began to see in this a limit to Miss Temple's virtue. She had seen, had deplored, had mitigated where she could, but for all that, she had condoned. You may object that she had had no choice, but choice is something women must somehow acquire – I know not how; my thoughts in this are vague and confused. There was a word I was looking for, and have found and have begun to hate. The word is *compliance*.

If Rachel had taken her talents to one of the great dress houses of London, she might have fared worse, I know, for the conditions of women working at dressmaking were never good; yet in the act of choosing her fate there would have been some merit, as there was a failing in Miss Temple's unquestioning acceptance of Mr Brocklehurst's authority.

I know that I ask for miracles. We cannot change society, but could we not change women and their view of themselves a little?

You lament that I had never told you the darker aspect of my life at Apsley Park, but in those days, I hardly knew it myself. It is only in the foreshortening of time which memory brings that one sees such things clearly.

I hope that you will have the best and happiest Christmas possible. How good it must be, to have the companionship of a child! You will be able to share the joy of the Christmas season with little Adele.

Your affectionate friend,
Mary Ann

White Hart
Worthing
30th January, 1855

My dearest Jane,

Thank you for your letter and your kind enquiries. You see that I am still at the White Hart, where I am feeling quite at home. I have, however, made a journey or two in pursuit of employment and have settled my future. I have even had some choice in the matter! But more of that later.

I had the most delightful Christmas. Having learned from Mrs Hagerty what dolls the little girls from London might possess, I made use of the skills I had acquired at Apsley Park to fashion frilled and embroidered pinafores for those miniature persons. For the baby boy I stitched a soft ball in bright colours – it was lucky that I had carried away my workbag with its scraps of material! Mrs Hagerty's sister was delighted with the baby's toy, and the little girls were so entranced by the pinafores that the five-year-old Sophie spent the afternoon sitting on my knee, while seven-year-old Catherine asked earnestly if I could make dolls' dresses too.

'That will be for next year, if Mary Ann will come to spend Christmas with us,' said Mrs Hagerty.

For that, I could have thrown my arms about her in gratitude. How precious is the offer of some continuity in the life of a wanderer!

To my astonishment, there were presents for me under the Christmas tree. Mr Hagerty had brought in a small fir tree in a tub, and our presents were set under it. It was a pretty sight, Mrs Hagerty having hung it with gilded walnuts and small confections baked in the shape of stars and fir trees. I had not seen this custom before. Mrs Hagerty's sister said that such a tree was set up for the royal children at Christmas, and that the fashion had been much taken up in London. When my name was called, I came to receive a small needle-case and a pin tray.

I had been to church in the morning, to celebrate Christmas in the true spirit, but I found as much sacred feeling at the inn, being taken in by strangers and given tokens of love, as I had found in the church. The family from the Manor was in the front pew, and I did in the spirit of Christmas succeed in shedding my anger, and prayed for their welfare, but with more effort and less joy than I found in holding little Sophie on my knee.

So, dear Jane, you have met Mr Rochester. From the detail in which you report that first encounter, it appears that the gentleman has roused your curiosity. It appears to me that Mr Rochester is very skilled in making himself interesting. This was the great game in the drawing room at Apsley Park, where gentlemen strove to fascinate the ladies and ladies returned the compliment. Molly, the senior parlour maid, all sober deference when she waited on the nobility and their guests, was nevertheless an excellent

159

mimic and would, with the help of Hugh the footman, repeat these scenes for us. There was no harm in these little manoeuvres, and the laughter in the servants' hall was kind. There are, however, those, among both sexes, who seek to be loved where they have no intention of loving. This is not listed as a sin in the catechism (unless it is bearing false witness), but I think it is a grave one.

There is no doubt that Mr Rochester seeks, perhaps simply from habit, to engage your attention. In the first place, he withholds his name, in a situation where any gentleman of proper manners would have introduced himself at once. But your Mr Rochester – how earnestly I hope that he is not your Mr Rochester! – must wrap himself in a little mystery, which will keep him in one's thoughts, for a time at least. Then, he asks about you – quite unnecessarily, for you had told him that you were the governess – of little Adele, knowing well that she will repeat the conversation to you.

Oh, Jane, have a care! I know the depth and the tenacity of your passions!

As for Mr Rochester's reserve, his air of gloom and despondency: he may indeed be gnawed by some secret sorrow; he may on the other hand have found this an effective way of touching the heart, particularly a heart of such ready sympathy as your own.

I repeat, dear Jane, have a care! Mr Rochester may have the best of reasons for wishing to gain your affection (I have already tried to convince you that you greatly underestimate your powers of pleasing), but if he is such a monster of vanity as would wish to capture any impressionable heart, I fear for you. I fear not for your virtue, but for your happiness.

If you find my letter impertinent, please judge me by my intentions and forgive me.

As for my future – I have made a decision which must astonish you. I intend to return to Lowood. Through the good offices of the Marquis, to whom I had, as usual, reported my situation, I received the offer of a post in a fashionable academy for young ladies, but I had also written to the superintendent to ask if there were a vacancy at Lowood which I might fill. She too offered me a post, much inferior in salary and conditions of course to the other – but I think there is work for me to do at Lowood.

I wait for news of you, dearest Jane.

Your affectionate friend,

Mary Ann

May Heaven armour me against the charms of Mr Brocklehurst!

White Hart
Worthing
31st January, 1855

Dearest Jane,

I have but now given up my letter to the post, and I sit down to write to you again, though there is much to prepare for the move to Lowood on Monday next.

It weighs upon me so much that I have left untold the story of my own unfortunate love, for I know well the sufferings which can follow the indulgence of a liking which cannot come to good. Shame has kept me from speaking, for the object of my affections was a married man. I could never have set out to love such, and can feel no pride in telling the story, yet I believe it may help you – and here I am, after all, pen in hand and determined to tell all, in the hope that it will be of service to you.

The post which Mrs Fordyce had found for me was pleasant, but of short duration, Miss Elizabeth needing only a companion with whom she might converse in French and somewhat improve her knowledge of literature before she left at the beginning of the next year to continue her education at an academy in Switzerland. I went from there to the Maynard household, where my story begins.

Mrs Maynard was an invalid, a frail, pretty woman who had not recovered her health after the birth of Gerald, three years before – a horrendous ordeal which she was inclined to recount in detail, though I think the practice was damaging to her health. She kept to her room, and usually to her bed, served by a personal maid named Agatha, who was something of a dragon, determined to protect her mistress from all demands on her energy.

My charges were the two elder children, two daughters, Arabella and Louisa – though little Gerald, too, would escape from his nurse, Ellen, to sit on my knee and learn his letters. Arabella was nine years old, Louisa seven. Since they were still in the care of the nurse, I dined alone with Mr Maynard. This was at first a cause of some embarrassment to me, but there seemed to be no possibility of any closer relationship, for he viewed the world and those in it from a slight but perceptible distance. I did not at that time find him pleasing either in person or in character. He could not be called handsome; there was about him a sleekness and plumpness which forbade the epithet, and as for his character – I took his continual amiability to be the shield of a detachment which made him indifferent to others, and most of all to his unfortunate wife, who seemed to live surrounded by every comfort but the sympathy of her husband. He failed in no attention to her, visiting her morning and afternoon to enquire after her health, but his very cheerfulness of demeanour appeared to make light of the sufferings she recounted. Agatha, indeed, thought it an insult to her poor mistress; she would direct at his back such a look of indignation as might well have bored two holes in his jacket. I learned later that Mr Maynard had tried to persuade his wife to dismiss Agatha and that this had brought on such a deterioration in the poor lady's health that the subject could never be mentioned again.

I thought Mr Maynard had been harsh in the matter, considering with what devotion Agatha tended her mistress, yet I too began to feel misgivings about the wisdom of the association, when I asked Agatha at what time of the day it would be best to bring the girls on their daily visit to Mrs Maynard, and saw the suggestion – it was something more than a suggestion, for I had taken compliance for granted – rejected on the grounds that the children tired their mother. There was perhaps no place for little Gerald in a sickroom, but Arabella and Louisa were quiet, affectionate, well-mannered girls. I felt strongly that the company of such daughters could do nothing but good to a parent.

I thought of protesting to Mr Maynard, but caution kept me silent. My protest might have seemed officious; this was not my concern, or was only my concern to the extent that the happiness of the girls might be affected. On reflection I saw that it was for their mother to demand their company, not for me to impose it.

I have never known a more promising child than Arabella – such delight in learning, such grasp of new ideas, such a capacious and accurate memory. Louisa, the younger sister, though less obviously gifted, had a sensitivity, a responsiveness which made her a delightful pupil, and Gerald at three showed the same readiness in learning his alphabet.

I begged of Mr Maynard that the education of the girls should be serious, not confined to the acquisition of a graceful hand and the accomplishments usually considered suitable for young ladies. I asked permission to introduce Arabella to the study of Latin, for I thought that to memorise its structures was an excellent discipline for a mind already giving promise of distinction.

I was astonished at the eagerness of his approval.

He said, 'If an intelligent woman cannot play a part in public affairs, her education should still make her a fit companion for those who do, able to listen with intelligent interest and give wise advice. Even in private life, a woman of cultivated mind raises the standard of conversation wherever she goes.'

The unusual animation of his tone made me feel that it reflected his own disappointment. Perhaps, I thought, his unruffled amiability was a shield, not for detachment, but for despair, and I saw in him a temperament which somewhat resembled my own.

He began to pay visits to the schoolroom, to show the little girls an affectionate attention which had until then been lacking in their lives, all Ellen's affections being centred on little Gerald. We agreed so well in matters of education – his only care being that I should not be too ambitious for the girls, that I should leave them what he called 'a little space for discovery'. I had somewhat sinned in this respect and found the advice wise.

Such an ease grew between us in our discussions that I began to talk to him of my life at Apsley Park, of Lowood and the scandal of the typhus, of Lady Forrester and her grievance and when I mentioned the circumstances of my birth, I saw him give a small, confirmatory nod, as if he had seen in me some signs of aristocratic blood.

And there, dear Jane, was the first sign of danger, in my being so gratified by the discovery that he had speculated on the subject.

When first he put a careless hand on my waist, I put it away quickly, saying, 'Sir, you forget yourself.'

'Oh, no, Miss Mary Ann,' he answered with his usual calm. 'I never forget myself. I am always the object of my most tender concern.'

At that, I smiled. I was aware that, though my words had rebuked him, my flesh had not. So I knew my danger and knew that I should flee it. This is to tell a woman benumbed with cold that she must stay far from the hearth because fire can burn. Is there not that lovely space of warmth and light where one can see no danger? We resumed our normal conversation, our plans for the girls. I hoped that the incident had had no meaning.

One day, he called me into his office, to tell me, regretfully, that I must not allow Gerald into the schoolroom, for Ellen complained that I was destroying her influence over the little boy. I objected that he was never there for long, being too young for more than a quarter of an hour's attention to his letters.

'I am afraid that we must respect Ellen's wishes, since Gerald is under her authority.'

'As I am under yours, sir!' I answered rather tartly, as I was vexed by the prohibition.

'Is that so, Miss Mary Ann? Then I bid you to come sit on my knee.'

'I was not employed to undertake such tasks as that, sir.'

'Oh, it would be a task then, would it?'

'An onerous one, sir, and quite outside my duties as governess.'

But at the word 'task' he had looked so comically woebegone that I felt a smile tugging at my mouth.

I condemn Mr Rochester for playing on the affections of an unprotected young woman to whom he stands in the responsible relation of employer, yet I found the same conduct pardonable in Mr Maynard.

And still I stayed! Oh, I deserve all the miseries that followed!

How laughter undermines the principles of morality. I see it as a bright, strong tide washing against the walls that prudence and decorum erect against chaos. My very resistance became an amusement; I could delude myself that this was harmless teasing. You and I should have exchanged temptations, my dear Jane. You would have been repelled by Mr Maynard's frivolity, while I think I could deal briskly with your Mr Rochester!

Of course the day came which must come: he called me into his office and said, 'Mary Ann, we must think of the future. We must live together or apart.'

Speaking with unusual earnestness, he told me that he could not offer marriage, but could make such a settlement as would give me security in the event of his defection – or his death, which he said would be the likelier.

I said in a whisper that it could not be. I felt all the weight of my guilt at that moment.

'Think, my dear. What would be changed, except that I should be happy, and you too, I think. I believe you are not indifferent to me.'

At that, I nodded. I had begun to weep. In my bitter tears he knew his answer, yet he continued to persuade.

'Our happiness could be our secret; everything else could go on as before.'

Even at that moment of deep emotion, I paused to wonder at the simplicity of this. Could he suppose that in a house full of servants such a secret could be kept? If the gentry and the nobility suspected how much their servants knew about them and with what detached amusement they held such knowledge, I believe the social order would begin to crumble.

The thought had steadied me a little. There had been no doubt of my answer; if my father's blood had prompted licence, my mother's fate enjoined prudence.

'Where one thing changes,' I answered, 'all things must change.'

It occurred to me that what we were contemplating was pure evil. If one resigns one's life to the guidance of a passion, where might that passion lead? First to the betrayal of that poor invalid, and then? Could I be brought to hate a human being who had done me no harm, perhaps to the point of wishing her dead?

It shocked me then as it shocks me still, that evil could have worn so fair a face. With more firmness, I said, 'This must never be spoken of again. We have been wrong in indulging our liking so long. We must do so no more.'

'Then, Mary Ann, I think we must part.'

I nodded, being unable to speak for weeping.

At last I said, 'Give me two days, to say goodbye to the girls and to pack my belongings. I shall stay no longer.'

We dined together, but we did not speak again until we said goodbye. He said, 'I shall supervise the education of the girls.'

I thanked him and contrived to smile.

'At least, my dear one, let me try to protect you from want,' he said as he handed me an envelope, which I found later to contain a draft on his banker for a sum of money which I could not have accepted from any other man.

Oh, Jane! Despite all the suffering, the longing and the loneliness which have been the penalty of my self-indulgence, I hope I may live to see in a man's eyes again such steadfast tenderness, such infinite goodwill!

What am I saying? Am I saying that, for all the unhappiness it may bring, it is worth all, to have seen love in a man's eyes, to know that love exists?

This is not the advice I intended to give you.

(Letter unfinished. Unposted.)

Lowood
8th April, 1855

My dearest Jane,

It is so long since you have written, that I fear you may be ill or have met with some other misfortune which prevents you from writing to me.

I have another fear, that I may have given offence – it is my misfortune sometimes to speak with apparent levity where my feelings are truly engaged.

If this is so, and you feel yourself offended, please forgive me and let me have news of you, at least to tell me how I have offended.

Your affectionate friend,

Mary Ann

Lowood
1st May, 1855

My dearest Jane,

I see, by your impassioned defence of Mr Rochester, that I have indeed offended! Yet I must cling to my opinion.

I know you, Jane. You do not love where your love is not invited. I know from what you have told me in your letters that Mr Rochester has set out from the first moment to engage your affection in a manner quite improper to an employer. If he had any other motive than sheer mischievous vanity, then there is some mystery here which I cannot penetrate. And that may be so, for it is difficult to believe that you would be captured by such a one as I must think him.

Since you are offended by my judgment of Mr Rochester, and I am, I must confess, angered by your humble opinion of your dear self, I think that we must for the time being correspond no more.

Jane – here perhaps I give further offence, yet friendship compels me to it – if ever you need a refuge, there is a bed to be shared at Lowood.

I get on very comfortably with the superintendent, Augusta Lingard. We agree on many points concerning the education of girls. I know she would welcome you.

If your situation changes, if you have news for me, please write to me. Until then, let there be silence between us – a loving silence, for my part. I wait hopefully for you to break it.

Your affectionate friend for ever,
Mary Ann

MISS PIPER AND EVERYMAN

Miss Piper was alone behind the Post Office counter, weighing a parcel for Mrs Newby and plodding through a conversation with her, when the stranger came in. With water running from his oilskin coat, his head bent as if he was still under the rain, he stood under the notice that said money orders 10 a.m. – 4 p.m. It was two minutes to four.

One of Miss Piper's moments was in prospect. In spite of a cracking headache and a swelling, floating sensation that made her feel like a balloon about to take off, she saw the moment coming and exulted. Slowly – customers could never complain that she stood idle while they waited for attention – she counted out change and pushed it across the counter, staring meanwhile at Mrs Newby's umbrella, which was spreading water comically, like a folded collapsible dog; and agreed that the river would be up if this rain kept on.

When Mrs Newby had gone, she approached the man even more slowly than her aching body required, looked tranquilly at the money order he held out to her, then at the clock on the wall and said, 'You're too late with that. Money orders close at four.'

The dismay on his face, the wetness of his coat, the continued supplication of his hand holding out the money order all increased her calm feeling of power. For a moment she faced his amazed, offended state, then he turned with a choking exclamation and went out.

Miss Piper had been wretchedly unhappy when she was young. She was middle-aged now and her life had shrunk to the level of comfort: her own little house, nice little fires, hot drinks, snacks and library books – with only one deep emotional satisfaction in being able to frustrate other people now and then. Watching the thwarted customer leave, she experienced peace and fulfilment.

Her headache however had grown worse. When the postmaster came in, he looked at her with concern. 'You'd better get along home. Or no. Not in this weather. Go inside and sit down till closing time and I'll run you home.'

She wanted no favours. 'I'm quite all right, thank you.'

'You don't look it, then. Well, suit yourself. If it gets too much for you, go in and wait for me. The offer's still open.'

At ten to five, she muttered, 'I think I'll go now,' and hurried out. There was no other way of avoiding the lift home which would have upset her moral balance. In the back room she put on her raincoat and took her umbrella, then she set out on foot under the saturating rain.

Once home, she fed the cat, drank some hot soup, filled a hot water bottle and went to bed, where she shivered in spite of the bottle.

'I have the flu,' she said to herself when she woke. Thick, soft rain was falling and the cat was crying at the door. She got up with difficulty, let the cat in, put torn-up newspaper in an old tin dish to make a lavatory for it, opened a tin of cat food – the smell of it made her retch, which hurt her head dreadfully – took aspirin, washed it down with a little fever-sour water, went back to bed and lay still until the evening, when she managed to drink some soup again.

That night she rode in the rattling, soaring car of fever. In the morning, after she had fed the cat, she mixed a jug of lemon drink, drank two glasses of it, took more aspirin and went to sleep.

In the darkening daylight, she woke in fear because the bedclothes were being pulled off her. She tugged at them and recognised the enemy by its weight: it was the cat, trying to climb into her bed.

'Stop it, Scratch,' she said wretchedly, but the cat persisted. She lay calculating the effort of struggling against the effort of putting it outside. The rain must have stopped, for she could hear only the low, steady sound of running gutters. She got out of bed slowly, picked up the cat – how heavy it was! – went to the door and opened it. She leaned against the doorframe, petrified. The earth was gone. The street was gone. She was standing on an island, water everywhere as broad as a sea but running as strongly as a mountain creek, skimming across the bottom step and deepening there visibly.

Though her mind nagged at her to hurry, she dressed languidly, pulling on socks, warm trousers, rubber boots, a sweater and a jacket. She pushed the cat onto the wardrobe, with water and more food – she would never buy that brand again.

She set off then, walking with the current, clinging to fences to keep her balance in the calf-deep water. In the twilight the world was grey, like a picture in a newspaper, and fear was more a landscape than a state of mind. The houses on each side of the street were empty. 'They did not know I was at home,' she told herself dutifully, but in the midst of her terror she felt a climactic pang of bitter pleasure at being forgotten by everyone.

A block ahead a man came from a side street and moved in a slow, plunging run through the water. She tried to run, but she could not. The man went into the empty warehouse on the corner of Station Street.

Refuge. She worked towards it slowly. Then the last fence was behind her and the current hustled her through the open doorway.

It was nearly dark inside the building. There was a long counter and behind it shelves lining the walls. The sound of voices made her look up to the highest shelf, where people were perched in a line like giant crows on a fence. 'Come on,' a voice called out to her. 'Want a hand up?'

She had thought, on the way there, that each step was taking the last of her strength. Now, climbing to the top shelf, she knew what those words meant, though she had accepted the helping hand and it lifted her strongly. She could not see the faces of her companions. Their voices approached and receded, talking of cars under water, of water depths, of landmarks drowned. In spite of her warm clothes, her body shivered, clacked and rattled.

'Are you all right, missus?' asked the man next to her.

'Flu. I'm sorry. Flu.'

'Gawd, what a night for it.'

It was a relief when they started to sing. She didn't have to pay attention then. Sometimes the singing stopped and she heard the soft chuckle of the water. Somebody shone a torch downwards and there was a burst of talk rowdy with anxiety. Silence then till one voice started singing and the others joined in.

In the middle of the night she died and went to Heaven. It was just like the warehouse, really, but she knew that she had died because the noise of the song they were singing – 'Oh Genevieve, sweet Genevieve – The days may come, the days may go . . .' – had dwindled and sunk away from her and she was drifting in space, though jerkily, with mysterious interruptions. She knew she was on the outskirts of Heaven, because of the voice. 'We're never going to be able to hold her on all night.' Imagine that. They have to hold you so you don't fall out of Heaven. What an awkward arrangement. You'd think they could do better than that. 'Can you hang on to her for a minute? I'm on a beam or something here.' Would that be a sunbeam? Not a moon-beam, not for Heaven. 'If I can change places, tie her on. Yes, there's a bit of a gap. I'm coming. Steady her.'

'Watch yourself.'

'I'm right. Got a hold on top of the wall. Ouch.' He made the groan comic, out of celestial politeness. 'Doesn't half cut into your knees, that edge. Get the belt out of my trousers, will you, mate?'

Of course it was an angel. How well they get them up, she thought, smelling flesh, feeling the stuff of trousers against her face, even the buried disc of a flybutton. The compact swag of flesh that hung above her collarbone should have been disgusting but was not.

The angel said to her, 'Now you shift along, love. That's the way. Don't worry, we've got you. Keep back against the wall as far as you can. Sick as a dog, poor little devil,' he reported with casual reproach to God. 'Lucky she's a little one. Give us a light here, mate, while I do up this buckle.'

The belt worried her, cutting into her ribs, but she did not complain, since the angel wanted it like that.

The rest of the night was darkness and singing, a bar of bone and muscle shutting her in like a gate, the undertone of the water, gabbling voices. Then nothing.

She came to in daylight, lying under blankets on the wet counter. A woman standing knee-deep in water said briskly, 'Hospital for you!' Two men waded across carrying a stretcher which they slid beneath her. As they carried her out, she looked around anxiously at the room behind her. It was empty.

While she lay – so comfortably – in bed at the hospital, she had a kind of dream again. It was not a real dream, for she was awake; besides, she had foreseen and dreaded it, struggled against it and tried to argue it away. She saw the angel's face. It was the face of the man with the money order. Of course it wasn't true, couldn't be true, but that didn't matter. While she didn't know who it was, it might as well be the man with the money order. She looked for clues in her memory, which offered only the surface of trousers, an arm and a voice. Anyone's voice. She hadn't thought it was a man, so how could she find out who it was? She could have believed the whole thing was a dream but for the long red mark the belt had left under her ribs. There was no escape.

Matron on her round said, 'The volunteer workers have made a beautiful job of your house. They dried everything out and cleaned it up for you.' Smiling so kindly while she told her that strangers had been in among her belongings. Or perhaps not strangers, which was worse. She turned her head away with such a defeated look that Matron said, 'You had better buck up, or we won't be letting you go home on Tuesday.'

The postmaster's wife came to see her and her neighbour dropped in to say she was feeding the cat. 'I didn't want you to be worrying about it,' she said with moderate friendliness. ('All the poor soul has got.' She had thought that before; for the first time, it was true.) The kindness would have embarrassed Miss Piper once. Now it seemed trivial.

*

177

Back at work, she fended off questions about her experience, so people left her in peace and talked about their own. Her eyes were on the customers. That one? That one? There was a hope that her rescuer might announce himself and clear her with the rest, but it was a small one, for she felt sure that he was a careless man who would not think of the incident again.

Grudgingly, she changed money orders out of hours, offered to fill in forms, gave advice, looked up postcodes, answered silly questions meekly and suffered constantly from the dullness of life.

At one moment she was nearly herself again. A woman came in with a parcel of books improperly wrapped. Miss Piper looked down at the parcel, controlling a smile.

'You can't send them through the post like that. The parcel has to be open at one end.'

Then she thought with a start of alarm that the woman might be his wife or his sister.

'Give it to me,' she said sullenly. 'I'll fix it for you.'

In the hot, bright air the fountain flashed pins and needles. The pins and needles melted into drops and fell in glistening rain behind the charcoal-coloured swans as they circled the lake. Tom and Alice had eaten their lunch in the shade of the giant fig tree that stood on a slight rise sloping down to the water. Alice folded her paper bag and put it in her briefcase. Tom set down his last sandwich unfinished on its wrapper.

'Swans,' she said. 'They're not calm at all really, not relaxed. Look at them, all controlled tension.'

Tom had been looking more absently than she at the dark marble and silver gauze that formed the living centrepiece of the lake. Now that his attention was drawn to the outside world, he had for it a smile of affectionate acceptance she knew well and loved, so that for a moment her look was a parody of his.

'Wearing themselves out keeping up the swan image,' he agreed. His discontented air returned as he added, 'I don't see why you're so set against coming.'

'Not set.' She was trying so hard to sound indifferent that she spoke as if she were dropping off to sleep. 'I told you, there's a family do I think I'd better go to.'

'I thought you said you didn't have a family.'

'Did I say that? I'm trying to cut loose. Can't cut them out entirely, I suppose.'

She was lying. She didn't intend to go near the family mansion, the glossy pile which represented everything she most despised. As soon as she'd got her hands on Grandma's money she had left it with joy. The room in Glebe was a staging post on the way to Bangladesh, where she would do real work among real people. Meanwhile she was trying the experience of poverty, for fear underfloor heating, spa baths and Mrs Potter's cooking had softened her bones. But that was all right; poverty didn't worry her.

'Can't you go there some other time?' One of the swans had come to shore and was trudging, flat-footed and swag-bottomed, along the edge of the lake.

'No. I told you. It's a do. Special occasion.'

Trying to contrive a plausible lie, she reflected that every occasion in that house was special. Nobody ever dropped in, there was never a snack meal, never a friend, only the right people, who usually turned out in the end to be not quite the right people.

Fortunately, he was not interested in the special occasion.

'Helen's been looking forward to meeting you.' She wished he could say that girl's name without wrapping it in velvet. Beautiful Helen. Helen, thy beauty is to me . . . She hadn't given a stuff about beauty, had never regretted her lack of it, seeing it as part of the rubbish Mum and Fiona cluttered their lives with, until she had fallen in love, up to her chin, her long, crooked, pointed chin, about which, as Mum so frequently lamented, nothing could be done. Not even then, not until she had seen the beauty passing at the other end of the Quad and heard a voice behind her say, 'Tom Allan fancies her, and no wonder.' She was glad the voice was behind her as she swallowed those words alive, and with them the sad discovery that young men who lived for Philosophy were moved by silky blonde hair and regular features, just as much as the silly young men who courted Fiona.

'Some other time, then,' she said. 'Look at that swan, will you? You only have to see a swan out of water to know what an illusion beauty is.'

'You'd enjoy it, you know, once you got there.'

'I doubt that. Not quite my thing, really.'

He said crossly, 'Take yourself seriously, don't you?'

No, she didn't. She used to take herself seriously, now she didn't. She had been the only person in that household she did take seriously, except for Mrs Potter the cook and maybe Dad, who worked hard and effectively at making money. Mum and Fiona put just as much work and worry into spending it, with little success, climbing a ladder which existed only in their minds.

She had taken herself seriously because of Bangladesh, code name for some yet unknown place in the Third World where she would spend Grandma's money and do it right, learn the language, live in the village, supervise the workmen, see to it that the well got sunk and the school got built.

'No, I don't. Some reason for taking myself seriously, that's what I'd like.'

You could be it. Bangladesh had receded. It was love that softened the bones.

He said nothing. He was disconcerted that she felt entitled to take herself seriously. He tore a piece from his unfinished sandwich and tossed it to the foraging swan, which killed it with one stroke, swallowed it and came towards them, the mean relationship between beak and eye suddenly apparent.

'You'll be sorry you did that. One moment of weakness and you'll find yourself supporting a swan for the rest of your life.'

He tore off another piece of bread and threw it as far as he could. The swan lumbered after it.

'The thing is that you're putting me in an awkward position. I thought we'd be working on the thesis, and when Helen mentioned the party, I said you'd be at a loose end, so of course she said to bring you. It's going to look a bit odd if you don't come.'

'Just tell her something came up.'

One thing, he wouldn't be pressuring her like this if he knew. She had promised herself that if he ever found out she was deep in love with him, she would take off at once. She'd never stand the humiliation.

Love! he was thinking. (Not only did he know; so did three librarians, the clerk who gave them numbered tokens in exchange for their briefcases in the lobby, and an old woman who spent her days in the library taking notes for a historical novel about the Young Pretender.) Love! What was the use of it if they wouldn't do the slightest thing you wanted? Helen had been difficult, too.

'Oh, not that awful girl!'

'She's not so bad when you get to know her.'

'I don't want to get to know her.' He had had to refer to the life-plan. A good thing about Helen was that she understood the life-plan without any discussion.

'She helps me a lot. She's typing my thesis for me. I couldn't trust anyone else with the job, and she's really useful in checking things. I couldn't get everything done without her.'

Helen had been waspish. 'How can she help you if she's in Philosophy I and you're doing an Honours thesis? I don't see it.'

'She reads everything up. She's only doing the donkey work, looking up quotes and checking references. It suits her; she wants to learn as much as she can in a year and I'm giving her a line to follow.'

'It sounds weird to me. What is she living on?'

He laughed. 'Mung beans and pita bread, I think. She's taken a year off work to live on her savings while she looks for some answers.'

He examined the word weird. It applied to Alice. Yet applied to Alice, it had some attraction, even a kind of poetry. He wasn't being entirely honest with Helen, either.

183

It wasn't just a matter of the life-plan. He liked Alice's company and didn't want to lose it.

Alice said, 'Here's your friend again. I warned you.'

This time, the swan had come closer. He hissed at it, glad of an outlet for his bad temper. It took a step back and two forward.

'Ugly thing,' she said. 'Go on. Get back in the water. Hide your feet. They do you no credit.'

He took up the last crust and threw it high and far, sending the bird trundling after it.

'You understand, I'm asking this as a favour.' The look he gave went through her like a large pin through a small insect. She thought, He does know. He wants a faithful Dobbin. To Alice, faithful Dobbin was one character in fiction who needed an analyst.

'Oh, look. Here it comes again!' She squawked in fear and jumped backwards, stumbling among the roots of the great fig tree and clinging to its trunk as the swan bustled forward and thrust its beak towards her, neck extended and wings spread.

'Don't panic!'

He took his denim jacket from the grass and snapped it at the swan, then chased it, flapping the jacket behind it, towards the lake, where it slid into the water, resuming its regal dignity at once.

How beautiful he was! Could she really leave him? As soon as the thesis is finished, she lied to herself.

He came back, grumbling. 'That wouldn't have happened if you'd kept your head.'

'Sorry, sorry. I dislike the creatures.'

'You made that obvious.'

'Well, if we're not going to be working on Saturday night, we'd better get back to John Stuart Mill. I could finish that book this afternoon.'

'Mmm.' He took out a cigarette and smoked in silence. At last he said, 'I'd just like to know what you've got against Helen.'

That was near the bone. Did he really expect her to tell him? He couldn't know; he must be saying that in innocence.

'I'd like to know why you're so keen to get me to the party.'

'I don't believe your excuse. You never mentioned that date before. I think it's inverted snobbery. You've taken against Helen because her father's a brain surgeon. Inverted snobbery, that's all it is. Maybe he's an effigy, but Helen's all right. You don't have to meet her parents anyhow. There's a big rumpus room under the house, that opens on to the pool. Helen entertains her friends in the rumpus room.'

She snapped at him, 'Games room!' then was appalled, because that was her mother's voice and she was after all her mother's daughter, sneering at unfortunate people who owned rumpus rooms. Words were the last things to go.

He was staring at her angrily.

She said apologetically, looking down at the grass, 'Games room. Games, you know. The billiard table and table tennis, and the darts board, which is a bit of decorator's whimsy because nobody plays darts; it goes with the panelled bar in the corner, mock-up from an English pub. If not, just basement will do.'

Nervously, she looked up at him. He was lusting, lips agape and eyes burning. She was describing his Heaven. What price Bentham? What price Socrates and John Stuart Mill? Lusting after a games room.

The silence was prolonged. She sank her head in her hands and her shoulders began to heave. Had he pushed it too far? Was she crying? Oh, God, was there going to be a scene? Why hadn't he let it alone, let sleeping dogs lie?

'All right,' he said. 'All right, forget it. Sorry I mentioned it.'

'Too late.' She straightened up, shaking her head, gasping with laughter. 'Too late. I saw your feet. Saw your feet.' She got up, still laughing, and picked up her briefcase. 'Sorry. I'm off.' She strode across the grass to the park exit.

Bangladesh, here I come.

THE PERFECT WOMAN

A score of passengers from the cruise ship had signed for the late sitting at dinner in order to accommodate a twilight tour of the foreign city. They were grouped around their guide in front of the Customs shed at the other end of the pier as Graham and Elaine came down the gangplank.

He said to her with amusement, 'We are observed.'

She turned and waved. How gracefully she moved!

Three old women in the group waved back.

'My Scrabble partners.'

'Odd company for you.'

'They are demon players, out of my class. It's good of them to put up with me. And they are good fun, really. Mrs Frobisher can be a trial, always complaining about Sylvia. Not very sensible, putting an old woman and a young one together. I think the real grievance is that Sylvia enjoys life. She isn't wasting her youth.'

'Nor the cruise, either,' he said indulgently.

'She comes in late and disturbs Mrs F. then won't get out of bed in the morning and wants to be waited on and expects Mrs F. to pick up after her. I suppose it is trying for an old woman, but the complaining does get tedious. It's fun to see how the other two keep her in hand. Last night when they decided enough was enough, Mrs Parker said to Mrs Robinson very seriously, "M3 – U1 – G2" and Mrs Robinson said, "Triple word score." I laughed and so did Mrs Frobisher, but she took the hint and got on with the game. No blood shed. I thought it was clever.'

Elaine was talking more than usual. Perhaps she was tense.

He felt a little tense himself.

He knew they were being watched not only by the three old widows but by the whole group because this was a significant moment. To take a shipboard romance on shore gave it a new importance.

Well, it was important for him and he hoped it was so for her too. All the omens were good; he thought the group watched them with sympathy. Their interest was not mere curiosity but a kind of well-wishing, which was a good omen too.

He could imagine their comments. 'Doesn't she look lovely!' 'I think he's a lucky man, all right. Such a nice girl, too.' 'Don't they make a handsome pair?'

He wished his sister could see them. That would put a stop to her sniping comments about ageing bachelors. 'I'm waiting for the perfect woman' was his usual answer. Well, here she was, and he had hopes of bringing her home.

She was a mystery to the gossips on board. He did not need to imagine their comments, for he had heard them all often enough, until they had begun to make the daily circuit of B deck together and the gossip had moved out of earshot.

'Such a beauty and unmarried – how old do you think? – early thirties, perhaps – you can never tell, these days – an unhappy love affair – marriage isn't what it used to be –'

Even to the elderly, the phrase 'on the shelf' was unacceptable nowadays, yet they skirted about it, tried to find substitutes: 'Odd, just the same, to see such a beautiful young woman travelling alone.'

He knew why she was unattached – the politest word the gossips could find to describe her unfortunate situation. Beauty, intelligence and grace had given her courage to wait for what she really wanted, just as he had waited. How fervently he hoped that he was the one.

They had left the pier and were walking towards the main street.

At the corner she paused and looked at the busy, crowded thoroughfare with a sigh of disappointment.

'All modern cities look the same.'

'What were you expecting? Temples? We'll see plenty of those tomorrow on the tour.'

To him, the black glass and the steel, the highrise hotels, the cars and the traffic lights, all the similarities made the subtle differences more exciting. The people were different, not only in skin colour and in feature, but in movement and gesture. For all their European clothes, the homegoing crowds were alien.

'The traffic lights seem to have much less authority here,' he said, watching the crowd advance in a slow wave across the roadway in spite of the little red man who, here as elsewhere, meant DON'T WALK. They walked nevertheless. That amused him.

'Yes,' she agreed. 'The people have it over the cars.'

'The more you look, the more differences you see.'

'And temples tomorrow, as you say.'

The purser had recommended a small restaurant on the ground floor of the International Hotel. It offered European cuisine. Graham did not intend to take risks with chopsticks and exotic dishes this evening.

There ahead of them, quite close, was the International Hotel.

'Would you like to walk along a bit? It's early for dinner.'

'Oh, dinner. We can explore later. Nothing to see here but shopwindows.'

Unlike many women on the cruise, she was not obsessed by shopping. That was another of her virtues. The window displays they had passed were truly international, without local flavour, offering expensive accessories in which she seemed to take no interest.

'You don't like window-shopping?'

'I do it when I'm looking for something in particular.'

She was always suitably and elegantly dressed. Now she was wearing a plain, straight dress of olive green silk, the colour well chosen to set off her medium colouring, a gold choker necklace, elegant town shoes in a colour he could not name – brown was probably as near as he could get, and very fine stockings which appeared to match the shoes. He knew the gold kid handbag she was carrying, but he had not seen the rest of the outfit before. Perhaps she came prepared for an invitation to dine in port with a hopeful suitor. The thought made him uneasy.

In the foyer of the International Hotel, which was smaller and narrower than he had expected, there were two lighted display windows set in the wall, like open treasure chests, one holding coloured silks, the other jewellery. Elaine gave them a brief, dismissive glance as she passed without slowing her step.

'You don't talk scandal, you don't window-shop, you are kind to old ladies,' he said, adding mentally, And tolerant of young ones. 'I should like to find you out in just one weakness.'

'Oh, I have plenty, but I don't advertise them.'

They were both smiling as he pushed open the swing door and followed her into the restaurant.

The purser's advice had been good. It was a small room of twenty tables, all empty at this moment, all shining with white damask and silver, offering an atmosphere of warmth and elegance which was personified in the beautiful young woman in scarlet tunic and trousers who came to greet them. She seemed without a word to recognise their status as new lovers and led them to a table as if she were taking part in a happy ceremony.

Graham asked himself whoever had introduced the notion that Asians were inscrutable.

'Do you think they are going to bring hot towels to wash our hands?' asked Elaine.

'I don't think so. I think they are being conscientiously European.'

'I rather like the hot towels. It makes me feel cherished.'

Was there a tinge of sadness in that, as if she had known little cherishing and must look for it wherever it could be bought?

'What are you thinking?' she asked.

The waiter had arrived beside them, offering the menu and the wine list.

'The fillet of beef is very good tonight, sir.'

They ordered the fillet of beef, with seafood cocktail as an entree.

'We might as well be having dinner in Sydney,' she said.

He hoped they would do that, too. The presence of the waiter prevented his saying so.

'Riesling or chardonnay with the seafood?'

'Riesling, thanks.'

'Oh, good. I never seem to get on with people who drink chardonnay.'

'Is that a political comment?'

'Oh, no. It doesn't affect my vote.'

This exchange and the laughter it brought were relaxing.

He ordered a claret to follow and they waited comfortably for the entree.

Instead, the waiter brought the fillet of beef for Graham's inspection, then set it on a lighted brazier on the counter to be roasted while they ate their first course.

'You see,' he said, 'it's the similarity that makes the differences so interesting.'

The waiter returned with the white wine in its ice bucket, and poured a little into Graham's glass.

He performed the absurd little tasting ceremony, the sip and the nod of approval and the waiter filled the glasses.

'Have you ever sent the wine back?' she asked.

'No. I wouldn't dare. Even if it tasted like vinegar, I'd think it was some wonderful vintage I was too ignorant to appreciate.'

'I find that hard to believe. I don't think you would ever be frightened by a waiter.'

That pleased him.

Conversation paused while they ate the first course. She took her food seriously. He liked that, too.

The waiter came to clear away the tall glasses set on small dishes of fine china and the elegantly wrought, delicate silver forks that had been used for the seafood cocktail.

It was the change in the waiter's expression that caught Graham's attention. For the first time he saw an Asian look inscrutable.

The fork which had been part of her place setting was missing.

It was, of course, on the floor. He thought he remembered an awkward movement as she had picked up her wineglass. It was so unlike her to be awkward that she might be too embarrassed to explain. It was correct no doubt to ignore the incident and leave the fork to be found after they had left, but he wished for a moment that she would laugh and confess and pull the folds of the tablecloth aside to show the fork on the floor. She had not noticed

193

the waiter's withdrawal; perhaps she had not noticed the absence of the fork.

The hostess took the fillet of beef from the brazier, brought it to their table on a warm platter, cut a slice from its centre to show the degree of pinkness, received their nods of approval and took it away to be served.

'They do make you feel well looked after,' she said.

'Cherished was your word. About the hot towels. They make you feel cherished. Do you care very much about that?'

'Doesn't everyone?'

'Some more than others. I think.'

The waiter came then to serve the second course. Another opportunity gone. Well, there would be time.

The waiter still wore his air of reserve. Graham decided to resist his impulse to dive and recover the fork. That would be absurdly undignified.

'Will you please serve the claret?' he asked in a tone which was polite but firm.

'Certainly, sir.'

The man took away the unfinished bottle of riesling and returned with the claret; the absurd little ceremony of pouring, tasting and approving was repeated; the man filled their glasses and withdrew.

Withdrew was the word for that departure. Graham revised his estimate of the tip he meant to leave.

The beef at least was excellent. They ate it with appetite and agreed that they relished the change from the meals on board.

'Would you like dessert? Or cheese?'

She shook her head, smiling ruefully over the quantity she had eaten.

'I'll help myself to one of those chocolates with my coffee.'

'What about a liqueur?'

She studied the level of the claret in the bottle.

'Come on. Live dangerously. I don't have to worry about the breathalyser for once.'

A liqueur and a little more personal conversation.

'Well, a Drambuie, then.'

When the waiter had served them and departed, he said, 'I know why I travel alone, but what about you? You don't look at all like a solitary person, you know.'

She was toying with the coffee spoon, probably reflecting on her answer.

'Is that such a hard question?' he asked, amused.

She dropped the spoon and looked up at him, startled.

'I'm sorry. My wits were wandering. What did you say?'

He felt sick. She had looked at that spoon as if she were saying goodbye to it. It was the same quick, dismissive look she had given to the windows in the lobby as she passed, not indifference but suppression of a passionate greed.

'I was talking about the advantages of solitary travel while you were admiring the silver.'

Her laugh sounded odd. She picked up the spoon again and replaced it with an affected gesture.

'It's a charming pattern, isn't it? I love silver.'

He thought he must be dreaming. Of course he was mistaken. If it hadn't been for the accident with the entree fork . . .

Nevertheless, he found conversation difficult.

Fortunately, she was taking the initiative, chatting easily about tomorrow's prospects, how she had been told they must not miss the Buddhist temple with its four hundred statues of Buddha.

'There's a legend that if you count the number of calm, smiling Buddhas you will attain tranquillity.'

There was no doubt whatever about the liqueur glass. He saw it go.

Silently, his heart like a stone in his chest, he called for the bill, paid it with his credit card, then added three English pounds.

The waiter thanked him without a smile. Graham thought he saw pity in his eyes.

'You tip lavishly,' she said.

He was thankful that the words in his mind had not been spoken.

They walked back to the ship in silence.

But I didn't, she thought angrily. I didn't do it.

The awful effort it had required to drop the spoon and leave it untouched in the saucer had gone unrewarded.

'Thank you for the dinner,' she said coldly when they had reached the companionway which led to her cabin.

'It was a pleasure,' he said formally.

So they parted.

In the cabin she sat on her bunk with a flounce, thinking angrily, 'What's the use?'

She was still tormented by her frustrated craving for the bright, delicate little spoon. She might as well have had it.

Well, she had the fork. That was something. She opened her handbag, wanting to fetch it out and fondle it, and stared in horror at the liqueur glass.

'Oh, no,' she whispered. 'Oh, no.'

I shall go to a doctor. As soon as I get home, I shall go to a doctor.

WASTE OF AN EVENING

Don had been practising the trick of widening his field of vision without moving his head so that he could see without seeming to look. That's how he saw the handbag. What a kick! There they were in the hall with Moira saying, 'Jane, this is Don,' and Jane looking straight at him while he took in the half-open door, the big bag dumped on the foot of the bed, zip open, a gift. It surprised him still that people could be such fools, but, after all, where would the smart ones be without them? It even gave him a kick that they let him in, not knowing, saying, 'Come along in. I hope you can find somewhere to sit. What would you like to drink? Beer or wine?'

Beer or wine. That placed them.

Moira had brought a six-pack.

'Beer, thank you, Jane. I'll get them and put these on the ice, shall I?'

'Yes, do that,' said Jane. She turned to the room and said, loud and calm, 'I know only one thing about good and evil. If you deny human equality, you'll pay. That makes a law of it, it seems to me. If you think one sex is better than the other, or a race or a religion, or the rich are better than the poor . . .'

'Or the beautiful are better than the ugly,' a young man put in.

'There sure is a lot of that about,' said Jane thoughtfully. She was thin, tall, long-nosed, pale. Not ugly. Not exactly.

'And you pay there, all right. That is the curse of matrimony.'

That was the fat girl in the corner. She shouldn't be drawing attention to herself.

There was an empty chair. Most of them seemed to like sitting on the floor. Moira came back with the drinks and they settled, he in the chair, she on the floor at his feet.

'Evil is an intellectual error,' said the boy in tee-shirt, jeans and thongs who was sitting crosslegged in front of the fat girl. 'We commit evil only when we can convince ourselves that it is good.'

Jane said, 'We're good at that, aren't we?'

He couldn't endure this. Disgusting, talking about themselves like that. It was like a strip show.

'Oh, yes. It's our special talent, all right. But it's an error of the intellect, fundamentally.'

'Human equality!' This was a scrawny, dark, sharp-faced fellow arranged like a tin god in a big armchair. 'I have news for you, Jane. People are not equal. They aren't born equal, they don't live equal. They may die equal, but I'm not even sure of that.'

There was someone with a glimmer of sense.

'You don't think, then, David, that anyone commits evil knowingly?'

This was a voice quite near, from the chair next to his. It came from a tall, blonde beauty sitting gracefully at ease. She had a narrow black bag on her lap. That was a pity. She looked well-heeled.

David was the one in jeans. He was older than he had seemed at first and the jeans were frayed and faded. The mug?

He said carefully, 'I wouldn't swear to that, on second thoughts, but I think the general tendency is to rationalise one's behaviour.'

Why didn't he get up and go to the john? Where was the john? If it was out the back, he was wasting his evening.

Jane said, 'Paul, prove it. Prove that men aren't equal.'

'My dear girl, I don't have to prove it. Look round you. Society is based on human inequality.'

Voices from all over.

'You're on to Lorenz now. Aggression and the pecking order.'

'Oh, that frightens me. What's the hope for us, if we are just animals in tight shoes?'

'There's reason. It's the faculty of reason that makes man superior to the animals.'

'I'll believe that when the animals start making bombs.'

The mug said, 'I think you have me there.'

'There is no hope for us,' said Jane. 'So who would like another drink?'

The conversation waited while she went out to the kitchen and came back with a tray of cans.

Sour as Don was with boredom, he smiled as he held out his glass and she smiled back warmly as she filled it. That made him feel better. The God-mask was functioning. It was his handsome, pleasant, serious face and the training he gave it that made the God-mask. It was functioning and he was snug behind it.

Filling Paul's glass, Jane said, 'I don't think that's right, you know. You're equating man's social role with his true value.'

The girl in the corner said, 'There is no superiority that matters, except the superiority of the heart, moral superiority, and who knows what that is?' She gave a witty yawn. 'The morally superior are probably all out whoring and unavailable for interview.'

Disgusting. That one didn't care what she said to get a laugh. He hoped it was her handbag. He gave the deadpan widescreen look. No go. It was there on the floor beside her. She was digging in it for a cigarette. Well, it didn't do to get personal.

'But what Lorenz was on about,' said the mug, 'was that if we recognise the animal, give it its due – once we learn to know it and respect it, we get out of our tight shoes.'

'That,' said Paul with interest, 'could be a very useful argument in certain circumstances. Have you ever tried it?'

'I only just thought of it, but feel free.'

'Thank you.'

Ah, there went the girl in the corner, out into the hall. Great. He had something to think about now and just in time. He couldn't stand much more of this.

And here was Moira speaking up. 'Love. What about love? Isn't love good and hate evil?'

'If that's right,' said Jane, 'it's a poor lookout. You can't depend on love. There isn't enough of it around.'

'And suppose you love what is evil?' Paul was looking at her with an air of tender superiority, his own favourite look for the girls. Save your trouble, chum. I've got a hold.

Moira gave way, but whispering, 'I don't think you ever could.'

'That would be intellectual error,' said the mug, but kindly.

Jane's eye was on him. 'What do you think, Don? What's your definition of original sin?'

He gave his easy smile, damning Moira behind it. 'I did have an idea ten minutes ago, but I couldn't get a word in and now I've forgotten it.'

'What a pity. It was probably the answer.'

That went all right and was all to the good, probably. You'd be conspicuous saying nothing in a mob like this.

'The free lunch.' That was the tall fellow in the yuppie shirt and pants. 'That's the original sin, wanting what you don't earn.'

Jane began to laugh. 'But that's privilege, and privilege is a denial of human equality! One to me!'

The girl was back now.

Somebody else would have to move soon, at the rate they were sloshing the beer. He had to pick his moment

202

carefully. Two more. Enough for cover and before the rush started.

Relax now. Take it easy.

Ah, there went Paul. A good, conspicuous one. The one he had picked for a mug didn't look like moving.

The beautiful blonde was slow but stubborn. 'I don't think it's out of the way for people to do evil knowingly. I think there's a lot of malice in people. I think malice is the original sin.'

'The cold intention to do harm. Yes,' said the mug, 'but I don't think it's a first cause, you know. Cruelty is the other face of pain. Malice is a form of revenge.'

The girl in the corner said, 'Ego. It's the wounded ego that's the dangerous beast, don't you think?'

That got them going among themselves over there, on and on.

Paul was back.

He wouldn't wait for another one. Two minutes. If nobody stirred in two minutes, he'd move.

He wasn't bored now, giving the widescreen look at them all, watching for anyone not listening, letting them buzz on, counting seconds, draining his glass, putting it down with a steady hand.

Now. Move easy, look casual. If you can't see them, they can't see you.

In the bedroom he moved fast, dipped fingers into the bag without looking, watching the door, felt for and found the catch of the change purse, felt notes, looked away from the door for a second: two fives. Paltry, an insult. He put them in his trouser pocket, resentfully.

203

This was the tricky bit, coming out. Get a laugh ready. 'Where's the john?'

The hall was clear. In the bathroom he put the notes in his wallet.

Funny how for a minute it stopped you peeing. Then the stream came. Relieving yourself, that was a good word for it.

Those fools. You do it because you can, because you've got the nerve, the speed, the skill.

He strolled back into the living room, said 'Thanks' to Moira seeing his glass full again, sat down and took a quiet mouthful of the beer.

This was usually the best part, sitting there knowing what they didn't know, feeling like God, really, feeling fond of them, fond of the one whose money was in his wallet, but even God couldn't love this lot. They were still at it. You could hardly believe it. The yuppie was saying, 'What about the golden rule? Do unto others . . .'

'The golden rule is fine so long as the others know it too.'

And on and on and on.

'Civilisation. Real civilisation, that's the answer.'

'Define!'

'You don't bomb your equals, you don't murder your equals!'

Instead of the God-feeling came anger. If it had been a real score, sixty or more, he could bear to sit here with a pleasant, intelligent smile on his face. It was against the rule to draw attention to himself by leaving early, no matter what the circumstances. He had to stay in training for the big score.

This mob were the exception; he wouldn't be likely to meet anything like them again, not if he could help it.

He murmured to Moira, 'Do you feel a headache coming on?'

She looked up at him, anxious and devoted.

'Do you want to leave?'

He nodded. 'Go and tell her you have a headache, will you? Cover for us.'

She nodded. 'I'll tell her.'

An entertaining idea had come to him. After all, she was one of them, wasn't she? Serve her right for bringing him here. He smiled at her, using his teasing smile.

'Go and fix your face. You have a shiny nose.'

'Oh.' She looked daunted. 'There'll be someone in the bathroom.'

That was right. They were on the move now. All the better. There'd be people in the hall to see her go in.

'There's a mirror in the bedroom, isn't there?'

'Oh, yes. OK. I won't be a minute.'

The perfect mug, and right beside him. She hadn't thought twice about doing what he wanted. She never did.

He watched her come back, carefully combed and painted, go to Jane and speak with her hand to her forehead. Why, she even looked shifty! She was a rotten liar.

He got up to join her, meeting eyes with Jane above her head, looked puzzled, then patient, gave a tiny shrug and walked out with her.

They walked to her lodging house. For a short time that clever little scene kept him amused, but then he thought of the tedious evening and the paltry score and anger came back, creeping along his bones till he felt like a tree of fire. All that for ten dollars, for ten lousy dollars. Insulting, just what you'd expect of that lot.

She must have had some idea of his mood, for she didn't try to talk, till they got to her front gate.

She said then, 'I'm afraid you didn't enjoy the evening.'

The light from the hall reached them. She turned towards him. He saw shock and terror on her face and understood, with horror himself, what was wrong. The God-mask was gone. Whatever she saw made her scuttle for the front door, claw in her handbag for a key, then press the bell in panic. As if he meant to chase her. Not likely.

She didn't matter, but the God-mask mattered. That had never happened to him before. It had been second nature to him; he had lived free and powerful behind it. His anger had consumed it. He walked away naked, bereft, analysing that terrible anger. It wasn't from boredom, resentment of her silly remark about love, or even the paltry score. It was the knowledge that you could never shut those people up. No matter how much you scored from them, fifty, a hundred, you wouldn't stop their silly cackle. You would never shut them up.

FACES AND VOICES

At that time I was living in two different worlds and neither of them was really fit for human habitation. I didn't think they had anything in common – not even that. They were two separate planets to me. If somebody from the staff of Brentwood Girls' High School had got by chance into the same compartment of a suburban train as Leo or Charles, Jackie or Francis or one of the others, or walked into a restaurant where we ate, I would have been surprised beyond reason.

At Brentwood I was responsible for class 1G. An hour in front of 1G was as close as one could get nowadays to an hour in the pillory, though of course in the pillory one didn't have responsibilities but could stand and suffer with an easy mind. Very little information passed between me and 1G and I tried to make a joke of that. Of that and of other things.

One day as I sat in the staffroom marking 1G's compositions I read aloud to Miss Hargreaves, '"Then I wathed the come and to went." What do you suppose Rhonda Munson means by that?' One wasn't supposed to talk in the staffroom, but Miss Hargreaves was friendly and the only other person there was Miss Mayne at a table across the room. 'Dear me, I'm not teaching them much, am I? I'm not cut out for this job, I'm afraid.'

No, I didn't feel any pity for Rhonda Munson. That was a separate planet again. A proper little orrery I must have had labouring round inside my head.

'You should marry that nice young man who waits for you at the bus stop.'

Dear innocent Miss Hargreaves. She took Charles for a suitor. That was far from the truth. I left 1G's compositions to calculate how far from the truth it was.

On the other planet that I called real life I was love-sick for a boy named Leo, a grey-eyed – but no, it doesn't matter what Leo was like. All I'm prepared to say about that passion is it had little to do with its object and less to do with love.

One night at Jackie's when Fred was playing guitar and the others were sitting on the floor smoking or singing a bit, Leo was acting out a sort of joking love scene with a girl called Narelle. I got up and went out, trying to fade quietly, but Charles followed me, put his arm round me in the garden and said, 'You poor kid. Come on, tell me all about it.' I was surprised, because Charles played the elegant untouchable, but I did tell him all about it. He met me sometimes after school and we went and sat in a cafe

208

to talk about Leo because he had appointed himself my comfort and support.

That wasn't true either.

Charles was forever asking questions about Leo's love affairs. I knew about them because Leo always told me – it was a token of friendship I could have done without.

'Does it occur to you,' Charles had said, 'that there may be a reason why Leo never commits himself to a serious relationship with a woman?'

Sure, I thought, glum and vulgar. Why buy a book when you can join a library? But I looked interrogative.

'Latent homosexuality.' He spoke lightly, handling a cigarette delicately while his eyebrows repudiated passion.

I'd noticed of course that Charles spent a lot of time thinking about Leo, and I'd felt the core under the wrappings of sarcastic appraisal, indulgent friendship, admiration and resentment. Now that the wrappings were off and it was like a little live suffering monster in the palm of my hand, I thought with a shock that unrequited love is an ugly thing.

'He's putting up a marvellous front then,' I said.

'They tend to, don't they? The Don Juan syndrome . . . It's one explanation.'

Don Juan catches all sorts. Charles and I were in love with the same man.

And that wasn't true either.

Charles wasn't a true lover. He wasn't saying yes to Leo but no to the whole homosexual thing. I wasn't like Charles, no, not I. I was a true lover, not a no sayer.

There was no doubt that I contributed to Leo's happiness. He came to see me when he was depressed and he

209

always cheered up in my company. Sometimes I looked up from reading aloud or getting the supper and saw him giving me a serious attentive look with a kind of brightness behind it that made me think I was more important to him than he realised.

Really, I think I was over it. Charles's conversation was the cure for love, all right. But if I broke away from Leo while I had something to give him, why then, I wasn't a true lover, was I? I'd be as bad as Charles. It sounds like something out of the *Women's Own Weekly Mirror,* but I'd reached the position after a lot of conscientious pondering, and I was so hung up on the difference between no sayers and true lovers that I was stuck with it like a religion.

'Charles is not the marrying kind,' I said to Miss Hargreaves.

Miss Mayne stirred and muttered '7 and 3½, 10½ plus 3', so I said no more for the moment.

It was hard to stay alone with 1G's compositions, and I'd just begun to read Miss Hargreaves another unforgettable sentence when the door opened wide and silent and Miss Ritter the headmistress stood there radiating malice. I've never met anyone who cared less about concealing rage and hatred than Miss Ritter. She walked about with a steady seventy watts of anger glowing in her unfocussed eyes. When their lighthouse beam first fell on me the wattage increased at once, as if I had been annoying her for years and this, actually seeing me, was the last straw.

She said, 'You will have less time to gossip in future, Miss Turner. I have arranged for you to spend your free periods observing the lessons of more competent teachers. You will attend Miss Wiley's second year History class in second period tomorrow.'

'Yes, Miss Ritter.'

All those corny words like 'icily', 'with a sneer', 'her lip curled' and so on – Miss Ritter was a living illustration of them all. Because of that, I looked at her with interest, frightened as I was.

'I shall have to answer to the inspectors for your incompetence, Miss Turner, if I do not take every possible means of dealing with it. You have no reason to consider yourself ill-used.'

I must have reached the point of revolution where there is nothing left to lose, for I clarioned back, quite out of character, 'You have no reason to suppose that I do!'

The effect of this was astonishing. The light went out in her face and for a second I saw an orphan child whose one beloved clockwork train has just refused to answer to its key. Then she covered desolation with a look of virtue misjudged, said bitterly, 'What a way to speak to me!', turned and went.

Miss Hargreaves sat burning quietly over the books she was correcting. It was Miss Mayne who said in a friendly voice, 'You poor kid! How she hounds you. It's a shame!'

I kept my head down, concealing my feelings while I worked at the job of incapsulating Miss Ritter in laughter. Then I said with a giggle, the best I could manage, 'Lucky she doesn't know I haven't marked the roll for three days.

She'd get so much fun out of that, it's a shame to keep it from her, really.'

I looked up then and saw Miss Mayne looking at me with Leo's eyes, bright, gentle and affectionate. Her expression moved me so much that I looked down straight away and submerged myself in 1G's compositions, afraid I might give way and create a scene.

Some time later, Miss Hargreaves said, 'Ellie!' and I looked up to see that we were alone. 'Ellie, will you promise to do something for me without asking why?'

'Of course I will.'

'Go straight round to your room and mark your roll.'

She didn't know, of course, about Miss Mayne looking at me just like Leo, or what that meant to me, but even so . . . I stared at her thinking how much I had liked her until then and how terrible it was that she should turn out sordid like the rest. Sometimes I felt as if I was living inside God's vermiform appendix.

'Miss Hargreaves!'

'Now do as I ask you, and don't waste time.'

A Girl Guide asked to dishonour her True Lover's badge, I said sullenly, 'I can't. They're at gym.'

'It doesn't have to be right, dear. Just fill in the spaces. You promised me, Ellie.'

So I went.

I was late back to the staffroom that afternoon, because I had been undergoing an emotional crisis in the upstairs lavatory, but Miss Hargreaves was waiting for me. It was her moment.

'Well?'

'Oh, yes. Miss Ritter came in and asked to see my roll. I'd just got it marked and back in the drawer. Miss Hargreaves . . .'

'That roll is a legal document. You can be reported to the Department if you don't mark it every day. It's the very worst thing that a teacher can do.'

Considering what I must have been doing to Rhonda Munson, I think that odd, but it didn't interest me then.

'Miss Hargreaves, she was sympathising with me! Drawing me out. Luring me to me doom, you might say.'

'Oh, yes. She's a very wicked bitch, that one. And Ellie . . .'

'Don't worry. I've caught on.'

That was all the thanks she got. I suppose the born teacher doesn't look for more.

I wasn't going to change towards Leo – not Ella, the constant lover, not me . . . just because for a minute Miss Mayne had looked like him, but I didn't want to see him that evening. It happened that he came. I was lying on my bed reading when I heard his step at the foot of the stairs, and I switched the light off straight away, but he must have seen it, for he knocked and called out 'Ellie!' full of confidence that I was there. I didn't answer. He knocked louder, saying, 'Ellie! It's Leo here.'

After a pause he repeated 'Ellie,' uncertainly this time. There was such a chill on his voice that I said to myself precisely, 'There goes another clockwork train,' and laughed aloud.

Leo ran away. I heard his footsteps rattle down the stairs as I lay in the dark, laughing and laughing.

It doesn't have much to do with love, as I said before.

THE WRITING DESK

The old woman seemed not at all perturbed by Emily's reaction. She said placidly, 'Well, you can't go up, but you can come down, that's what I always say.'

'How far are you prepared to come down?'

Not very far, it seemed. She stood firm at forty dollars, which was extortionate. Emily hesitated, but she could not resist the promise of that pool of light and silence which the writing desk offered. Having experience in this matter, she said firmly, 'It is a very high rent, but I shall expect it to cover the cost of electricity. I shall be wanting to work at night.'

The old woman considered this for a moment, apparently with discontent.

'Don't you do your schoolwork at school? They give you time off for that, don't they?'

You truly are an extraordinary old party, thought Emily, as she answered, 'Not enough. I have to bring corrections home. Besides, I am doing a special job.' She knew that it would be unwise to mention novel writing, which would mark her out as an oddity to become the talk of the town. 'I'm writing a thesis. A university thesis. That's why I'm leaving the boarding-house. I want somewhere quiet to work.'

'I wouldn't want anything going on in my house that wasn't respectable.' The old woman seemed to suspect some danger even in a thesis. Perhaps the word 'university' had bad connotations. 'Our name stands high in this town.'

'Not for generosity,' thought Emily. She answered, 'I shan't be doing anything to disgrace you.'

'It'll be payment by the fortnight in advance.'

Emily handed over the eighty dollars, with regret, consoling herself with the thought of that lovely, silent, lighted place which was to be her own.

'I never would have thought of taking a lodger, if it wasn't for the emptiness of the house. If there was anyone, anyone living in the place, even a child . . .'

The misery in her voice was moving; it would have affected Emily more deeply if it had not been for the forty dollars paid fortnightly in advance.

'I'll move in, then, on Monday and the rent will be covered until the second Sunday. Monday to Sunday, all right?'

'I suppose so.'

The old woman put the notes into a deep pocket of her skirt and the interview was over.

*

The first shock hit Emily five minutes after she had moved in on Monday. Having put her suitcase on the floor and opened it ready for unpacking, she opened the wardrobe and stared in amazement at the jackets and trousers which crammed the hanging space. She pulled open the drawers and found them filled too with a miscellany of objects: ties, odd socks . . .

She found her landlady in the kitchen.

'Mrs Britton, you have forgotten to clear out the wardrobe in my room.'

Mrs Britton did not answer at once. Emily now looked at her attentively; till now she had been the fortuitous owner of a room with a writing desk, conspicuous only for her love of money. She was a soft-fleshed, bulky old woman, with white hair dragged back into a knot from a round skull. She had a plump face with neat small features and very pale eyes. At the moment her face wore a look of strange, obtuse calm, like a beached sea-creature pondering new surroundings.

'I did not know you would be wanting that.'

'I did not think I had to mention it. It is generally understood that the rent of a room includes the use of the furniture.'

'Those are Kenny's things. I wouldn't know what to do with Kenny's things.'

'But I must have somewhere to hang up my clothes!' Emily heard and deplored the pleading note in her voice.

'Can't you keep them in your suitcase?'

'No, I can't. Certainly not. I must have the wardrobe cleared.'

217

'Well, you can't have the cupboard. You can have the wardrobe, I suppose, if you can't do without it, but I can't have you using the cupboard. I need that for storage.' People who required a wardrobe to hang clothes in were clearly monsters of selfishness who needed a firm hand. 'I can't see to it now. I'll have to find some place for Kenny's things. I suppose you can keep your clothes in a suitcase for a day or two.'

This she said with a sneer.

'Oh, yes,' said Emily feebly. 'Just when you have the time.' She expected this remark to elicit a sniff, and so it did.

Why, thought Emily, she's malevolent, a real witch. It's a wonder she stayed civil long enough to collect that rent.

Back in her room and fearing the worst, she pulled open the drawers of the writing desk. Sure enough, the space she intended for her novel outline, her notes, typing paper and carbons, and the chapters as they were completed, was already taken by old account books, worn ink-stained rulers, blunt pencils, eroded rubbers, rubber bands, a set of geometrical instruments. No hope of getting rid of that lot, with permission. She would empty the contents into a couple of cartons and hide them under the bed.

'I'm a rabbit. An absolute wimp. What I ought to do is empty the stuff into cartons, carry them out and say boldly, "What do you want done with this stuff, Mrs Britton? It was in the drawers of my writing desk."' But she knew that she would not.

She had expected some coolness from the old woman after the disagreement over the wardrobe, but she found her affable and ready to gossip as she showed her the arrangements for cooking and washing. This burner for simmering, that for quick boiling, heat up water on the fuel, electricity too expensive, this accompanied by information about her husband's last illness (cancer right up the fundament), the iniquitous bill for twelve hundred dollars sent by Doctor Burbage to arrive three days after the funeral – 'after I had told him again and again to send me a bill by the month and he took no notice. Three days after the funeral. The heartlessness of it!' She spoke of the misdeeds of the Huntleys, who rented from her the house down the road, and had the chip heater roaring every day, so that you could hear it from here, pumping away like a steam engine. 'There'll be a new lining needed for the heater soon. Always needing something, that lot. I'll swear that most of the stuff they complain about is their own doing, or the doing of those children. I'll never let to people with children again, that's certain.'

Mrs Britton indeed covered a lot of ground, showing equal enjoyment in the misdeeds of the Huntleys and the heartlessness of the doctor, among other minor sufferings, as she showed china, cutlery and linen.

'I'll have to keep out of her way,' thought Emily. 'I can't let myself be trapped like this again.'

When Mrs Britton asked her what she meant to cook for her dinner tonight, she was glad to be able to answer that she would be dining out.

'I've been invited out to dinner at a friend's house.' And no, I'm not going to tell you by whom, she silently answered the flash of anger which followed the old woman's disconcerted air.

219

'I hope you won't be coming in late.'

'No. I don't keep late hours, especially when it's school the next day. Ten o'clock at the outside. Can you give me a door key? I wouldn't want to disturb you coming in.' Reluctantly the old woman got up and fetched a large key from a nail behind the kitchen door.

'Surely she isn't going to tell me that I'm not allowed out to dinner,' thought Emily with amusement. For a moment it seemed that the woman was on the point of doing so.

After a cheerful dinner with the deputy and his wife, she walked back to the house and put the key in the door with unease at her strangeness in these surroundings. She opened the door quietly, felt for and found the light switch and pressed it down. That to her surprise required considerable strength. The switch yielded with a loud spanging noise which startled her and might well be enough to waken the old woman.

Damn. Who would expect a light switch to explode with such a crash? She went to her room, turned on the lamp over the writing desk and was comforted at once as it shone down on what was to be her private working space.

Ready for bed, and back in the hall, she tried to work the switch more gently, out of respect for the old woman's sleep, but there was no help for it. The switch resisted, then yielded with the same loud spang as before. Maybe she is used to it, she thought, yawning. She set her alarm clock, put out her light and fell asleep.

A worse shock came next afternoon, when she set up her typewriter on the desk, fed in the first page of her novel

220

and set to work. It was a moment of special joy, but it did not last long. The old woman rushed into the room, looking wild-eyed, hands covering her ears, crying, 'Stop it! I can't have that noise! I won't have that terrible noise in the house! It goes right through my head! As if the noise you made coming in last night wasn't bad enough. I can't put up with this. I can't stand that noise. It's giving me a terrible headache.'

Emily might have known that it was all too good to be true. That lovely well of light and silence the desk had promised could not be for her.

'I'm very sorry. I did take it for granted that I should be able to type. If I can't type, then I can't stay. I'll stay for the fortnight, of course, because I have paid the rent, but meanwhile I'll look for something else.'

She said later, as she described the scene to her friend Miriam, 'If ever you saw two eyes convert into dollar signs before your own . . .' Mrs Britton had taken her hands from her ears. Her headache appeared to have abated. She stood hesitating. Emily seized the advantage.

'I'll get a piece of felt to put under the typewriter. That will cut the noise a lot. And I'll keep my door shut. If at the end of the fortnight you find you can't bear it, then I'll leave. What about that?'

'I suppose it's worth trying. If you must.'

Emily gave up typing for the afternoon, for the lack of the felt baffle. She applied herself to cleaning out two drawers of the desk and boldly stacked the contents in the corner of the room, ready to be packed into a carton. The old woman would certainly investigate and find them tomorrow. Emily thought she would not care to mention the matter.

Nothing more was said about the typing. Perhaps the noise, dulled by the layer of felt and the wooden panels, did not reach the old woman, whose habitat was the kitchen. Perhaps, on the other hand, she was daunted by the fear of losing the rent. Emily finished her first chapter, so long planned and written in longhand, and at the weekend, started on the next. On reflection, she put the top copy of the first chapter into a folder and took it to her friend Miriam, the only inhabitant of the town who knew of her serious literary ambitions. She handed her the folder, saying, 'Do me a favour, will you? Look after the top copy of my novel for me, I just don't trust my landlady. Silly of me, but I'd be happier if you looked after it for me.'

'I'd love to. May I read it?'

'Of course you may. You and Mrs Britton. I'm dead certain that as soon as I leave for school she gets into my room to find out what I'm doing. I can stand that. I haven't much choice. But . . . I don't know. Just look after it for me. And I hope you will read it. I do want to know what you think of it, but don't tell me till it's finished.'

Miriam took the folder.

'I'll look after it for you. I wouldn't trust her either. She's the meanest old snake in town. All her children have cleared out, and no wonder that poor Stella ran off with a man of seventy. Mrs Wingrove next door said the old woman never let up on the poor girl, and they used to hear her crying. But a man of seventy! And now she has a baby girl. Imagine, she'll have a husband over eighty and a child under ten – what a future! But better than life with mum.'

'She does her own share of crying. If you try to argue with her and she can't get her own way, she absolutely breaks down, sobs like an infant. Like over the noise I made coming in that first night. The light switch makes an incredible spanging noise, enough to wake the dead, I agree. So I disturbed her sleep. She held on to her grievance till the next time I went out, then she said, she couldn't stand having her sleep disturbed by noise at night and she hoped I'd be more careful in the future. I thought, "Oh hell, the light switch!" and I said, very reasonably, I thought, that I could not understand why anyone so sensitive to noise should have light switches that went off like a bomb, and she started to cry. "The boys fixed them like that, for safety." Insoluble problem. You want the safety, you take the noise. Though really, I'm buying a torch to get around with at night. No point in making any trouble.'

'Why on earth did you go there? I could have warned you.'

'It's only till I finish the book. I've won the point about typing. That's the main thing. She did try to stop it.' Emily described the scene and made the remark about eyes which turned into dollar signs.

'It's lucky I made an absolute point that forty-dollar rent would have to cover the use of electricity, because I meant to work at night. Of course I don't type at night, but I'm doing the first draft by hand, and I leave my corrections till after dinner. So there's plenty to do.'

She did not mention the private place, the little lighted room formed by the lamp and the wings and back of the writing desk. Nomads find homes in strange places.

It was lucky indeed that Emily had insisted that the forty-dollar rent covered the use of electricity. She discovered in the following weeks that there were many things it did not cover: toilet paper (Sorry, I'll buy a roll.), washing-up liquid (Sorry, I'll get myself a bottle tomorrow and you can use some of mine.), laundry soap (Sorry, I just didn't think. I won't do it again.), floor polish (Okay, I'll get my own.), sinful and extravagant use of the chip heater for a daily bath (It's a wonder what some people do to get so dirty.). That one Emily preferred to ignore, since she had no intention of giving up the daily bath.

'She hasn't thought of wear and tear on the broom yet,' said Emily to Miriam. She was laughing, for she had decided to classify Mrs Britton as a comic character.

'I don't know how you put up with it. I'd love to have you here, you know, but Graham says it isn't possible for a doctor to take in lodgers. He says it's a confession of failure. Well, why doesn't he admit he's a failure and take a salaried job in the city? He says it's my fault, because I don't socialise, but Mary Burbage is no angel and Burbage's practice goes along all right. But that's Graham, always someone else's fault, never his own.'

Emily, who did not wish to be exposed every day to Miriam's bitter unhappiness, said that she could see Graham's point of view, 'in a place like this, where everyone is out to make the worst of anything.'

'Besides, it really suits me. If she wasn't so poisonous, I might feel I had to socialise. As it is, it's minimal exposure. Well, I do see her at breakfast, and then I get a few remarks about the dirty habits of those who find it necessary to bathe every day, but I let that pass in silence and get on with my cornflakes. And I don't cook dinner, just have cold cuts and salad. I don't eat till seven o'clock and by then she's out of the kitchen. I've had a few remarks about eating at a reasonable hour, and I point out in a reasonable tone that I like to do my typing at a time when I know it won't disturb her.

'So I type from five to seven, then I eat and wash up, then correct essays and maybe begin a new chapter. I don't care for anything, so long as I finish the book. I'm fired up. I've been thinking about it, planning it for so long and never had the chance, never had a place where I could sit and work and know I won't be interrupted. Two hours a day and most of Saturday, when I've done my washing and cleaning, and just about all of Sunday. You can't imagine what it means to me.'

'Oh, I think I can.'

'Yes. I know you do. I'd put up with anything, just for the chance to write in peace.'

'It's a wonderful book. I finish one chapter and I can't wait to get the next one.'

'I hope some publisher agrees with you.'

'Oh, they will! They must!'

'Well, it's worth putting up with the old lady and that dreadful rent I can't afford, just to have this one chance.'

'Have another cup of coffee.'

225

'No. I'd better be getting back, or there'll be remarks at breakfast about people who come in at all hours without consideration for the sleep of others.'

'And this using a torch! You shouldn't have paid any attention to her moaning about the light switches!'

'I think she lies awake, waiting to see if I do anything to wake her up. Don't worry. I'm bearing up. Honestly, it's a bit of a laugh.'

'When do I get the next chapter?'

'Next Friday night, if you'll be home.'

'Sure. I'd love to see you.'

When Emily arrived on Friday evening with the new chapter, she found Miriam in distress.

'I have to talk to you. Thank God, Graham's out visiting a patient. I don't want him in on this.'

'What's the matter?'

'Oh, that Rhoda Britton! I was at the Burbages' on Tuesday afternoon, playing bridge. It was fundraising for the Red Cross, more people there than usual, not all friends of Mary's. Otherwise the beastly woman wouldn't have been there. Mary would never have invited her. She was telling the world what a bad character you were, how poor Auntie was at her house crying about it. She'd taken a lodger in for the company after Uncle Fred died and you just ignored her. I was so furious, I said, "Took her in for company, indeed! Took her in for forty dollars a week, you mean. Charging an exorbitant rent and doing nothing for her. If she wanted company, she should have halved the rent and offered a bit of service." I don't believe Rhoda knew about the rent, and it shocked her. It shocked everyone. Jane Croft said, "Why, you could get a self-contained flat for that." I said, "And if you did let a self-contained flat, would you expect the tenant to come and keep you company in the evenings?" Rhoda didn't know what to say. I suppose I should have left it at that, but I couldn't help myself. I said, "If your aunt had been looking for company, perhaps she should have chosen someone a little more on her own intellectual level."'

And there went Graham's practice again, thought Emily. Miriam did not know where to stop.

'She'd have said it anyhow. What she said. Of course I'd got under her skin. She isn't exactly proud of Auntie. And said it somewhere where I wasn't there to argue.'

'Miriam, what did she say?'

Miriam braced herself.

'She said you might be doing better than staying in your room day and night drinking.'

'*What!*'

'Yes. That's what I said. I said you didn't drink. She said, "Oh, yes she does. Auntie has seen the bottles." Emily, I know there's no truth in it.'

'There's an atom of truth in it. I sometimes drink a glass of sherry at night. It puts me to sleep. A bottle of sherry lasts more than a fortnight. Of course she's seen bottles, two maybe in eight weeks.'

'If a thing like this gets around in a town like this, your life won't be worth living.'

'It would get around the school, that's the problem.' Emily was engulfed in depression. 'I thought I could put up

227

with anything, to get the book finished, but I can't let this pass. I'll have to tackle her and make her retract. So she'll put me out. No help for it. She's got to give me notice. I won't budge till the end of term, that's three weeks. There are the term papers to mark. But I won't give up work on my book if I have to sit up all night. Damn the old wretch and her electricity bill.'

'Can't you work in the holidays?'

Emily shook her head. 'I'll be staying with Diana. If she knows about the novel, she'll never let me help out with the kids. And with two toddlers and a baby, she needs all the help she can get.'

'It seems to me that you could do with a break.'

'My sister Diana is about the closest person to me on earth. I don't grudge it, I assure you. She'll be there for me if I need her. Meanwhile, I have to think how to handle the old party.'

Next morning, carrying writing pad, envelopes and pen, and armed with resolution, Emily advanced on the enemy in the kitchen.

'Mrs Britton, did you give your niece Rhoda reason to understand that I drink to excess?'

'She's not my niece, she's my second cousin!'

'Did you give your second cousin reason to understand that I drink to excess?'

The old woman was flustered but defiant. 'I didn't say anything about excess!'

Emily sat down opposite her and prepared for a long struggle.

'And I didn't say "said". I said "give to understand". If you say that a person drinks, the implication is that she drinks to excess. That is certainly how Rhoda Britton understood it and communicated her opinion to a number of people at Mrs Burbage's house last Tuesday. Her words were that I sat in my room all day drinking, and that you had seen the bottles. Did you think to tell her how many bottles you had seen?'

'A young woman like you shouldn't be drinking alcohol at all.'

'I have my own ideas about what people should and should not do. We can discuss that some other time. How many bottles?'

The old woman withdrew into silent resentment.

'How many bottles?'

'How would I know?'

'Too many to count, was it? That was the impression your relative gave the company. I'll tell you how many. Two. Two empty sherry bottles in eight weeks. Do you call that heavy drinking?'

'I suppose not.'

Emily put the pad and the pen on the table in front of her. 'Now you are to write to your relative. You are to tell her that you did not mean to give the impression that I drank to excess, that in the eight weeks I have lived in your house you have seen only two empty sherry bottles in the bin and have no reason to suppose that I spend my time in my room drinking. I want you to do this now.'

'Why should I?'

'Because if she doesn't get a letter from you, she'll be getting one from Frank Brown, the solicitor, and so will you. You'll both be facing a charge of slander.'

The word 'slander' stood like a solid object in the old woman's path. She eyed it with caution.

'I don't mind putting Rhoda right. She had no right to repeat what I told her in confidence.'

'What you had no right to say in the first place.' With every statement Emily's voice grew firmer. 'Start writing, please. And start with the date. "Dear Rhoda, it has come to my attention that last Tuesday . . ."' I am enjoying this, thought Emily. Bullying people is fun. It could get to be a habit. I must remember that.

She dictated, the old woman wrote. She stopped over the word 'implication'.

'Rhoda will know I never wrote that.'

'I am sure that Rhoda will understand the situation perfectly. Go on, please. "In the eight weeks she has lodged in my house, she has . . ."'

'I can't stand this! I can't stand this!' Tears of aggrieved and bullied childhood rolled down the old woman's face.

'I can't help it. If the story gets to the school that I am a secret drinker, then my career as well as my reputation will be ruined. I have to protect myself against slander. Go on writing, please.' Her voice was gentler, for the old woman's misery was genuine. Emily told herself firmly that it did not spring from remorse.

They finished the letter. 'Now I am going to type a copy of this, and I want you to sign and date them both. If Rhoda does not do as you've said, and speak to Mrs Burbage, then I'll have to make sure that she gets the information.'

She was glad to escape from the scene of the old woman's destruction and her own deterioration.

She brought back the letter and the copy.

'Now sign the copy, please, and date your signature.'

As the old woman wrote, she cried out in a moaning voice, mournful as a dirge.

'If you knew what it was like, living with someone who doesn't have a word to throw you from morning till night. If I get "Good morning" and "Good afternoon" from you, it's as much as I'll ever get. You'd give more thought to a dog than you give to me. And no consideration, not a thought for my sleep, coming in at all hours . . .'

'I don't use those light switches. I use a torch.'

'You have a particularly heavy tread.'

'Well, thank you for letting me know. Now, if you address the envelope, I'll post it.' She was thinking with horror, 'She wanted love. She wanted me to love her. That poor, mean-tongued, avaricious creature. She wants love.'

'I can't even look for a word over the dinner table. Eating that nasty cold stuff at any hour, like a gypsy.'

'My diet is healthy and adequate. I think that you have expected too much of a lodger.'

'I'd have been ready to cook you a bit of dinner, if you'd asked.'

'I wouldn't want to put you to the trouble. Come on, address the envelope and we'll forget all about it. I'll never use that copy unless I really have to. You just have a word with Rhoda and tell her she has to kill the story, that's all.'

Her voice was almost as sad as the old woman's, weighed as it was with the burden of all the unloveable people who yearned for love. If she could not give love, she would at least give forgiveness.

'I can't understand,' said Emily to Miriam, 'why she has taken it so quietly.'

A week had passed and the notice of dismissal had not come.

'Rhoda hasn't taken it quietly. She gave me a poisonous look at the last Red Cross committee meeting. The old lady is probably frightened.'

'It's more than that,' said Emily. 'She looks somehow . . . thoughtful. Subdued, but – I would have expected her to be more resentful.'

'You had to do it, you know,' said Miram firmly.

'Oh yes, I know.' But I shouldn't have enjoyed it. She felt nauseous, remembering the pleasure she had felt in watching the old woman write at her dictation. Once or twice she had had to impose her will on refractory children, though not often. She was lucky in that; she could not herself explain why a noisy class would become quiet when she entered the room. When other teachers asked for the secret, she would answer, 'I don't know. I suppose I just expect it.' She could not imagine taking pleasure in dominating and humiliating a child. If it had to be done, she could do it, but to enjoy it . . . the thought was disgusting. I shall never seek power over another human being again, so long as I live.

Aloud, she said, 'Well, it doesn't look as if she's going to put me out. That's the main thing. I'll know by the end of the term, when I pay for the fortnight's rent for the holidays. If she doesn't tell me to pack my bags then, I'll know that she's decided to swallow it.'

'It's a bore having to pay when you're away.'

'That's the big drawback about renting, but it means I can leave my things. Don't have to clear the room out. That's something.'

'I'll store your stuff for you, love, if she does throw you out.'

On the last day of term, Emily handed eighty dollars to Mrs Britton saying, 'I'll be off tomorrow morning and I'll be back on Sunday fortnight. Probably in the morning. I'll take the night train.' The old woman did hesitate for a moment. Now was the moment to say, 'I don't want you to come back.' The sight of the money must have been too persuasive. She took the money without a word. One would wonder, thought Emily, with an inward grin, at what some people are prepared to swallow for forty dollars a week.

For the first week of the vacation, Emily managed to put the novel out of her mind. At the first sight of her younger sister, thin, wan and prematurely ageing, she had exclaimed, 'Di, you look terrible!'

'The baby's sleep pattern isn't established yet. I haven't been getting much sleep. Peter does help at the weekends,' she said, forestalling criticism of her husband, which Emily might entertain, though she would not express it. 'He has

233

to have his sleep during the week, so he wears earplugs and I cope. Derek and Edgar keep me going during the day, so there you are. It's a bad spell.'

'I'll take the boys over. You look after the baby. You sleep when he sleeps. You have to get some rest.'

Diana nodded, saying, 'It's not much of a holiday for you but . . . I'd be grateful.' The manner which imposed discipline on the rowdy classes had no effect on four-year-old Derek and two-year-old Edgar. Emily ran, caught, washed, fed and entertained, balancing on a knife-edge between affection and exasperation. The undoubted charm of the human infant was, she decided, a survival mechanism. Without it, one would certainly throw them out of a high window onto their fragile skulls.

Diana, meanwhile, ate breakfast in bed and went back to sleep till the baby cried for its ten o'clock feed. She relaxed. Peace and a little colour came back to her face; observing the change, Emily thought of her efforts as rewarded.

Peter also balanced on a knife-edge between gratitude and resentment. The young women were closely bound in affection, having been allies in the difficult household of their father's second marriage. Peter did not care for that closeness; most particularly, he did not want Emily to regard his house as her home. This attitude, never expressed in words, was however clear to Emily. At the weekend the cool wind of courtesy blew. Emily thought, 'All the home I have in this world is made up of a writing desk, a reading lamp and a typewriter.' The thought started a concentrated longing for that small private place.

234

When she took breakfast to Diana on Monday, she sat on the bed, saying, 'Love, I've got something to tell you. Better take my chance while the kids are watching *Play School*.' She laughed at the sudden attentiveness in Diana's face.

'No. I have not met Mr Right. Forget him. I'm writing a novel.'

'Oh, Em!' Diana's start of delight jiggled the breakfast tray and spilled coffee into the saucer. 'That's wonderful. I've always known you should do more with your life, you just have it in you to be something special. You're not just anybody. This is it.'

'I've proved nothing yet. What I want to say is, I'd like to go back early. You are looking better. A couple of days should set you up.'

'Peter's getting a student to help for two hours after school. That's crisis time, when I'm trying to feed the boys and get them ready for bed, and Jeremy is very unsettled. It is going to make all the difference.'

'How to repel invaders,' thought Emily.

'It's your doing,' said Diana, answering the unspoken thought. 'When he saw how worried you were, and ready to give up your holiday. I truly am so grateful!'

Emily answered only with a smile.

'It's all right, then, if I leave on Wednesday? But you have to make the most of me until then. I'll get back to the boys now. Don't worry about the tray, I'll get it later.'

'Give me a hug.'

Emily obliged and went downstairs to resume her duties.

*

235

In the night train she planned her next chapter and wrote the outline and certain pithy expressions which must not be forgotten, before she got into the sleeper – a necessary expense, rather than a luxury, after ten days of looking after her nephews. She slept soundly and woke happy, thinking of duty done and Diana restored, relishing her freedom and ready for work. She took a taxi – or rather, the taxi took her – to Mrs Britton's house.

There was a car in the drive. 'Early in the morning for entertaining,' thought Emily, but she was pleased that the old woman had a visitor. She could go straight to her room without announcing her arrival.

The bed was unmade, a slept-in bed, which told the whole story with shocking suddenness. She looked about. Her typewriter was not on her desk. Instead there were a stranger's brush, comb and mirror, face powder, face cream – evidence enough of settled occupancy.

She sped to the kitchen, where Mrs Britton sat with another woman at the breakfast table. It was not a moment for introductions. Emily fixed her eye on Mrs Britton and shrilled in fury, 'Who has been sleeping in my room?' Later, she thought that she could have been trying out for the part of Father Bear in the Christmas pantomime, but at the moment fury ruled.

Mrs Britton answered in indignation, 'You're not supposed to be back till Sunday.'

'That has nothing to do with you. While I pay rent for the room, nobody else has the right to use it.' Her voice rose to a shout. 'I demand an explanation.'

236

A wail of fright from a small child startled her. She looked at the third person present, a youngish woman with a worn, gentle countenance which was in itself a reproach. Emily now saw that she was holding a baby girl on her knee. The little girl was whimpering as she stared at Emily.

'I didn't mean to frighten the child, I'm sorry. But this must not happen again.'

'It's my house, I suppose.'

'If you had wanted to use the room, you should have asked my permission. Well, I should have given permission, but I shouldn't have been paying rent for the room while someone else was occupying it.'

'I didn't ask you for the rent. You gave it to me.'

'Oh, come off it. Did you think it was a present?'

'Kept your things there, didn't we? Nothing's come to any harm. It's not like renting.'

'If it comes to charging for storage, perhaps I should be charging storage, too, for the cupboard you have crammed with your stuff in my room. You can just get your stuff out of there.' Emily's tone was dulcet, out of consideration for the baby. She perceived that the scene was becoming comic.

Mrs Britton stiffened, set her lips and communed with some inward presence who understood right behaviour.

The young woman spoke. Her voice was as gentle and as worn as her face.

'Miss Balfour is right, Mother. You should not have taken the rent and I think you ought to give it back.' As she made this audacious suggestion, her voice quavered.

Her mother turned on her.

'Don't you use that tone with me!' The tone had been mild to the point of extinction, but by objecting to the tone, Mrs Britton could of course avoid discussion of the meaning. 'Lucky I'm prepared to have you in my house at all, after you've made me a laughing stock, running off with your old Romeo. Dirty old man!'

The baby girl who had been frightened by the anger in Emily's voice appeared to be soothed by her grandmother's tirade. These must be the sounds of home, too familiar to be threatening, and this must be the daughter Stella.

'Jack is a good man, a good, kind man, and we are happy together. And I will not have you speaking ill of her father in front of Philippa.' With this protest the young woman seemed to have reached the limit of her courage. Emily sensed that she had been using physical strength to force out every word.

'Father indeed. Great-grandfather, more like!'

Any pity Emily might have felt for Mrs Britton was extinguished. She said, 'Mrs Britton, will you please listen to me? You do not seem to understand anything about the law. You have taken money under false pretences, and that is called fraud. I cannot take action against you, because I don't have enough evidence that you took the money.' The old woman's expression relaxed. There, thought Emily, went her last chance of getting her money back. 'But in the future you will sign a dated receipt for every cent I pay you. Then, if there is any more fraudulent conduct on your part, I shall have evidence and I shall know what to do.' After this pompous speech, which she knew to be perilously close to the ridiculous, she waited for the woman to say, 'Don't bother. You can pack your things and get out.' That seemed to be the only possible answer. The old woman however chose not to answer at all, except with the all-purpose sneer. It was the daughter who bowed her head under the weight of the humiliation and stared scarlet-faced at the tablecloth.

Stella looked up at length and said, 'I'll drive out and spend a few days with Gwen and Harry', got up and carried the baby into the invaded room. Emily followed. Stella had set the child on the floor and was gathering up her possessions from the desk and putting them into a travel bag.

'You would have been welcome to stay as my guest,' said Emily, 'if I had been asked. It was a shock, coming in and finding the room . . . really, I am sorry. I know you did not understand the situation.'

Stella said indifferently, 'I'll change the sheets.'

It was no use. There had been too many tirades, too many humiliations. Emily could hope only that Jack was indeed a good man who had brought the poor woman some happiness.

'Where is my typewriter, please?' she asked diffidently.

Stella winced before she answered, 'On the top shelf of the linen press. I'll fetch it.'

'I'll go, I'll get the sheets.'

Stella accepted the offer of help with the same indifference. She nodded and began to take clothes out of the wardrobe. It was clear that her only thought was to get out of the house as soon as possible.

It was done, the room cleared of strange possessions, the typewriter back in its place, order restored. Stella had responded with a silent nod to Emily's farewell and departed. Emily sat down at the desk and waited for her hands to stop shaking. She typed. 'The qrick brown foz fumped . . . the qr . . .' How could any woman love money so much, more than dignity, more than self-respect, more than . . . It wasn't need, according to Miriam. Mrs Britton was a rich woman.

It's nothing to do with me, thought Emily firmly. She got the notes for the next chapter out of her travel bag, the world of her novel closed round her and she began to type.

She bought a receipt book. When on Sunday she paid for the rent she presented the receipt book and a pen and watched Mrs Britton fill in the receipt – date, amount and signature. After all, it was a normal procedure, wasn't it? She should have done this in the first place.

'How did she take it?' asked Miriam, who had listened with delight to Emily's account of the confrontation and the history of the receipt book.

'Oh, no fuss. She didn't seem to mind. In her place, I should be seething. I'll never know why she didn't tell me to leave after the row.'

'With her standards, she probably took it for normal conversation.'

It was Emily who minded. Whenever she presented the receipt book with her rent, she remembered how she had stood over the old woman, dictating the letter to Rhoda. The satisfaction she had felt then became uglier in her memory; she applied to it words like 'gloating' and 'glee'. That satisfaction had been followed by a nauseous reaction;

whenever she watched the old woman sign the receipt, that nausea returned.

She came back from school one day to find the cupboard in her room open and empty. When she told Miriam this, she said, 'I wish I could get out. If it weren't for the novel . . .'

'What's the matter with you? Why aren't you pleased? She should have cleaned out the cupboard in the first place.'

'I don't want the wretched cupboard. I don't want her trying to please me, that's all. Ever since she started signing those receipts, she's been like a different person. No complaints about the bath heater, no complaints about noise.'

'You've got her frightened. She's always dominated everyone in that house, the old man too. He was a sour old cuss, but he never stood up to her. Now you come talking about slander, talking about fraud, letters from solicitors, receipts. Now she knows there's an authority bigger than she is, and she doesn't know quite how big it is. So she's wary.'

Emily nodded.

'I did say something about using my room for storage. She might think there's some law against that. But it's not just that. She's almost friendly. Offered me a cup of tea the other day. You'd think she was glad to meet someone who stood up to her.'

'Isn't that all to the good?'

'As if she was glad to be stopped. You meet children like that sometimes, really bad children, who hate and despise you because you don't know how to stop them.'

241

'Why does it worry you?'

'Bullies create toadies, but toadies create bullies. Every time I watch her sign a receipt, I feel more and more of a bully.'

'You are entitled to defend your interests.'

'At what point does defence become aggression? The big international question. Power over another person I simply don't want.'

'It's not a very great power, is it?'

'All power corrupts, and all corruption is absolute. I don't think that woman is capable of feeling shame, and she has a wonderful knack of making you feel it for her. I noticed that with the unfortunate daughter, who couldn't be blamed for the situation, crimson with shame and misery over her mother's behaviour.'

'But that's different. You do feel like that when your parents or your children disgrace themselves. You identify. But not with a landlady. It seems odd to me, that you can't simply pay your rent and do your work and leave it at that. Why do you have to involve yourself at all?'

'Oh, yes. Why does one? That's the mystery. Well, it won't be long now. As soon as I finish the book ... well, it'll be nearly the end of term and that will be the end of it. No more of Mrs Britton, thank goodness.'

As Emily put together the pages of the final chapter and secured them with a paperclip, she felt the chill of homelessness take possession as it always did at the end of the year, stronger this time than usual. She stroked the writing surface of the desk, thinking, 'You've served your turn, and now goodbye.' Her sense of loss was acute and startling. She closed her eyes over ridiculous tears. Well, after all, some quite grown-up people go gaga over teddy bears. No, not a teddy bear. More like a ship. It was quite respectable to cry over a ship. She patted the right-hand panel, thinking, 'Some day, if I can write books that sell, I shall have a place of my own, and in it there will be a desk just like you.' Then she wiped away the two tears with a finger and set off to take the chapter to Miriam.

As soon as she arrived at the house, Miriam seized the pages, saying, 'I can't wait. I'm going to read this straight away. You go and make yourself a cup of coffee.'

Emily drank coffee, looked at a magazine, fidgeted and waited, till Miriam looked up, laughing.

'You've sprung a surprise. But when I look back, yes. I shouldn't be so surprised. It's all there. Emily, it's marvellous. You must have a wonderful sense of achievement.'

'Well, yes. At finishing it at all. Whether it's any good . . . that's for others to say. I hope you are right. But I feel sad. It's sort of a safe house, writing a novel. You're in your own little world and you control it and can shut out everything else. So I feel kind of homeless. And I haven't made any arrangements for the holidays. So in practical terms, I am homeless.'

'How did it happen, Emily? It seems so dreadful, to have no home.'

'Dad left the house to Delia. Right and proper, she was his wife. To Dad it was the family home and we were all one family. He never knew how bad things were between

243

Di and me, and Delia and her kids. I don't think he ever dreamed that Delia would get rid of us.'

'His own children!'

'I wouldn't want to live there anyhow. I have a corner of the basement where I keep possessions in a tea chest and an old trunk, and I go there when I want something. I suppose I could have a bed there if I were desperate, but it would be a last resort. It's all right. I'll have Christmas with Peter and Di and the children. That's acceptable. And then I'll find something. Have to find something for next year too. Maybe I'll get a move.'

'Oh, Emily, no! If you go, there'll be nobody in this bloody town to talk to.'

'I'd miss you, too. But teachers don't get much choice, you know.'

Emily paid the last fortnight's rent and collected the last receipt.

'I shan't be wanting the room next year, Mrs Britton. I'll take all my things and leave the room free for a new tenant.'

It took Mrs Britton more than a moment to put a decent face on astonishment and dismay.

'That's a pity. Just when we were getting into each other's ways.'

This is something I've been carrying alone for forty years, something I wanted to say and never had the chance to say it. There's not much point in it now. Charlie's been long dead, Lilian died two years ago, and yesterday I saw that woman's death notice in the paper. *Dexter, Damaris, aged 68, at St Catherine's Hospital, after a long illness. Mourned by Peg and Bobby.* So she'd never married. Sixty-eight years old – older than she had looked, then, forty years ago, when it all happened.

That was the first thing I said about her, when I saw her crossing the home yard to the schoolroom with the children.

'Is that the new governess? A bit young, isn't she?'

'Yes,' said Lil. 'That's Damaris. Got that out of a book, I think. Christened Madge, I shouldn't wonder.'

A bit too young and a bit too pretty, is what I thought. Seeing that moment again just as it was, the sunny day, the girl with the neat round head and the long neck – not so pretty, really, but neat, and there was something about the way she moved that took the eye – I thought, 'Why, nothing had happened then. The world was something it could never be again.' Somehow I felt as badly as I'd ever felt about it, after forty years. As if it was a whole world killed.

She wasn't so pretty when she left, poor wretch.

What's the point of talking about it now? As I said, they're all dead and who's interested? But I'm interested still, interested in getting it off my chest. I wanted someone to share it with then and I still have that same nagging feeling, resenting being alone with it.

From that first moment, when I ran into the wash house and found the poor creature screaming and writhing on the floor, clawing at her eyes, and Lil shouted at me, 'Get water! Get water!' I've been alone with it. They made great play with that at the trial, that Lil had screamed 'Get water!' but it wasn't like that. She was glaring at me as if I'd done it, as if she could hand the whole thing to me. 'This is your business, not mine,' she was saying.

I couldn't put that across in the witness box. I didn't want to, either. But I wanted Lil to know what I was doing for her.

The barrister, the counsel for the defence, said to me, very quiet and friendly, 'Now, Mrs Ferris, I want you to give the court your account of the events of that morning. From the moment you heard that screaming.'

'It came from the wash house. I ran in and I saw Damaris rolling backwards and forwards on the floor, clawing like at her eyes. Lil was standing still, with an open tin in her hand. I think she was too shocked to move.'

'Objection!' said the other fellow.

'Upheld,' said the judge.

'You must tell us only what you saw and heard,' said our man, kind and regretful.

'Well, she was stock still and staring, and white as a sheet,' I said, and a bit of a smile went around. 'She yelled to me, "Get water! Get water!" She was standing in front of the washtubs, so I couldn't reach the taps, but the water in the copper was still cold and clean and there was a dipper on the edge of it, so I scooped water out of it, and sluiced it over her eyes, time and again, fast as I could.'

It's an odd thing that when you're doing something like that, you get a feeling for the person you're trying to help, that has nothing to do with right and wrong. Much as I hated that wicked girl I was handling her as if I was really fond of her, murmuring to her, 'Still now. Quiet now,' as if she was a little kid. She must have felt it, for she whimpered to me, 'Twice. She did it twice.'

Of course that settled it. Once could have been an accident – though I don't know what sort of accident gets caustic into somebody's eyes – but not twice. There was no doubt about it. That was how we saved the other eye. She had had time to shut it. She had shut it so fast that she couldn't open it herself and when I got a wet cloth out of the copper and kept rinsing and then found another wet washcloth and held that over it – no use thinking about the other eye, I don't even want to think about it – but how I was praying that this left eye was all right, as

much as if she was my own child. When at last I got the
muscles relaxed and she opened the eye, there were little
white lines of unburnt skin like a great white cobweb on
the red flesh. That's a sight I'll never forget. And then it
was nearly all undone, for she put her hand up to the eye
and of course the stuff was on her hands too. I grabbed it
just in time. Then I started to wash the stuff off her hands
and I began to think I could do with some help.

'Give me a hand here, Lil,' I said.

After that first moment I hadn't looked at Lil. Now
I did, and pretty sharply. Then I saw that she was in a
very bad way. She hadn't stirred, was holding that tin still
and staring in front of her.

I wasn't going to touch the thing with my bare hands.
I wrapped the wet cloth round it and lifted it out of her
hands. That was when I saw the state of the glove. I had
sense enough not to speak. The other one was calmer now.
She was sitting up, holding the washcloth to her eyes, but
her ears were open. I looked at the glove, I looked towards
the tap, and then at Lil. She got the message. I don't think
she had the sense then to act without prompting. She turned
on the tap, held the glove under it and rinsed it clean. Then
I set the tin on the bench, found the lid sitting there and
rammed it on.

It must take a while to realise that you've committed
a crime. If Lil was used to it, she would have washed
the stuff off her glove right away, while I was busy with the
other one. The whole palm had been smeared; you could
see that she had held a fistful, a real fistful. So much for
her story that the lid was hard to shift, that she'd got it off

with a jerk and lost control so that it spilled. The other one had been kneeling in front of the copper setting the fire under it. She had looked up unexpectedly and got the spilled stuff in her eyes.

The other one told her story first. She was wearing dark glasses. She took them off to show the jury the damage. I was glad I couldn't see that; the look on some of the jury was enough. She put the glasses on again and they looked relieved. She said she had been kneeling in front of the copper setting the fire. Mrs Harrison had been filling the copper with a dipper from the washtub. Suddenly Mrs Harrison had said, 'Look here!' She had looked up and got a handful of the caustic in her face, blinding her right eye. She had begun to scream from the pain and put her hands up, but it had happened again. She had thrown another lot. Funny, she wasn't allowed to say 'handful' and 'thrown'. Lil's man objected and the judge said he was right. Was 'handful' an estimate of quantity? She supposed so, though how the poor girl could estimate quantity when she was rolling on the ground screaming, I don't know. He brought that out, and she admitted she couldn't have known how much paste there was, so the word 'handful' had to go. The story that comes out in court is made up of your answers to the questions they ask, and they have the choice of that, so it's not like telling a story as it happens. Not that I wanted to, on that occasion.

They don't take much account of your feelings, either. Lil's man wanted to know if she had been lying still and got out of her that she was shaking her head and rolling from side to side. The paste was semi-liquid? Yes. Was it not possible that the paste had spread from the right eye to the left? 'She threw it!' 'But your eyes were shut?' 'Yes.' You could see that reliving it was making her feel sick. She was white and trembling and perhaps she gave up easily on that account.

Then came the motive. Had she any reason to suppose that Mrs Harrison would wish to harm her? Yes. Mr Harrison was in love with her and had asked his wife for a divorce, which she wouldn't give him. Of course it wasn't Lil's man who brought that out. It was the other one, establishing motive. He asked very quietly, what her relations with Mr Harrison had been. Had they advanced as far as physical intimacy? So that's what they call it, I thought. Yes, she said, they had. But she didn't tell about moving into the bedroom, which was the thing that had maddened poor Lil to the point where she'd lost control. Perhaps she wasn't brazen enough to say it right out in court, and it seemed to me that in a way she was pleading guilty. You could see that there was something she didn't want to talk about, and that told on the jury. I suppose her man didn't bring it out because he wouldn't want to lose the sympathy of the jury – and maybe she hadn't even told him – and Lil's man wouldn't, because it would strengthen Lil's motive. But perhaps he didn't know, either. Lil wouldn't be saying what drove her to it while she was sticking to her story of accident. I knew then that Lil was safe.

I wondered if Lil was worrying about me. I wasn't going to tell about the glove, but I'd seen it and Lil knew that I had seen it.

I had said, 'I'd better get Charlie,' and when I added, 'Are you all right, Lil?' I meant, was it safe to leave the girl alone with her. I think she understood me, for she nodded. I said, 'We have to get her to a doctor.'

I helped the girl up. She'd be better able to look after herself standing. Then I ran to where the men were at the sheep run.

'You'd better come,' I said to Charlie. 'There's been an accident.'

They made a lot of play of my saying that straight away, that it was an accident. What was I supposed to say? Your poor wretched wife has thrown caustic into your floozy's eyes and blinded her and now I hope you're satisfied with what you've done. That's what I would have liked to say. I think perhaps he heard it in my voice, because he ran back with me in a hurry.

I'll never know what happened between Lilian and Charlie. He took one look and ran to phone for the ambulance. I said to Lil, 'I'll get the children and take them back with me.' I was thinking, That's the end of poor Lil. He'll never forgive her for this.

The children were doing their correspondence lessons in the schoolroom. They were good enough children, the boy Gavin seven and the girl Iris five, doing what they were told without fuss. They looked at me in surprise. I must have been a funny sight, drenched as I was with the water from the copper.

I said, 'There was an accident in the wash house. Miss Damaris got burnt.'

They thought it must be from the copper fire and they didn't ask any more. They weren't inquisitive children. I find with most children that they're interested only in what affects them. Everything that had been going on in the house had gone right over their heads, I think. They might have noticed that Lil was snappier than usual, that's all.

'Miss Damaris has to go away to hospital, so you're coming to stay with me for a while. Come and show me where to get your night things.'

I took them to the front of the house, away from the wash house. They fetched their things and I hurried them into the car and back to town.

I still think I was right not to tell about the smear on the palm of the glove or of her saying to me, 'Twice.' After all, I couldn't say, 'Yes, she did it, but she was driven to it.' Sometimes you have to tell a bit of a lie to get near the truth.

As for what drove her to it, I wasn't supposed to talk about that. Only what I had seen and heard myself.

'Had you ever seen any signs of discord between Mr and Mrs Harrison?'

Well, of course I hadn't. I never saw them together. Charlie was always out on the farm when I visited Lil. I heard plenty, though, but for some reason what Lil said to me didn't seem to count. But from the start of the affair I'd listened to poor Lil and tried to give advice. I think I gave the wrong advice. I told her to sit it out. I said Charlie would wake up to himself, he was just at the age when a man tends to make a fool of himself over a younger woman, but it never lasted.

'Have you talked to Charlie?' I asked.

252

'He doesn't hear me. He doesn't even see me. He's like a man asleep, having a lovely dream.'

'He'll wake up,' I said.

But Charlie didn't wake up. He asked Lil to divorce him.

'As bold as brass,' she told me with the tears running down her face. 'No shame in either of them. That wicked little bitch, I curse the day she came here.'

'She'll pay some day,' I said. I wish I hadn't said that.

Lil had said to him, 'You can't divorce me because I'll never give you grounds, and I'll never divorce you whatever you do. You'll never drive me to it.'

This is the only place where I think I might have done wrong. I encouraged her. I said, 'Don't let them drive you away from your home and your kids. Just wait them out.'

It might have been the wrong advice, but I don't think Lil would have gone anyhow. It's my opinion that she loved that land more than she ever loved Charlie. She was the one who kept it together through the bad times and she wouldn't let Charlie owe the bank when things were good and he got grand ideas about expanding. He had cause to thank her for that.

They took Lil at her word. She had to leave the house to go to a CWA meeting and when she came back she found all her belongings in cardboard boxes outside the bedroom door, which was locked. The other's room was stripped bare. She had moved in to Lil's place.

Lil swallowed it. She had no choice. She moved her things into the other's room. But when you think what it must have been like, seeing that locked door every night and knowing what went on behind it ... you can forgive Lil a lot, if not everything.

Our man made a great play with the fact that the two women were working side by side in the wash house. Would that have happened if the two women were enemies? I looked at this gentleman who had probably not rinsed a shirt in his life and wondered if he knew how life was lived. Friends or enemies, the washing had to be done. It was too much for one. They could hate each other as much as they pleased so long as the men's work clothes got onto the line.

On the stand Lil was quiet and dignified, not showing much emotion. It was true that she had had words with her husband over his attentions to Miss Dexter. She thought it was harmless but it was easy for a young woman to make too much of such a thing. There had never been a question of divorce. If they had had a serious relationship, she hadn't been aware of it.

I couldn't help looking at the other woman. She sat calm and easy, as if this didn't matter to her at all. The dark glasses must have helped. I thought it was Charlie's words she was hearing, not Lil's, and she was hiding her feelings, out of pride. You couldn't but be sorry for her at that moment.

It had been a shock to me, too, that Charlie had changed sides. I had expected him to go with the woman in the ambulance or at least to believe her and turn on Lil. I had said the word 'accident' and they both stuck fast to it and so, I suppose, to each other.

At first it had looked as if that was the end of it. I kept the children for two days, then Lil rang, as calm as you please, to say that she would call for the children to take them home. The other woman had been taken to Sydney to the eye hospital and they had got in touch with the insurance company. All the employees were insured against accident, which was fortunate.

I think she was taken aback when the police came. The other woman had laid charges. Lil had to go with them to the station in town to make a statement. Then she had to go before a magistrate who said there was a case to answer and she was committed for trial.

Lil's friends blamed the gossip for that. Of course everyone knew what had been happening and the talk, for and against, was ferocious. Lil's friends said she should never have been brought to trial. It was all the work of evil tongues.

This was when I began to think that I wasn't any longer one of Lil's friends. In a way I could understand it. You could never wipe out that moment when I had seen the smear on the palm of the glove. Our eyes had met and she knew that I knew. Better to keep me right out of it. But I was the one who could have done with a bit of support. She would know that I meant to stand by her, but it was a hard thing to carry alone.

That trial was a long time coming. It must have been a terrible time, like having a debt that had to be paid sometime and having it weigh on you. I'd like to have helped Lil through it by letting her know that I was standing by her, but she never asked. Perhaps she took it for granted. I hoped so. Nobody else ever spoke to me about it either, though I believe they never talked about anything else to each other. They weren't supposed to. It was something called sub judice, but tell that to the gossips. Everyone knew I was bound to be a witness, so I had a kind of official position that cut me off from the rest. I don't think I've ever been lonelier.

Lil said, No, she didn't regularly use caustic in the copper. The men's clothes were particularly dirty because of the sheep dipping. The caustic hadn't been used for some time, so the lid was stuck fast.

If the other fellow had known his business, he would have asked why the paste was so loose then. Why hadn't it dried out? Any woman would have asked that. Of course the stuff dries out and the usual thing is to mix it up with water just before you use it and stir it in with an old spoon or something that you keep in the wash house. It's not stuff to take risks with, as we all know. So I asked myself that question, and I didn't like the answer. I could understand Lil losing control and throwing the stuff into the woman's eyes instead of into the copper, but getting the stuff ready beforehand, opening the tin and mixing in the water to make it the right consistency – that was hard to take. Lil said that the lid came off with a jerk so that she lost control and almost dropped the tin. She caught it but not in time to stop the caustic splashing out. She thought she must have made a sound when it slipped, so that Damaris had looked up and got it in the eyes. Saying 'Damaris' must have been the hardest thing about that.

Everyone who had turned up to watch was waiting to hear Charlie, but he didn't give evidence at all. The crowd was disappointed, and so was I. I knew he was going to support Lil and lie about the affair, but I wanted to hear him lying, and I hoped I'd at least see him squirm. Well, I did, not long after.

As for me, I didn't even have to lie. They didn't ask about the glove. If they had, I meant to say that I hadn't noticed, but I didn't need to. Well, they're the ones who ask the questions, and if they don't ask the right ones, that's their lookout.

So Lil was acquitted.

That was when I thought my lonely time was over. I went up to Lil and Charlie where they were standing by their car. There weren't any people around, congratulating them, I noticed. The general feeling seemed to be that it was a good thing Lil had got off, but nobody was going to stand close to her when she had a tin of caustic in her hands. They didn't seem to care, they were wrapped in each other, but I had been a true friend to them and I thought they might thank me for standing by them.

I said, 'Well, that went all right, didn't it?'

They turned round and looked at me and I've never looked into colder eyes.

Lil said, 'What do you mean?' and Charlie carried on for her. 'You heard what the judge said. Isn't that good enough for you?'

I could see that I was never going to be forgiven for what I had seen and heard. I was never going to share that dreadful moment with anyone. I turned away, feeling sick, and there behind me was the other one. I think she was showing herself to them with me on purpose, because she and I were the ones who knew. It was a kind of demonstration.

'The doctor said that it was you who saved my eyesight, at least what is left of it. You saved the left eye and there's some residual vision in the right eye, though the eyeball is badly scarred. I thought you would like to know.'

'I'm so glad,' I said. 'Lucky I got there in time.'

We were ignoring the others. I suppose they were just waiting for us to go away.

'I'll always be grateful to you,' she said.

Suddenly, as quick as a snake striking, she was facing Charlie, wearing a neat little smile and taking off her glasses. It was an obscene gesture, and Charlie, all unprepared, jerked his head away like a frightened horse. So he had to face the moment, after all. She put the glasses back on and walked away. As I watched her go, I realised that she was the only one I could have shared that moment with and I'd cut myself off from her. I walked away too towards my own car, still alone with it.

I didn't see much of Lil and Charlie after that. Sometimes I thought they couldn't have hated me more if I had told the whole truth.

I've never liked secrets. I've never wanted to have one, but I was stuck with that one. Until now, when they're all dead, and who's to care? Except me.

THE SURVIVORS

It was hot in Len Fuller's shop, but worse outside. At the screen door flies kept buzzing and battering, wanting refuge from the sun, and beyond it one saw the sharp knife-edge of the summer light. Kevin paid for his cigarettes and pocketed his change slowly, leaning against the counter, looking in his mind for a word or two to say to the shopkeeper.

The girl came in carefully, opening the door just wide enough – and that wasn't far – and slipping in quickly to foil the flies. She put her grocery list on the counter and waited.

'Hello, Gloria,' said Kevin. That'll give you a start, said his tone, full of self-contained amusement.

She turned her head and seeing that he was a stranger turned quickly away, leaving the memory of light grey eyes in a small pale face, a child's face with an old pattern of sorrow set in its bones. Not too bad, he thought, looking at the long fair hair that clung wet with sweat to the back

259

of her neck. The cotton dress clung too, so that he could see she had a bit more figure than he had thought at first. Not too bad at all.

'Ma says she doesn't like that brand, Mr Fuller.' She spoke with poise and propriety. 'All juice and no fruit, she says. Do you have another brand?'

It was Len Fuller who had told Kevin her name, a couple of days ago, meaning no harm. Now he was sorry. He put the tin of peaches back on the shelf with a bad-tempered thud.

'Tell your Ma I'm not responsible for what's in the tin.'

'She ain't blaming you, Mr Fuller. Just wants to try a different brand, that's all.'

She knew Kevin was there, all right. His mouth stirred to a smile that did not disturb the rest of his regular, neatly upholstered features, but reappeared as a gleam of pleasure in his brown eyes. When the door had shut behind the girl he moved, followed her out to the road and walked behind her along the bottom of the ocean of burning air, not hurrying but gaining on her all the time.

'Hi, Gloria!'

That stirred her, but it didn't surprise her. His smile widened.

'Hi, Gloria!' Now he was walking level with her. 'Carry your bag?'

She shook her head, though the bag of groceries was weighing her down and she drooped in the heat.

He didn't mind the heat just then. The hot, soft dust that rose round his thonged sandals moulding his feet, the sweat at his hairline, the burning streak of sunlight across his shoulders and the shirt clinging wet to his ribs made him more conscious of himself as the object of the girl's attention. Caring no more for the flies than a statue cares for pigeons, he walked slow and complacent beside her and left the next move to her.

'How did you know my name?'

She had meant the question to be severe, but shyness won out over severity.

'Ah, that'd be telling.'

Now she let him take the string bag and began to brush away from her neck the flies that were looking for shelter under her hair.

'Go on. How did you know?'

This time she was sharper, having let the bag go.

'You got nice hair.'

'The flies like it all right.'

'They got good taste.'

For Kevin, that was a flight of fancy, which made him feel inspired. It left her speechless, too. Uncertainly and after too long a pause, she said, 'I don't know you.'

'Well, I know you, don't I? Gloria.'

Now she looked troubled. They were coming to the corner where she would leave the main road.

'Tell you what. You ask me my name and I'll tell you. We'll be square, then.'

At the corner he said, 'Stop a minute,' and she stopped. After all, he had the string bag.

'What's your name then?' she asked.

'Kevin. Kevin Drinan. And now you know.'

261

Looking back later, with pain and difficulty because looking back did not come easily to him, he thought, 'That's where I made my mistake. Joe Blow I should have said.' But he did not know then how long things were remembered.

With her eyes on the bag, she said, 'You new here?'

'Staying at my uncle's, out at Finney's Corner. Giving a hand on the place.'

'I'll have my bag now, thanks.'

'Come and get it.'

'Oh, give it to me. I got to go home.'

'What's your hurry? Plenty of time.'

She made a pass at the bag, but he swung it away out of her reach.

'Oh, come on. My Ma will see me, and I'll get into trouble.'

Just the same, she was laughing a bit.

'Give it to me, go on. You got to give it to me. I got to go home.'

'Where do you live then?'

'Just down the road there, in the house with the lattice.'

As she spoke, she fixed her eyes on his, keeping them away from the bag. He saw through that and when she lunged he was ready and got both her wrists in one hand.

He laughed at her while she struggled and she laughed too, without knowing why, though she wailed, 'You're hurting me.'

'Keep still then. You're hurting yourself.'

Then she stood still and tried asking again, softer this time.

'Give it to me, please.'

In one of the wrists he was holding, he could feel a pulse leaping like a flea. 'Oh,' he thought, 'I'd give it to you, all right. All right.'

'Promise to come for a walk this evening, then.'

'I wouldn't be let.'

'You don't have to say where you're going. Say you're going to see your girlfriend. Be a sport.'

Gloria didn't have a girlfriend. Young sisters and brothers, a mother who was the nearest thing to a friend she had, and a father to be feared like a bad-tempered dog.

She stood quiet, looking perplexed, her wrists relaxed in his hand.

'Can you whistle?'

Puzzled, she shook her head.

'I can. Like this, see.' He whistled four notes. 'Got it?' He whistled again. 'If you hear me whistling outside your place tonight, you better come out or you don't know what might happen.'

She took the bag and left without answering, but he knew that she would come. What else did she have to do?

When she had gone he considered the problem of filling in the next four hours, calmly, because he was hardened to the emptiness of life. He would miss his lift back to the farm – too bad; the less he saw of that dump, the better. Something to eat wouldn't go astray, though. He didn't bother looking in his pocket – all he had there was the price of a beer and if that went his self-esteem would go with it. Just the same he went to the pub, because that was where the life was, and he struck it lucky, because the pub-keeper wanted a hand in the cellar, and he got a meal and a few drinks and the promise of a bed in exchange for a few hours' work. He might have forgotten all about the girl if it hadn't been for the good-looking waitress who was eating her dinner in the kitchen when he went to get his. He tried to chat her up but there was nothing doing there. He felt restless then and walked out into the hot, dark night, finding his way without thinking to the side road and the house with the lattice.

When he whistled, she came out so fast that she was there in the dark close to him before he expected her. It gave him a start.

They got clear of the house without talking, and he was still silent when they came to the main road, but she had plenty to say, explaining that she wasn't really coming, only she thought her mother would hear, and he mustn't come round again – all the time leading him away from the road into the thin belt of trees and down to the dry bed of the creek. There they stopped and he got hold of her. She started to squawk and cry but she didn't try to get away, and then he had her down on the bristling grass and was working away for dear life, and her squawking was something different that had to be stopped, so he got his hand over her mouth. It was always like that, the way they went on. It frightened him and he would have liked to get away but it was too late to stop. Stop your bloody screaming, he thought, or perhaps he said it, because she was only whimpering now. Then he forgot her altogether. Ah, ah, ah.

Then all of a sudden she was friendly, though she complained about the mess she was in. 'Look at my dress,' she said, 'what am I going to do?' As if he cared. He thought girls were mad, but he didn't let their madness worry him.

He went back the next night, then the job at the pub ran out and he had to go back to the farm where they weren't pleased to see him, and that was putting it mildly. He stood that for three days, then he got out. His uncle gave him nothing either except a few dollars for his train fare and hard words with it. He went back and tried his luck at the pub again but all he got there was the promise of a bed.

He went out and whistled the girl but this time she didn't come running. He had started to walk away when she came after him and started in on him because he hadn't come before.

That was a laugh. He'd only come now because there was nothing else doing, and he walked straight ahead while she chittered around him like a self-important insect. He thought that at any moment he would lengthen his stride and be rid of her, but the desire that came from having nothing else to do was just as strong, after all, as the desire that came from real need, so he interrupted her to say, irritably, 'You coming down to the creek, or aren't you?'

She shut up then and he slowed down so they were walking together. She kept looking at him sideways, but the look on his face stopped her talking. He liked that. In his depression it was a comfort to be having an effect on somebody, even on a girl he'd had, which was the next thing to nobody at all. As they slithered and scrambled down the dry bank, she put her hand on his arm and he let it stay there, feeling lordly.

They sat down on the grass and he rolled over her and pushed his tongue into her mouth, fierce with boredom and misery. Tonight she wasn't complaining. It annoyed him that she softened every ferocious movement with her yielding and clinging. He had liked it better the first time.

'You coming tomorrow night?'

'No fear. I'm getting out. Getting the train tomorrow.'

That stopped her all right. She was quiet for a long time.

'How long are you going for?'

'Going south. Get a job picking fruit. Nothing doing here.'

'Going for good, do you mean?'

'Be back next year for the shearing.'

Then she flung herself on him, put her arms around his neck and kissed him, pushing close to him, and he was just as scandalised as if a strange woman had jumped him. Gawd, he thought, Gawd, too shocked to push her away. At last he got to his feet, shedding her as he went, and set off for the road, leaving her to scramble after him. When they got to level ground, he said loudly, 'So long,' quickened his pace and was gone. He couldn't get out of there fast enough.

It was made up of a lot of things, the magic of the shearing season, and though Kevin didn't know it himself, but cursed his aching back and grumbled about the food and the quarters, the work might be the best part of it – the work and the company. He and Lin were forever talking about the breaks in town and looking forward to them, but sometimes they were a disappointment. There was that first minute, though, when he came into the bar, after he'd had a shower and put on his town clothes, the money in his wallet spreading a feeling of ease and freedom right through him – there was nothing to beat that. He had an idea, with not a drink taken and not a card turned, that he was nobody at all, and he was sorry, in a funny sort of way, to be spoken to and to start being Kev Drinan again, though there was nobody he'd rather be.

He went into the Public and found three of the gang there already, set up with schooners in front of them: George with the sad, wiry face and the line of teeth glistening between his thin lips, Blue Avery and Jack Wrightson. There was nobody else in the bar, so the publican Karl was standing chatting with them.

'You ain't wasting no time,' said Kevin.

'We got none to waste,' said George. 'Karl here's got a message for you, Kev.'

He didn't care for the look on George's face, which was always half a grin and might be a bit more than half at the moment.

'Schooner of old, thanks, Karl.'

As he drew the beer, Karl said, 'Been someone in here looking for you.'

'Is that right?'

'Fellow named Thomas. Roy Thomas. You know him.'

'Never set eyes on him.'

Kevin lifted his glass steadily. He was beginning to see the drift of the conversation and suspected Karl of handling it in a particular way. He was a funny fellow. Known for it.

Sure enough, the glass was right at his mouth and they were all watching him when Karl said, 'Got a daughter, Gloria. You know her?'

The glass never budged and he drank a couple of ounces before he put it down.

'Could do.'

'Some fellow knows her pretty well. Too well, I reckon.'

'It don't have to be me.'

'Well, her father's looking for you, that's all I know. And I think he means trouble.'

'Carrying a shotgun, is he, Karl?' said Jack Wrightson, grinning.

'Not that I saw. Behind his back, maybe.' Giving up the pretence of joking, he added, 'I don't want any trouble in my pub.'

'I'm not aiming to make any trouble. Trouble comes looking for me, that might be different.'

Delivered with insolent calm, this answer inspired visible respect in the other members of the gang. Karl turned away with as much discontent in his face as a publican cares to show.

Kevin had a wonderful time at the crown and anchor game that night, a run of luck that was still running strong in his head when he got back to the hotel, thrust the wallet full of winnings under his pillow and fell asleep on it.

Somebody came to fight him for it, and when he struck out at the thief the room filled with shouting and laughter.

'Look at him. He's a game one.'

'Watch out, now. He's dangerous.'

268

'Hey. Wake up. Wake up, mate.'

He opened his eyes to the face of his friend Lin, round and grinning like a kid's picture of the sun, with his gold eyetooth shining like another little sun inside it.

'Full of fight, ain't he?'

He sat up in bed, hiding the fury he felt at being handled, and shook himself awake.

'You're in strife, mate. Wanted man.'

There were four of them, the three young men and George, all grinning in spite of the warnings they hurled. Lin offset the seriousness of the situation further by handing him a glass of beer.

'Sitting out on the landing, we was,' said George. 'Jack had got around Karl to open the bar and we was sitting there having a beer, when this fellow comes into the yard, looking up at us, see, and he calls out, "Is Kev Drinan there?" It was on the tip of me tongue to say you wasn't up yet, when it came into me head what Karl was saying yesterday about the girl's father looking for you, so I says, "Haven't laid eyes on Kev Drinan this season. Must be working with another gang," I says. Didn't I? And I look round at the others and they back me up. "You got any idea where he is, then?" So we all shake our heads.' George shook his with a solemnity enlivened by enjoyment. ' "You tell him I'm looking for him, then, if you see him. Thomas is my name," he said. So I was right, wasn't I? That was the name, all right. I says, "If I happen across him, I'll tell him." So he went off, but I ain't saying he's satisfied.'

Lin said, 'You better lay low for a while.'

'Does he know you by sight?'

'Not that I know of.'

The conversation spun a warm cocoon around him: lay low – stay out of sight – ah, it's all talk – I wouldn't be too sure. He lay secure at the centre of it, smiling faintly at the ceiling.

'You're a cool customer,' said George with admiration.

That afternoon, they smuggled him out in Lin's car to the pub at Spiny Creek, all of them laughing, George acting like a two-year-old and wanting him to get down on the floor of the car till they got out of town, but he wouldn't come at that, having a fine feeling for the moment when he would become the butt of the joke, instead of its hero.

That happened, of course. By Sunday afternoon George, tormented by boredom, was nagging at Karl to tell Kevin that the girl's father wanted to see him outside. Foiled there, since Karl refused to treat the affair as a joke, he went to the door of the back room where the poker game was going on, calling out, 'Feller here to see Kev Drinan,' then advancing his savage, delicate clown's face into the room to see Kevin jump and withdrawing it, discomfited by his failure.

'It'll die down,' said Lin, who was watching the game for want of anything better to do. He spoke to console Kevin, but he need not have troubled. The sky could fall on that fellow when he was playing cards and he'd never notice.

It didn't die down, for someone was keeping it alive. The enemy stayed out of sight, but the name Kev Drinan travelled ahead of its owner, had been before him into one little pub outside town and was recognised two weekends later by a stranger in Karl's bar.

'Are you Kev Drinan? I met a friend of yours, Roy Thomas, out at Murrigong. Says he's keeping a lookout for you and he'll see you before the shearing's over.'

It was George that led the laughter, and Kevin kept his countenance, but the situation was beginning to bug him.

'Did he say what he was going to do when he saw me?'

'Nothing to do with me,' said the stranger, turning away.

'He can do plenty,' said Karl, 'seeing that the girl's under age.'

Lin said, 'Gawd,' and round Kevin there was a silence as if a cloak had fallen away and left him naked.

'She never told me she was under age,' he said later to Lin. Nobody else was interested now. They sat on Kevin's bed and smoked, Lin keeping a thoughtful look on his face out of respect for Kevin's difficulty, though he didn't know what good thinking would do.

'Stands to reason, if he was going to the police he would've gone by now. They'd be looking for you, and if they was, well, they would have found you, wouldn't they?'

Angrily, Kevin repeated, 'She never told me she was under age.'

Till now Lin had supposed that the poise he admired in Kevin sprang from worldly wisdom. He looked at him with surprise and sympathy.

'It don't make no difference, mate. Wouldn't even matter if she swore she was twenty. I dunno. Judge might take it into account in the sentence.'

At the word 'sentence' Kevin stirred irritably.

'I tell you, mate, if she's under sixteen and you did her, you've had it. If I was you, I'd run for it. Get the train. That's what I'd do.'

Kevin looked sour and said nothing. The clatter, heat and the grease of the sheds, the fierce competitive movement and the pungent smell of the sheep rose with such power in his mind that Lin's words sounded far away. It was short enough, the season, compared with the empty height of summer and the hungry winter.

'She was ready enough,' he said fiercely.

'It don't make no difference,' said Lin with a little too much patience. 'Ah, forget it. He hasn't been to the police and that's the main thing. He might be after you to marry her, though, if she's gone sixteen. He might be thinking you're more use to him married to her than in jail.'

'I don't see it. If I didn't know.'

'No, it's tough. That's the law, though.' For all Lin's sympathy, Kevin heard in his voice the complacency of security. 'Ah, he won't do nothing. Like I said, forget it.'

That was the advice Kevin was waiting for. His face lightened as he said, 'Coming down for a beer?'

He did forget the affair, almost completely, but was haunted now and then by the troubling thought of a small monster, something alive that ought not to be alive, whether it was his own name, travelling out of his reach, or a piece of the past that would not die as it should.

The thing materialised three days later outside the shearers' quarters at Andersons'. Kevin was lying on

272

his bed waiting for the evening meal, holding a comic to the fading daylight that came through a window high in the wall behind him and hearing in the background George with his bookie's cry: 'Stew, five to four on. Sausages, even money. Even money, sausages. Rump steak, a hundred to one.'

Outside, there was an unexpected outcry, and his own name hung on the air with obscenities flowering like rockets around it. Then Mr Anderson's voice sounded, firm and sharp.

'Watch your tongue.'

'Get out of my bloody road. I know the bastard's in there. Drinan! You come out here, you hear me?'

'You're drunk. You're in no state to talk to anyone.'

Lin got up from the next bed, put a foot on a beam and pulled himself up to the window. He nodded to Kevin and stepped down to leave him the place.

Kevin peered down at the enemy: a little puffy fellow with a scalded complexion, weeping eyes and a fat belly pouring over his belt. He was drunk all right, reeling about and flailing with his short arms as he shouted in a voice more powerful than his frame.

'I'll kill the bloody dirty swine. You let me in there. I'll have his balls.'

Kevin sank down from the window and sat on his bed. He seemed calm under the eyes of the others. His mind was a blank.

Mr Anderson's voice sounded. 'I'll hear no suggestions from you in the state you're in. If you have anything to discuss, come back when you're sober.'

273

Frank called out loudly, 'Drinan's not here!' and the other men took up the cry. 'Not here! Drinan's not here!'

The relief was so great that Kevin couldn't help smiling. It was like a game, him safe and snug in his hideyhole and so close he could have reached out and touched the other man, if it wasn't for the wall.

Frank got up, opened the door just enough, slid out and shut it quickly behind him. The voices began to move away. Whether they were getting around Thomas, or, drunk-like, he'd forgotten what he'd come for, he was whining now instead of shouting, and then the voices died away altogether. Frank came back in. Kevin grinned. He was never the first to speak, but this time it was up to him to lead the joke.

'Christ, that was a close one.'

Nobody answered. He looked around at them but nobody met his eye. Lin said awkwardly, 'Close all right. I thought you were a goner.'

'Sure thing,' said somebody else, but perfunctorily.

Frank said, without friendship, 'Mr Anderson told him you'd go and talk to him. He says he'll drive you over there tomorrow night.'

This thing. You dealt with it and it came back again. You killed it and buried it, and you turned round and there it was.

'What am I supposed to talk about?'

'You'd know that better than I would.'

The other men, lying on their beds, heavy with the fatigue he shared, pretended to pay no attention. He fixed his eye on the old tobacco tin full of hand-rolled butts giving off a cold metallic smell, but it was dark midnight for him and the properties of the day, the drift of comic books and crime magazines, the naked wood of the walls and the pack of dirty playing cards looked fantastic and gave him no reassurance.

'You might as well have let him in.'

'He was drunk enough to get nasty. We don't want any trouble in the sheds.'

Too cocky by half, Frank could be.

'He'll have forgotten all about it in the morning,' he said in a whine of anger.

'You can take a chance on that if you like. If I were you, I'd talk to him before he talks to the police.'

There was that bossy, self-righteous tone in Frank's voice that the others didn't like; perhaps they weren't liking it now, but they showed nothing. It was their silence that beat him.

When Lin said, in a respectful murmur, 'Are you going?' he shrugged, but he knew that he would go.

'You don't have to marry him if you don't want to,' said Gloria's mother as she pierced a sausage and watched a stream of grease spurt from it into the pan.

It was she who had kept the search for Kevin alive. Being an expert in survival, she had kept Gloria safe by finding employment outside the house for her husband's rage. She had jumped between them, driven by fear to desperate jeering. 'Go on, then, tell him about it, will you? What do you mean, you don't know where he is? Haven't started looking either, that I can see. If you was a man you'd find him all right. Play the big fellow around here, oh yes, that's easy.'

She didn't expect for a minute that he'd find Kevin. She had driven him on, feeling confident that he would fail in anything he undertook, unless it was murdering Gloria. And given the smallest bit of help from this Drinan, she would have got away with it, but this fellow was a bigger fool than Roy, and that was saying something. 'Another fool in the family,' she thought bitterly. However, she wasn't referring to her grandchild.

'You want to think about it,' she said, but without confidence, for Roy was as drunk on his success as he had ever been on beer and he was down at the pub reinforcing its effect, so he wouldn't be easy to handle.

'What's come over you?' said Gloria. 'I thought you was all for it.'

Mrs Thomas stopped moving the sausages in the pan to give her a sharp look over her shoulder.

'Get your feet off the rung of that chair, I keep telling you.'

Gloria did not stir. With her heels propped over the rung of the chair, she curled like a thin shell round her swollen belly. Her body was pathetic, but the look on her face was maddening. She had got off too easy and now she had a headful of silly notions. The word 'marriage' had hold of her, and if she only knew what it meant, if you could ever tell them anything . . .

'If you don't want to do it, nobody can make you,' she said, with a shabby idea of handing over responsibility.

'And let Kevin go to jail, I suppose,' said Gloria, handing it smartly back again.

I don't know why you care about him, thought the mother. He don't care much about you. But she didn't say it, out of pity, thinking what the poor little devil had in front of her.

'What about Dad, anyhow? I'm not going to stick around here forever putting up with his abusing and threatening. It's been bad enough having to run and hide and putting up with what he says about Kev.'

'We don't know much about him and what we do know ain't much good.'

Gloria met this with a closed, superior look, just as if Kevin had been turning up every Saturday night to take her to the pictures.

'Go and call the kids for their tea,' her mother said, banging the lid on to a saucepan in a fit of temper that sent Gloria pretty promptly to the door, calling out, 'Mi-ike! Charley! You're wanted!'

Kevin was determined not to marry her. He meant to use the power of silence. He had sat through enough diatribes, staring ahead of him, closing his ears, not caring. He had this great power of not caring, withdrawing inside himself, waiting them out; when he could, he walked away and when he couldn't he sat it out. It had always worked before and it would work this time. So he had the dead look on his face already, from resisting in his mind, when he got out of Mr Anderson's car outside the house, but the father was too pleased with himself, fairly quivering with triumph, to pay any attention. At the sight of him Kevin went deeper into his own thoughts, where absolute resistance welled steady and quiet. His mouth sagged slightly, his eyes brooded. When he followed the father into the dining room and he saw the mother get a real shock at the sight of him, his face took on a sheen of satisfaction without moving a muscle.

'Well, here's your son-in-law,' the drunk was shouting.

She gave him a scared look that made him feel secure in spite of everything.

'Take a seat. Go on. Sit down.'

They all sat at the table and the shouting started.

'Well, when's it going to be, eh? No use sitting there like a bloody image. That ain't going to do you any good. When's the wedding, eh?'

Kevin, facing the door, was staring straight ahead of him, but he was aware of the fidgeting, worried mother getting up courage to speak and he was giving her time.

He wasn't thinking about the girl at all, words like son-in-law and wedding coming at him like fists from nowhere, and there she was in the doorway, the past on her face and the future in her great belly, and it shattered him, for he didn't give thought to either but travelled in the lighted cabin of the moment.

'Come on, now. You know the score. You'll be inside looking out, mate, unless you do the right thing and do it fast.'

With his eyes on the girl, he stammered, 'I can't get married. Got nowhere to take a wife.'

'You should've thought of that before. I'm not having any bastards in this family, do you hear me? Or you'll pay for it if I do. In jail you'll pay for it. So make up your mind. What's it going to be?' He was winning and he knew it, his voice twanging with triumph like the strings of a hideous guitar.

'Got to start at new sheds Monday.' Kevin sounded sulky and helpless now.

The mother opened her mouth, but she hardly got a word out.

'You get out. Go on, out. Go and put a cup of tea on.'

The girl hadn't said anything. She stood there with her eye on him, and now she came silently and took the chair next to him. It was a sign to him that he was beaten.

Oh, Gawd, the mother thought, but young girls were silly. There he was with a face like cheese and looking as if he wished the ground would swallow him up and she looked at him like she was expecting love-talk.

No use talking to her, no use talking to anyone. The mother was full of guilt and misery as she stood watching the kettle on the stove, and still she didn't see what else she could have done. The most you could do about trouble, it seemed, was put it off as long as you could.

Gloria waited with her father and mother in front of the church, which stood isolated on the highway that served as the town's main street. The church was a small wooden building, painted with a dignified lack of pretension in the colours of dust and raw wood. The mother, aiming at neatness as a tribute to solemnity, had polished her shoes, put a new ribbon on her hat, set her hair and pressed her good dress. Having a true sense of occasion, she would not have done better if she could. Gloria had a new dress that made her furiously sulky. She glowered, looking down the road along which Kevin would come.

'Not my fault you're getting married in a maternity dress. You're the one that seen to that.'

Her mother didn't understand. The important thing was that Kev should look at her. He hadn't looked at her yet and when he did everything was going to be all right. Surely, when they faced each other in the church, when the minister was marrying them, he would have to look? For the occasion she needed a miraculous dress that would make her as she used to be, and here she stood in this great pink bag, the hem not even straight.

'Could have done a bit better than this,' she muttered.

At least she had got that silly look off her face that would get her murdered one of these days. Just as the mother was telling herself so, back came the look again. Roy, who had been fixing his steady, narrowed gaze at the length of the road, relaxed with a smirk of triumph. The bridegroom was coming.

The mother turned and faced the road. A friend with him, and both of them as full as boots. They paused ten yards away on the other side of the church. The bullet-headed best man was grinning, silly with drink, his golden eyetooth shining as he came towards them.

'Pleased to meet you. Pleased to meet you. Very happy occasion. How do you do?'

In the silence that met him, he realised he was alone. He looked round and saw that Kev had stayed where he was, uttered a wild giggle and turned back. Kevin took no notice either of his going or his returning but stood wrapped in a haze of alcohol, wearing a gentle, dreamy air.

Just as the minister's car was coming, he whispered in his friend's ear and they disappeared round the side of the church with Roy after them.

They were only going to the outhouse, after all.

Embarrassed, the mother offered the minister a writhing smile. He came and took her hand with a politeness that approached affection, and that made her feel worse than anything up to now. The effort should have come from somewhere else; with him it was only religion, when all was said and done, and the kindness in his face was desolating, because you saw your need for it.

The men came back with the father worrying at their heels like a sheepdog and the best man's face pinned in a silly smirk which the mother tried not to see. She had endured great injuries and forgotten them, but she remembered that smirk with resentment till she died.

It was a consolation to find that the words of the marriage service were the same as ever. The mother wouldn't have been surprised if there had been a special, humiliating version for these circumstances, but the words came in their old order, sober and sustaining, and caused her to hope that things might after all go well. If only the pair of them was really listening.

The bride's father made a speech in the road outside the church.

'Now piss off, you two. And don't come back.' As they stood undecided, the words producing no change in the bridegroom's gentle, stupefied expression, he roared, 'Piss off, you hear. Get going.'

The bridal party began to move off towards the pub, farewelled by a moan of dismay from the mother that would have been ridiculous if it had been intended for anyone's ears.

The bridegroom was moving fast, so that the bride had to scurry to keep up with him, and when she did she was still alone. Lin walked beside them persevering with a smile that kept fading. He liked to think that life was a joke, but he had trouble fitting Gloria's father to his theory.

'Gawd,' he said with awe. 'Your old man, eh? Gawd.'

Mrs Drinan, Mrs Drinan, Mrs Drinan, she was thinking. Say Mrs Drinan a hundred times and everything will be all right. She gave Lin an abstracted look that did nothing for him. It was too long since he had had a drink, besides, and he was sliding into depression when they came within earshot of the cheering Saturday afternoon clamour of the pub.

'Well, let's go and have a beer. Celebrate, eh?'

Gloria said, 'What about me?'

She didn't weep easily, but the circumstances were trying.

'Well, we'll go to the Ladies' Parlour, then.'

'I can't go into the pub at all. I'm under age.'

'Well.' Lin could work his brain no further and Kevin still seemed to be miles away.

'I suppose I can sit in the yard. There's a seat there under the tree. So long as you can put up with the flies.'

'They don't drink much,' he said, and her face lit with pleasure at the joke.

That was enough to cheer Lin. It never took much. She led them through a side gate into the pub yard, where there was a picnic table and benches of wood weathered to the colour of iron and sprinkled with shade from a tall gumtree.

'My shout.'

Lin left them sitting at one of the benches, Kevin with his soft, stupid gaze set on the ground and the girl with a tight little smile, and that was exactly how they were when he got back. The girl looked a proper freak in the pink cotton dress that hung loose everywhere else and curved smooth over her big round belly, and the rest of her so skinny. Not what you'd call a girl at all. It made Lin feel comfortable with her.

'Here you are, Tiger.'

He sat down opposite her. The beer he had put in front of Kevin was half gone already. Before he touched his own, he poured a dribble of it into her lemonade.

'Got to have a drink on your wedding day.'

Wrong thing to say. There was Kev like turned into lead and heavy enough to sink into the ground. But the girl played up to him and made a funny little face, sipping it. You could see her asking herself what she thought of it, so he poured in a little more, and then more. They got a real giggle out of it, considering they were sitting at the same table with what you might call a dead man, except for his thirst. Kev had drunk his beer in two goes and now he was sitting glooming behind the empty glass.

His turn to buy, thought Lin, spinning out the game, pouring so much into her glass this time that she got a real taste of the beer, screwed up her little monkeyface and said, 'Good lemonade spoilt.'

That was the last mouthful of beer he had poured into her glass, so, playing for time, he took a mouthful from hers, rolled the sweetish shandy round his mouth with a horrible grimace, spat it out on the ground and said, 'Bloody good beer spoilt, you mean.'

She really laughed, she wasn't putting it on. She was a caution. One of his own mob.

It must be the first time since he'd known him that Kev hadn't been willing to stand his turn. Look at the girl though and the fix she was in, and she could still raise a laugh. Lin gathered the glasses, saying, 'Same again?' This was the last one, anyhow. They had a long way to go.

'See if my Dad's in there, will you? I want to go home and get some things.'

'Don't worry. If he's in there, I won't wait. I'll come running. I'll go for my life.'

'Go on. I bet you'd wait and get your beer.'

'Depends. If he had his back to me, I might risk it, but I'd be quick about it, I can tell you.'

'Oh, go on. You ain't frightened of much, I bet. Anyway, Dad won't take any notice. So long as he's got his beer, that's all he cares about.'

284

'Well, here goes. If I'm not back in two hours, come and get me.'

'No fear.'

Looking round the bar, Lin saw the thick soft neck and the pink ears of Roy Thomas who was shouting away in some argument above the noise of the race commentary. The girl was right: there wasn't much danger there. Lin thought, if Kevin didn't have such a case of them, he'd be enjoying this. It was just the sort of thing that gave him a laugh. And then, it wasn't the kid's fault was it? Not any more than Kev's, anyhow.

He got out unobserved and coming back across the yard he hunched his shoulders, looking cowed and putting on a real clown's act for the girl.

'He's in there, is he?'

'He sure is. Didn't see me, though. We better make this the last. You got to get your things and we got a long way to go.'

Kevin met that with a look of deep rage that startled them both. Having drunk the first beer so fast, he took this one as if he had a bet to make it last an hour. Lin and the girl sat it out quietly for twenty minutes, then he gave her the nod to get up and they walked to the car and waited for him there. That did the trick. He came after them – in his own time, but he came.

Next time one of the gang got married and wanted a pal to stand by, it wasn't going to be Lin.

*

If Lin had only heard about that wedding cake wilting under the muslin cloth at Thomases' while they were down at the pub, he would have thought it a very funny joke. Seeing it was different. It wasn't a very showy cake, and only the eyes of Gloria's skinny fair-haired brothers and sisters, directed at it from various heights around the table, showed that it was anything special. Gloria's mother knew how far she could aspire without making herself ridiculous and was besides quite indifferent to the neglect that met her efforts. It was the dignity of that indifference that daunted Lin. He found himself embarrassed by the behaviour of Kevin, which drew not one sidelong glance from the others – Saturday afternoon was the time for men to sit swaying from the hips, looking dazed, saying nothing – and to make up for it he tried to be jolly, stuffed his mouth with cake, praised it and blew wet morsels on the tablecloth, while the mother, with worry drawing her face like a headache, said to Gloria, 'You got to watch the real hot weather and cover everything from the flies. And see it gets enough to drink. You got to give it boiled water as well as milk. You boil it up in the morning and keep it in a jug with a cover over it. Don't give it to him too cold though or you'll give him the colic.'

'All right. I know, Ma.'

Gloria, who had been so patient at the pub, looked bad-tempered now. She had given up any idea of shining as a bride but she still didn't want to share the day with the lively load in her belly. She had made a vague appointment with it for a day in the future but she had other things to think about just now.

'You know. You know everything, I suppose,' the mother said angrily.

In a minute she was off again. 'If the heat's real bad you wet the mosquito net before you put it over him. Keep on wetting it, that'll keep him cool. Don't go off in a dream and forget about it, and don't put any clothes on him if it's that hot. Just lie him on his napkin.'

'Well, we better be going,' said Lin. 'Got a way to go.'

'You write and let me know. Don't take too much notice of your father. He's just . . .' She didn't finish the sentence but with a sour look at the young men got to her feet, saying, 'I packed your things.' Buggered if I'm going to carry them, thought Lin, wounded by the look, but when the mother brought out a big battered suitcase with a strap round it and a couple of paper bags, Kev got up and walked to the car without even a look at them, so Lin came after him loaded and looking like a real Charlie, telling himself he would never get into anything like this again.

Even at the door, the mother was still giving advice and had enough in stock to keep them there till midnight. Lin got the engine running, then gave a toot on the horn that brought Gloria scurrying to take her place in the back seat.

When they started off for Sotherns' Kevin was sitting beside him like a block of wood, but little by little he was creeping out of his bolthole of drunkenness and just before they got to the turnoff for Sotherns' he said, quiet and sober, 'Keep straight on to the next turnoff. Going out to my uncle's.'

'Well, thanks for letting me know,' thought Lin. He wondered if the kid knew where she was going, then he pounced on that uneasy thought and squashed it like a running insect. He should mind his own bloody business. Not his affair whether she knew or not, or how she felt about it.

It was getting dark when they stopped in the road outside the farmhouse. This time Kevin moved fast, jumped out, opened the back door and threw the girl's bags out, saying, 'You get out here. Go on, get.'

She got out, but then she hung back keeping her eyes on him.

'Go on. Get moving.'

He was in a temper, all right, but the Fury in his voice was put on to frighten her away. She stood still, her peaky little face shining like bone in the half-light. Someone in the house had heard the car. A door opened and showed the outline of a short, stout woman on a background of yellow lamplight.

'Get,' he repeated. He climbed in beside Lin again and said urgently, 'Get going.'

Then for a moment nobody moved. The stout woman paused in the doorway, the girl stood watching them beside the car and Lin in the driver's seat found it impossible to stir.

The woman came out of the house, calling as she came, 'Who's that?'

Kevin spoke in Lin's ear, this time with a bit of a laugh, 'Quick. Get going.'

Lin sat staring at the dashboard as if he had forgotten how to start a car. This was a hell of a day, with the beer wearing off and leaving him cold and sour with a headache knocking gently at his forehead. Should have got a couple of bottles at the pub.

He muttered, 'We got time,' and then felt the air going out of Kevin, caught the edge of his puzzled stare and felt just as puzzled, and ashamed of himself as well.

The woman walked past Gloria towards Kevin. He got out of the car as if there was some way of warding her off.

'Oh, it's you, is it? What the hell do you think you're doing? You're not coming here, I can tell you that. Your uncle's had enough of you, loafing about eating your head off.'

The indignation that possessed the woman was almost too much for her small fleshy body to contain. It sprang and quivered as she shouted.

Desperation made Kevin shout too. 'It's not me. It's the girl. She's got nowhere to go. Her father threw her out.'

She turned round to look at Gloria and said, 'Looks as if he had his reasons, too. Like your bloody hide trying to dump your girlfriends on us, got enough to do to feed our own kids not going to be landed with your bastards don't you think it for a minute. Get going.' She scurried round to get between the girl and the house, looking like something out of the circus though Lin never felt less like laughing, then she started to dog her into the car step by step, face stuck out like a bum and yelling, 'Get out of here, do you hear me? You dirty trollop.'

Lin muttered, 'Can't help hearing you, Ma.' It was so much like a row in a pub that it was terrible to be sober.

Kevin got back in and slammed the door. The girl picked up her suitcase and heaved it into the back seat, then she came scrambling after it, carrying the paper bags.

The woman's battle cry turned into a song of triumph.

'Been the same ever since you was born, you bloody lazy no-hoper, coming here taking the food out of decent people's mouths and never a tap of work. Never want to set eyes on you again you thieving loafer.'

A cluster of children who had been visible for some time in the lighted doorway advanced now and stood listening respectfully a short distance away.

'Oh, for Christ's sake,' Kevin muttered.

Lin started the car, but he had to turn and drive past her again, the fountain of abuse playing triumphantly as they passed.

What with getting drunk and sobering up, taking this trip for nothing and having the long drive back to Sotherns' ahead of him, Lin found this day too long for his mind to measure. He was troubled by the pangs of an empty belly and a full bladder and depressed by the disgrace of having let Kevin down. He didn't know why he'd done that. When Kevin said, 'Quick. Get going,' his hands hadn't moved and he didn't know why.

The road ran for miles through a treeless region. It was fairly dark now, and when they came to a group of spindly trees that offered a conventional idea of shelter he stopped the car, walked across and relieved himself behind them without worrying too much about the girl. Kevin came after him and they stood there crossing swords without speaking. Kevin was shirty with him and no wonder.

There was something else nagging at him, more than hunger or guilt, with the irritation of a word on the tip of his tongue but out of memory's reach. He thought, if he could remember it he would cheer up.

'If Sotherns' don't give her a bed, we'll borrow a couple of blankets and she can doss down in the car.'

He felt better after he said that. It was weird: like there was a fire somewhere on a cold night, you didn't know where and came near it accidentally, feeling the warmth of it, then next minute in the cold again.

The hell with that. He shut his mind to what he didn't understand and told himself that women were to blame for the lot: his hunger, his headache, Kevin's sulks, the lot. Where you had women, you had trouble.

Mr Sothern answered the knock at the door, but when he saw Gloria, looking saint-like from tiredness and hunger, he called, 'Josie! Come here a minute,' and his tall, calm-faced wife appeared, a being so alien to the young men that they hung back, too shy to speak.

There was no need to say anything. Mrs Sothern drew Gloria inside as if she was rescuing her from them. 'You poor little thing. Now you mustn't cry. You're tired out, aren't you?'

Mr Sothern picked up Gloria's luggage and followed them in. Kevin and Lin drove to the quarters to park the car and went to the kitchen looking for something to eat. When they came into the lighted room, Lin noticed that Kevin was wearing a cheerful little smirk. He bounced back fast, all right, the old Kev.

*

Mrs Sothern drove Gloria to town next morning, took her to the doctor and left her at a friend's house. It was just as well, for the baby boy was born four days later. Mr Sothern came to the quarters to give the news, bringing a quart of scotch to wet the baby's head.

Kevin was squatting on his heels playing poker with three of the others in the space between the door and the first of the beds. He had just discarded three cards – actually his hand was king high but he had kept the nine of spades as well as the king; no point in telling the others his business – and Jack was dealing again when Mr Sothern came in. He never got to look at his cards.

'Well,' said Mr Sothern, 'you're a father. It's a boy. Six pounds, two ounces. Born at five o'clock. He's no heavyweight but he's healthy, the doctor says. Your wife's very well.'

The other men were slapping Kevin on the back, with goodwill but too heartily, as if he was the baby and they were smacking him to start him breathing.

'Good on you, mate!' 'A boy, eh?' 'Teapot!' 'Good for you!'

'Bring up your glasses,' said Mr Sothern.

The cards were trampled and scattered. Kevin might have brought a flush to those spades. He felt it in his bones that he had. He'd never know now.

Blind Freddie would have known she was under age, thought Lin. More like twelve than sixteen. Whenever Kevin spoke to him the thought came and blocked his answer, turning it into a vague mumble that put an end to conversation.

The night before they were paid off at Sotherns', Frank caught him crossing the yard and said, 'Lin, I'd like a word with you in private.'

Lin said warily, 'This is as private as you'll get.'

'About Kevin's wife. The men have put a bit of money together for her and the baby. We want you to give it to her.'

'Why me?' Lin was surly. Wasn't he Kevin's mate?

'You're the only one who knows her. And it's for her and the baby, you understand. You could explain to her. It'd come better from you.'

Fair enough. It was their money; they didn't want to see it go across the board at the crown and anchor. It shook him though, to see what they all thought of Kev. He couldn't say that they were wrong. No saying that they were right, either. He put the money in his pocket but he thought he might tell Kev about it just the same.

They got into town about five o'clock the next day.

'You going up to the hospital?' Lin asked carelessly as they went up the pub stairs together.

The look on Kev.

'What the hell for?' he asked, each word separate, and spitting them out as if they were poison.

Oh, all right. All right. Lin was aware of the bulky envelope in his inside pocket. He'd take it up to her then. One thing, there wasn't any chance of running into Kev.

Kevin went to the pictures first and then to the crown and anchor where he had a bit of luck, enough to cheer him up. He got in at two in the morning and woke up late and feeling fine. He got dressed and went down to the bar looking for Lin, to have a beer before lunch. Lin wasn't there. Jack and Blue and George were just finishing a beer. Jack said, 'Well, here's the new father. We'll have to have a drink on that. Same again, all round, Karl. And have one yourself. Special occasion.'

George raised his glass and said, 'Here's to you, Dad.'

Kevin turned on George the cold furious look that used once to bring silence. They laughed. They knew now that he was harmless.

Jack pushed the beer across to him, still grinning.

'Better drink up, Poppa,' George said, pulling the lion's tail.

'Enjoy yourself while you can,' said Jack, winking at Karl.

'Sure enough.' Even Karl was grinning. 'Soon you'll be walking the floor with him at three in the morning while he cuts his teeth.'

Meekly he drank his beer, allowing the look of rage to dissolve slowly into vagueness.

A fly in a web would know his feelings.

Sitting up in bed, pale but cocky, with a shrunken cardigan over her cotton nightdress, she looked as young as ever. Younger.

'Hi, Lin.'

'Hi. I got something for you.'

'From Kev? Didn't he get in?'

'Yeah, he got in. The whole gang's in. Finished at Sotherns'. No, it ain't from Kev. It's from the gang.'

He put the envelope in her lap and she peeked at the wad of notes.

'Gor. Ain't that nice of them.' She stared with awe at the envelope.

'Listen. What they want. They want you to put the money away. For the baby, like. I mean,' – here it came, against his deepest feelings – 'they'd just as soon you didn't say anything about it to Kev.'

There was a long silence while he allowed her to frown over that.

'What I mean is. What they think. Kev's a gambler. You couldn't talk sense to him while he's playing cards. He might take the money and think he was doing you a favour, thinking he'd bring it back double.' That sounded hollow. He never did know much what Kev was thinking, but he doubted if doing favours came into it.

She had been listening carefully and now that he had finished she nodded without any fuss and put the envelope under her pillow.

A nurse pushed a rumbling trolley into the room. When she stopped beside Gloria's bed to put a glass of orange juice on the bed-table she gave Lin such a dirty look that he and Gloria got the giggles and couldn't stop.

'Thinks you're it, don't she?' Gloria snuffled away tears of laughter, then joyful pride took her face over entirely.

'You seen him?'

He shook his head.

'Oh, go on. Go and have a look on the way out. The nurse'll show you. He's lovely, he really is.'

'Get me arrested, you will.' At this they crumpled again.

'Go on. Have a look at him, do.'

'Garn. I bet he's as ugly as sin.'

'No, he ain't. He's cute.'

'When do you get out of here?'

'Wednesday. Mrs Marsh is coming to get me. She's Mrs Sothern's friend. She's lovely. I can go and stay at the pub and do a bit of work for me keep. Just helping with the breakfasts and the teas. People are real nice. Lin . . .'

'Yeah?'

'He ain't coming, is he?'

'Search me. Doesn't tell me everything he does.'

That told her though, all right. Lin wished himself anywhere else, for the minute, and wondered with anger how he came to be in this spot. Always the mug, he said to himself, looking at her with a painful fixed grin.

'Well, thanks for coming. And the money. That was lovely.' She perked up all at once. 'Don't forget to have a look at him.'

The following Monday the men started work at Wrights'. It was out of sight out of mind with the girl and the baby. George tried to get some fun out of calling Kevin Daddy, but he gave it up as Kevin refused to be drawn. Lin didn't say a word about it. He stayed close to Kevin and they chatted along quietly about this and that, mostly good times they'd had and funny things that had happened. They weren't good sheds at Wrights' and the food was terrible, but Lin liked the spell they had there. It was the last in the district. After this, they moved south-east.

They cleaned up late on Friday and checked in at the pub early Saturday morning. Karl's wife Mona was handing out the room keys.

'I've moved you into 16 with Gloria, Kevin. It's a double with room for a cot. I've moved in an old cot that you're welcome to borrow . . . Don't mention it,' she called after him furiously.

'Hasn't settled down yet, Ma,' said George. 'Still got the honeymoon jitters.'

'You mind who you're calling Ma.'

In the corridor Kevin walked into Frank who was coming from the bar with Karl.

'Couple of bills here, Kevin, that you might as well settle out of your cheque. As we're moving on.'

He looked mild and unbelieving at the two envelopes Karl held out to him.

'Do you have a bank account here? I didn't think so. Karl can cash your cheque for you and make a couple out. That'll be the best way.' Pretending to be helpful. Moving in on him. Living his life for him. A man would have done better to go to jail. It was a life sentence. For twenty minutes, a life sentence.

Between the beds in room 16 there was a cot with a teddy bear propped up in one corner and underneath it a baby bath and a potty, both in blue plastic. Kevin showered and changed and got out fast. The less time he spent there, the better he'd be pleased. He went down to the bar and had a pint with the flies, spinning it out till a couple of the others came in. He had a few with them. When he went across the yard to the Gents before lunch he saw a canvas crib near the kitchen door and seeing was as sharp as touching, but he was insulated by then.

No Gloria in the dining room. She must be eating in the kitchen. She was laying low, he thought, and that restored some of his self-respect.

In the afternoon they played poker and all the time he was conscious of having less money than the others. It didn't affect his play – he always played cards as if his back was to the wall – and he came out ahead, but he felt it.

When the game broke up he took his winnings and joined Lin at the bar.

'What are you doing this evening?' he asked while Karl served him a pint.

Lin was about to say that he thought he'd give the girls a treat and go to the dance, but sentiment stopped him. He and Kev had always gone to the dance together, and this might be an indirect plea for his company.

'Dunno. Haven't thought about it.'

'What about coming to the dance, then?'

Lin had a funny expression on his face as if he was trying to look two ways at once.

'Might go out to Spiny and have a couple of beers with old Walt. Seeing as we won't be back for a while.'

Kevin's face tightened with temper. A new girl, that was what he needed. He wanted to go to the dance and pick up a new girl, somebody with real class. Not just for the night, either.

It was no use going without Lin. They were hard cases, the town girls at the local dance, and it was Lin who knew how to chat them up. Kevin tagged along and did all right, better than Lin sometimes, but he was no good by himself.

They went out to Spiny Creek but it wasn't much of an evening. Walt was kept busy because the cricket team was in. The cricketers were having a fine time but the joy didn't spread as far as Lin and Kevin. They dragged it out till closing time and they ended up looking in at the dance when they got back to town, but it was too late to do any good then.

When Kevin got back to the room she was awake feeding the baby and she stared at him, all eyes, not saying anything. The look he gave her made her duck her head as if he had raised his fist. That made him feel a bit better.

Karl and Mona made such a fuss of the baby that they would probably have given Gloria a permanent job to keep it there. Kevin wanted Gloria to ask them but he couldn't speak to her, the silence between them having set as hard as steel. He always knew what she was doing in spite of that because she told the baby, chatting to it in an even quiet voice as if she was talking to herself. Like a bloody madwoman.

When he woke up, the morning they were leaving for Willow Creek, she was standing at the dressing table doing her hair up and talking to the waving legs on the bed. 'Don't mess up your new suit now that Auntie Mona give you. You're going down to stay with her while I put the stuff in the car. You be good now and no yelling. Come on, then, we got a lot to do.'

All the stuff was gone when he came back from the bathroom, so he knew what to expect, but the situation hit him just the same when he came out into the hotel yard. Mona was standing by the car holding the baby while Lin and Gloria, as thick as thieves, were trying to pack the boot of the car.

'Try the crib in the boot,' said Mona, 'and put the bath on the back seat. Put the pillow in it and you can lie him in it. You'll have a nice sleep then, won't you, pet?'

'A travelling circus, this is,' Lin growled. 'All because of you, mate.' He threw a punch in the baby's direction, but it was Kevin who felt the jolt of it. When Lin said, shortly, 'Come and give a hand with this stuff, Kev,' he went unresisting, and all the way to Willow Creek he sat pensive, too discouraged to be sullen.

Raking the ashes of his temper for a little life-giving warmth he thought of the scene at the car. Everything about it annoyed him: the sunlight, the silly look on Mona's face when she talked to the baby, the tone of Lin's voice and the sight of Gloria so pleased with herself and done up to the nines. She had a new dress on and new sandals too. Where the hell did she get the money for new clothes?

The question was so interesting that he repeated it in a different tone. Where did she get it then? From her mother? Not likely. The old girl wouldn't have two cents to rub together. From Karl and Mona? What a laugh. Her board, she was working for, and Mona had made a sharp remark or two about that. Not to Gloria, of course. To him.

Minding his business, like everybody else. The bath and the teddy bear – who paid for all that? He meant to keep a good lookout till he found out.

At Willow Creek, remembering the mean note in Lin's voice, he unpacked the car without waiting to be told and stacked the stuff in the lobby outside the office. Gloria waited to talk to the pubkeeper's wife and he waited with her though he resented it, the woman's indifferent glance marrying them again as he stood there.

'Do you need any extra help in the kitchen? I want to earn my keep if I can.'

'I could do with someone full-time to do the rooms. You don't look very strong, though.'

'I'm wiry.'

'How old are you?'

She lied, 'Seventeen.'

'Are you feeding the baby yourself? I think it might be too much for you.' Harried and listless as the woman was, she smiled when she looked at the baby. 'Well, every little helps. We'll see how it works out. How long are you staying?'

Gloria looked at Kevin, who had to mutter, 'Five weeks.'

'But the men will be at the sheds most of the time.'

They had almost had a conversation, and he still didn't know if she was going to earn money. She was like a spider, tossing her soft, sticky threads round him, and the whole world helped her at it. Soon, he knew, he would have to give in.

The country round Willow Creek was livelier than the West. They went to Thompsons' first, six miles from Pike's

301

Crossing where Dan Bryan kept the pub and his daughter Moira ran the bar. The gang was known there. Lin and Kevin drove over the first night and found it just the same as last year, quiet and pleasant, with one or two men from the farms round about talking shop over a pint and Moira behind the bar with her knitting.

'Hello, you two. That's another year gone then.' She set down her knitting and took their order.

'That's right. You don't look a day older, though.'

'Thanks.' Moira drew their beer without smiling.

'That the same old pullover you was knitting last year, Moira?' asked Lin.

'Have to do something to pass the time. I can't travel round like you lot.'

'There ain't so much to travelling around,' said Kevin. 'Not when you've got a nice little spot like this. You don't want a barman, do you? Permanent, live in.'

Moira couldn't count the number of times she'd heard that one. Some of them had meant it, too. She had waited a long time for a man who would offer to take her away from the bar, but they always wanted to join her there.

'See enough of men from where I'm standing, thanks.'

Kevin didn't leave it at that. Next time they ordered, he said, bright-eyed and with the teasing look that brought his face alive, 'Come on, Moira. What have you got against men? We ain't such a bad lot.'

Looking downwards, Moira communicated her opinion of men to the tap of the beer pump. Delighted to see Kevin himself again, Lin said, 'We ain't all the same,

302

you know. You meet one or two that's no good and you take it out on the rest of us. Is that a fair go?'

That was the sort of thing they could keep up forever, and they did keep it up for the rest of the week, Kevin being so animated and so friendly in his teasing that at last he had Moira smiling and Lin wondering what he was up to. It wasn't like Kev to go to so much trouble for nothing.

Willow Creek was too far away for a weekend, so they went to the local dance at Pike's Crossing on Saturday night. They picked up a couple of nice little birds there and had a wonderful night. It was just like old times.

From Thompsons' they went to Carrs'. There Kevin took to the cards again and played as if it was his life's work to lose money. He had had runs of bad luck before and lost money but never like this. It looked as if he wouldn't believe the cards. He would go the limit on two pairs and look as cool as a cucumber when somebody put down three tens. Lin lay on his bed and watched, depressed by Kevin's bad luck and awed by his mild indifferent expression. After three nights' play he borrowed fifty dollars from Lin against his cheque.

'I don't see it,' said Lin. 'What you get out of it. If you drink, you get something. You get your skinful anyhow.'

But the mystery filled him with respect and Kevin's self-control with admiration. He gave the money willingly, telling himself with pride that Kev never welshed on a debt. Though a funny fellow in some ways.

After they finished at Carrs' they went back to Willow Creek, Kevin sitting silent in the car, showing no emotion but seeming to fade a little. The marriage that was old talk to everyone else was new again to him.

That night Gloria tried to get into bed with him. He thrust her out furiously with his hands and feet so that she slid to the floor, and she got up and scuttled back to her own bed, but he knew he had made a mistake. She had seen the worst he could do and it wasn't bad enough. He could not deal a blow; his hands stayed still when they should strike out. She had his measure now.

Sure enough, she got nasty.

The incident had broken the silence. In the morning he opened his eyes when she was feeding the baby and instead of closing them again and shamming dead he said, 'Where's the money coming from?'

'What money?'

'That dress. The shoes. The bloody teddy bear. Where are you getting the money?'

'Not from you, so mind your own business.'

'What about your bloody doctor's bill? I paid that, didn't I?'

'Too bad. It'd have all gone on the crown and anchor by now so you're no worse off.'

She sounded just like his aunt punishing the ears of his meek, defeated uncle.

'Where is it?'

'Where you won't find it. And I ain't going to tell you so don't wear yourself out asking.'

For an answer he seized the shabby white handbag she carried with her everywhere and shook its contents out onto his bed. Though the dismay in her face had made him

304

hopeful, he found only a dollar bill and a few cents – which he took just the same. It was not for the sake of the money.

He was too afraid to speak to her again. His only refuge was the dark cave of sleep, his only defence the glass wall of silence.

He kept up the search for the money, which was also a substitute for conversation. It had rules, like a game. He never looked behind her back and if she was in the room he always looked, even if he wasn't serious. As they lived, to turn a picture and run his fingers over the paper backing was as much as saying hello. When he had more time he searched seriously and she watched him without ever changing her expression. Once he thought, She wouldn't make a bad poker player, and that was the friendliest thought he ever had about her.

One night when he was drunk he came up from the bar and turned the whole room upside down without a word: emptied drawers onto the floor, dragged out suitcases and opened them, shook out her clothes and felt hems and pockets. The only time her face changed was when the baby woke and cried, and even then she didn't move but lay in bed looking at him. He came for the bed then and she slid out, throwing the pillow towards him as she went. Nothing there, nothing under the mattress. He gave it up and went away, trying to convert the disorder he was leaving behind him into a triumph.

Gloria began to clean up without too much distress. Oh, well, she said to herself in a tone she had learnt from her mother, while he's doing that he's not doing something worse. He must think though that she'd never heard of banks. There was a cache in the room where she kept her marriage certificate (for fear he made the baby illegitimate by tearing it up), her bankbook (because what he didn't know didn't hurt him), and any money she needed to have in cash, but she made sure that was as little as possible. The publican's wife would have minded her money if she had explained the situation but she didn't feel inclined to do that. Having the position of a married woman was all the pleasure she got out of life, except for the baby, and she didn't want to spoil it. When she started work full-time as a housemaid she had said, 'Don't tell Kev,' hoping they would suppose he thought the work too much for her. Ha ha.

At Harriotts' where the shearers went next there was poker every night again. Kevin won at first and acted as if he would go on winning forever, playing high and annoying the others by forcing up the bets. Then he started to lose and lost even faster than he'd won, but with such a steady look on his face that it took a while to realise how silly his play was.

Though he didn't show any feeling, Lin got the idea that he didn't enjoy the game any more. It had got on top of him.

'Why don't you give it away, mate?' he asked one night as Kevin got into the bed next to his.

'I like it,' said Kevin, with a yawn intended to express indifference.

Lin thought, 'You don't play as if you liked it.' He watched Kevin come to the card table every night as if it was some sort of test.

'You must hate money, to throw it around like that.'

'Luck's got to change.'

It wasn't a matter of luck any more. If he did get a big run, it would only make more of a fool of him. Lin made up his mind to refuse to lend him money if he asked. To his way of thinking, that was what a good mate would do.

Kevin didn't ask Lin for money. Instead he tried to put an IOU into the centre. It was Jack who had raised the bet, and seeing the slip of paper he said quietly, like a priest interpreting a point of religious procedure, 'Take your stakes back. I'm putting my hand in.'

George who was standing behind him reported later with awe, 'A full house, he had. Three aces and two fours.' So the worth of his gesture was known. It imposed on the others then, and in a moment only the fallen cards, the last of Kevin's cash and the embarrassing slip of paper were left on the table.

As he gathered them in he said, 'You should let me chase my money,' covering himself with a show of anger.

'It takes money to chase money,' said Jack. To mend the situation, he added, 'You're staying over at Willow Creek for the weekend, aren't you? What about a game on Saturday night? You can have your revenge then.'

That was the end of the poker game. Kevin had so much feeling to hide that his face looked frozen when he came to lie on his bed and read a magazine.

'Wouldn't play with them if I was you,' Lin murmured, under the pretext of consoling him. Great hopes.

*

There wasn't a crown and anchor game at Willow Creek. On Friday night Kevin went down to the two-up school hoping to get back some of the money the unseen power owed him. He lost again. Though it wasn't his game and he had meant only to give it a flutter, the effort of getting away with the remains of his cheque was so great that he came away shaken, knowing for the first time what a hold gambling had on him.

It was only nine o'clock, which left a lot of the evening to fill in. He would have liked to spend it quietly, drinking a few cans with Lin in his room, for instance.

Lin must be in the bar with the rest of them. It would be a big night because the gang would start to break up tomorrow. As soon as he thought of that he knew he had better turn up there and look pleasant if he didn't want to lose face forever. His position with the gang was shaky enough as it was. He was puzzled and dejected at the change that had come over his life. That marriage – he took no account of it, yet ever since it had happened he found himself doing what he didn't want to do, as if, once you gave away one little bit of your freedom, you lost the lot.

At the noisy, crowded bar he stood next to George, who asked, 'Where are you heading for, Kev, now that the season's over?'

He didn't know. He hadn't thought about it. That meant he would drift back to Murrigong to Gloria's family – which didn't bear thinking of.

Why didn't he shoot through tonight, go to Queensland, change his name?

He couldn't be bothered.

His reckless fit was over. When he sat down to the poker game on Saturday night he was calm and careful, ready to get the best out of the cards. The hands he got weren't bad either, not wonderful but a lot better than he had been getting. The trouble was that, not having a big enough stake to start with, he couldn't afford to back a good hand when he got one. He let himself be bluffed out twice when he had the winning hand. Though he played as well as he knew how, kept his head cool and went slow on the beer, all he could do was lose as slowly as possible. By midnight he knew that his money wouldn't hold out and he would have to leave with his head down and his pockets inside out.

Not him. Not Kev Drinan. The beer he had been drinking had reached him by then, so that he looked with amusement at this prospect. It was time. Time for something.

The winning idea came suddenly and lit his face with a gentle smile.

He got up, saying, 'Deal me out this hand, will you?'

They thought he was going to the Gents, but he went up to the bedroom and switched on the light. That woke her up and she was out of bed in a flash when she saw where he was heading, but he got there first and picked it up. It came neatly out of the blankets wrapped in a cocoon of flannelette, but it was nasty to touch, wet and warm, soft

309

and alive, like somebody's insides. It was harder to hold than a string bag, wobbling and sagging everywhere, but he got his hands under it and raised it over his head.

'Put the baby down, Kev,' she said in a full-toned whisper.

'Where's the money?'

She stared at him and her lips moved, but this time nothing came out. She wasn't so sharp now, not by a long way. Smiling at her, he began to take little steps backwards towards the balcony door. He thought it would be a nice touch to stagger a bit, but that was a mistake. Though he wasn't reeling drunk he wasn't sober enough to put it on and he almost went over.

'Come on. Where's the money?'

'Put the baby down,' she whispered as if she was making love to him. 'Put him on the bed. You can have the money.'

He shook his head and backed again.

'Put him down, Kev.' She was licking her lips now. She wouldn't make a poker player after all.

Without taking her eyes off him, she felt inside the cover of the mattress in the baby's crib and took out a plastic bag. He could see ten-dollar notes through the plastic. She threw it on the floor at his feet and said, 'That's all I've got. Put him down.' She might have had nothing at all. She had kept her last fortnight's wages in cash for the journey.

'Come and get it.' He raised it higher, grinning at her, thinking he'd get into bed with her when he came back. Might as well. Then it stiffened and squalled. He got tired of the game at once and lowered his arms. She was there and snatched it, and he picked up the money and went.

His luck really turned when he got back to the game, so that he could have cleaned them all out if he could have kept them playing but Lin came in with a girl about half-past one and the others made that an excuse to break up the game and get away. Lin and the girl were both at the giggling stage. Lin had a bottle of whisky and he wanted Kevin and the girl to come up to his room for a drink, but the girl saw through that, not being as far gone as she looked, so they sat down at the card table and drank the whisky out of beer glasses. After three sips, the girl said, 'Excuse me one moment,' in a modest tone that suggested she was off to the Ladies, went away and didn't come back. Kevin said, 'Ah, it's the oldest trick in the book,' but Lin thought she might have passed out somewhere, so they went to look for her and outside the smoky room the cool night air struck Kevin down. Lin got him to his feet and up the stairs.

'This has been one hell of a season,' he thought in dejection as he steadied Kevin down the corridor to the door of his room and went away to his own.

Far gone as he was when he fell on to his bed, Kevin must have noticed something, for his sleep was filled not with a dream but with a strange dreamlike atmosphere, as if the walls had come down and he was sleeping in his bed in the middle of a great plain.

When he woke up, she was gone. The crib, the teddy bear, the blue plastic, the clothes, the baby – all gone. He felt the great stone slide off his shoulders, closed his eyes again and slept till late in the morning. Next time he woke, he thought it was a funny thing she had left just when he gave in. Well, who cared? That was his good luck. Wide awake now, he looked at his watch and wondered if Lin was ready for a hair of the dog. 'Better get dressed,' he thought, and then, 'Hell, I am dressed,' and started to laugh to himself, though the laughter nearly split his head open. Have to tell Lin that. He got up and washed his face in cold water, had a shave and went off to find Lin.

Lin was gone, luggage and all.

At Murrigong Lin pulled up outside the Thomases' house and the sound of the car brought Mrs Thomas out. She paid no attention to Lin and not much to Gloria, but put her arms out to take the baby, settled him in the crook of her arm and fixed her whole attention on him.

'Mum, I've left Kev.'

'Not much like you, Glor', is he? Got a bit of a look of Charlie.'

'Mum, I've left Kev, if you're listening. And you might say hello to Lin, who's driven me all the way from Willow Creek.'

He hadn't had much choice, thought Lin. He had had a terrible night, finding Gloria and all her gear in his bedroom, Gloria at the sight of him starting to howl and climbing up his arm like a monkey, begging him to take her home till he had to promise, to shut her up. He didn't know what it was about, either – only that Kev mustn't know. Just as well, because the way Kev was it would be hard to tell him anything. Four hours' sleep he had had on the sofa in

312

the lounge and she had grudged him that. Now he had a headache, a bad taste in his mouth and a feeling that he'd been taken for a mug since he first laid eyes on Gloria. Not only by Gloria, either. Why did they all pick on him? Didn't they know he was Kevin's mate?

Used to be. Kev would be looking for a new mate now all right.

Lin had gone wrong somewhere right at the beginning, and things had never gone right since.

Mrs Thomas gave him a sour goodday and he returned it just as sourly. Gloria took no notice. She knew how he felt and she didn't give a damn.

'What about Dad, Mum? Will it be all right?'

'Never mind your father. I'll look after him. What's this rash he's got on his neck?'

Lin had the luggage unloaded, for the last time.

'You'll come in and have a cup of tea?' said Gloria.

'No thanks. I'll be on my way.'

He looked back before he got to the highroad. Mrs Thomas was still looking at the baby as if they were the only two people alive on earth, but Gloria gave him a wave, and, after all, he waved back.

Once a mug, always a mug.

Text Classics

textclassics.com.au

Amy Witting
I for Isobel

INTRODUCED BY CHARLOTTE WOOD

Text Classics

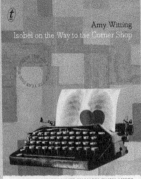

Amy Witting
Isobel on the Way to the Corner Shop

INTRODUCED BY MARIA TAKOLANDER

Text Classics

Amy Witting
The Visit

INTRODUCED BY SUSAN JOHNSON

Text Classics

Amy Witting
A Change in the Lighting

INTRODUCED BY ASHLEY HAY

Text Classics

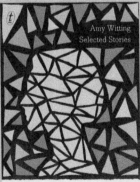

Amy Witting
Selected Stories

INTRODUCED BY MELANIE JOOSTEN

Text Classics